Kelly Caldwell's *Apple of His Eye* is a heart-warming story of faith, family, and renewal. The story will delight fans of Amish fiction and readers who love an endearing romance.

—AMY CLIPSTON
BEST-SELLING AUTHOR OF *THE FORGOTTEN RECIPE*

Kelly Caldwell's debut, *Apple of His Eye*, will please so many longtime Amish fiction readers. This crafted story is deliciously entertaining. Caldwell has outdone herself on this sweet-as-pie romance!

—ELIZABETH BYLER YOUNTS
AUTHOR OF THE PROMISE OF SUNRISE SERIES

Kelly Caldwell has penned a sweet, tender story about strong faith, family ties, and gentle love. It's a beautiful book you won't put down until you've read the last word.

—KATHLEEN FULLER
AUTHOR OF *A RELUCTANT BRIDE* AND *AN UNBROKEN HEART*

Apple of HIS EYE

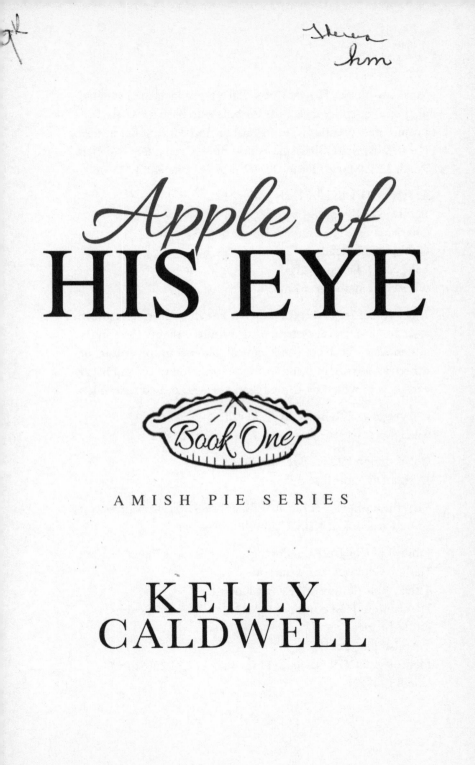

Book One

AMISH PIE SERIES

KELLY CALDWELL

Most CHARISMA HOUSE BOOK GROUP products are available at special quantity discounts for bulk purchase for sales promotions, premiums, fund-raising, and educational needs. For details, write Charisma House Book Group, 600 Rinehart Road, Lake Mary, Florida 32746, or telephone (407) 333-0600.

APPLE OF HIS EYE by Kelly Caldwell
Published by Realms
Charisma Media/Charisma House Book Group
600 Rinehart Road
Lake Mary, Florida 32746
www.charismahouse.com

Cover design by Lisa Rae McClure
Design Director: Justin Evans

Visit the author's website at kellycaldwellbooks.wordpress.com or on Facebook at Kelly Caldwell Books

Library of Congress Cataloging-in-Publication Data
Names: Caldwell, Kelly, author.
Title: Apple of his eye / Kelly Caldwell.
Description: First edition. | Lake Mary, Florida : Realms, [2016] | Series:
  Amish pie ; book 1
Identifiers: LCCN 2016002134 (print) | LCCN 2016006202 (ebook) | ISBN

9781629982311 (softcover) | ISBN 9781629982328 (ebook) |
ISBN
9781629982328 (e-book)
Subjects: LCSH: Amish--Fiction. | Mate selection--Fiction. |
Man-woman
relationships--Fiction. | Triangles (Interpersonal relations)--
Fiction. |
GSAFD: Christian fiction. | Love stories.
Classification: LCC PS3603.A4365 A87 2016 (print) | LCC
PS3603.A4365 (ebook)
| DDC 813/.6--dc23

First edition

16 17 18 19 20 — 987654321
Printed in the United States of America

AUTHOR'S NOTE

IN RESEARCHING THE Amish way of life, I discovered that Amish communities differ from one to another. In fact, it would be difficult to find two Amish communities exactly alike.

For instance, there are dialectical differences in the spellings of some words. This is why you may see *dawdi* (grandfather) also spelled *doddy* or *daudi*, depending on the region in question. You may even see a grandfather referred to as *da*.

There are more substantive differences as well. In some communities, like the one in this story, courting is done at night. In still other communities dinnertime prayers may at times be voiced when a particular praise is offered.

While all Amish communities may share basic beliefs and values, diversity still exists. This diversity makes for a rich culture, and it is my honor to present within these pages some small glimpses into their lifestyle and traditions.

CHAPTER 1

Mid-February
Paradise, Pennsylvania

T HE TALL, DARK-HAIRED Amish man stood amidst
the piles of aromatic wood shavings and ran his
callused, sensitive hands down the oak cabinet
front. He closed his eyes, feeling for the slightest imperfection in the wood, but the burled grain was sanded smooth.
John Miller was satisfied.

He lifted his lashes as the wood shop door banged open
and his best friend, Rob Yoder, entered, rubbing his hands
together in an obvious attempt to warm them.

"Brrrr," Rob muttered. "Still cold out there and I forgot
my gloves."

"You're late," John said mildly, turning the heavy cabinet
he held with ease.

"I know—I always am. But today I've got *gut* reason."
Rob paused for effect, and John arched a dark brow. "I've
met a girl."

John groaned and looked away.

"*Nee, nee,*" Rob protested. "I mean it—there's something about this girl."

"This girl, huh?"

Rob grabbed a brush and a jar of varnish from the work bench. "Don't give me that look."

"What look?"

"The one where you think I'm about to do something *narrisch.*"

John had to smile. He was twenty-six to Rob's twenty-three and was the more quiet and serious of the two—he knew Rob's penchant to flit from girl to girl, thinking himself smitten a good number of times per year. "Not crazy," John said. "Just repetitive. Let's see...who was it last week? Lily? *Nee,* Ruby, and Susan, and Mattie and—"

"I think I'm in love with her."

Rob's quiet words silenced John's bantering, and he stared at his friend. "You're serious?"

"*Ya,*" Rob laughed uncomfortably. "I guess I do sound *narrisch,* but it's true, and for once I have no idea what to say to a girl."

John put aside the heavy cabinet he held and went over to lean his hip against a worktable near his friend. "Surely if you're in love with her, you'll find a way to talk to her. Who is she, anyway?"

"Tabby Beiler."

John tilted his head in confusion as he thought of his young neighbor. "Tabitha Beiler? But she can't be *auld* enough for courting..."

Rob blew out a sigh of clear exasperation. "John...sometimes I wonder where your head's at. Tabby Beiler is nineteen and beautiful to boot."

"Nineteen? Who'd have thought?" John murmured, seeing in his mind's eye a young girl with unruly blonde hair, *kapp* askew, and a schoolgirl's dress. "I would have thought her to be twelve or so."

"Twelve?" Rob snorted. "John, you only think Tabby's still a kid because time stopped for you the minute Phoebe—"

John tightened his jaw and stared down at the wood of the table beneath his hand. He sensed Rob's discomfort but didn't look up.

"Sorry, *auld* man," Rob muttered.

John did lift his eyes then and gave a slight nod. "It's all right...I—well, never mind. Why don't we come up with a plan on how you can talk to Tabitha, especially if she might be your future wife one day."

Rob grinned. "That actually doesn't sound too bad."

"When you would have run for the hills if I'd mentioned the word *frau* with any other girl?"

"Yep."

John reached out and shook his friend's hand. "Well then, Tabitha Beiler has got to be something pretty amazing indeed."

"Your eyes are like twin blue pools of delight." Rob kept his voice low and level, a well-practiced inflection of tone. But he realized too late that even though he and John had discussed talking with Tabitha, he did not quite know how to actually talk with a beautiful girl—only how to give her compliments. It was one thing for him to be an acknowledged flirt to the females of his community but quite another to find himself in the rather awkward position of actually being in love with a girl. All of his facile charm seemed rather idle—even to his own ears, and he wondered what she thought as they sat together on a bale of hay in her *Aenti* Beth's main barn. He'd snuck in while she was doing the milking and had been pleased by the delightful flush that had stolen to her cheeks at his sudden presence.

"Is that what you really think of my eyes?" Tabitha queried demurely, breaking into his thoughts.

He hesitated a fraction before answering, then quickly recovered. "*Ya*, but I could go on..." He trailed off suggestively, sure she'd want him to continue, like other girls might. But to his surprise, she sighed instead.

"What's wrong?" he asked, his quick mind running the conversation backward to see what he might have said.

"Nothing," she hastened to assure him. "I—it may sound like vanity, but I am proud to have my *mamm's* eyes, though I cannot remember exactly what they looked like."

He suppressed his own sigh of relief, feeling back on level ground. Comforting a sad or distressed girl was one of his specialties, but he was surprised at the genuine pang of emotion he felt when he searched her pale face.

"That's right," he murmured, inching a bit closer to touch her small hand. "Your parents died when you were very young."

"*Ya*, and you lost your own *daed* when you were but a child."

"Yes." He thrilled to the fact that she hadn't moved away from him. "So we have a bond, you and I."

She lowered her eyelashes against the cream of her cheeks to nod in silent agreement. Rob decided at that moment that it was time to close up shop; it wouldn't do to give any girl, even one he was in love with, too much of a thought life about togetherness—just in case something didn't work out.

So he got to his feet, towering above her but still holding her hand.

"I'd better get going, sweet Tabby," he said, and she rose to her brief height beside him.

He looked down to where a few tendrils of blonde hair escaped her white prayer *kapp* as she lifted her face to meet his gaze. He dropped her hand with an abruptness he didn't feel, narrowly avoiding the desire to sneak a kiss on her cheek. Instead, he took a step away from her and clapped his black hat on. "Until later," he whispered.

She smiled at him with true beauty, and he had the satisfaction of knowing that she must surely be in love with him as well—perhaps even a bit more than he was with her. It was something to consider. *Always keep one step ahead in the game, in love or not, Robbie*, he told himself, then sketched her a brief bow and made his way out of the barn door without looking back.

❦

"*Ach*, Letty! I'm so in love with him." Tabitha couldn't help but twirl on the rag rug in her best friend's bedroom. Then she fluttered her arms in a graceful arc. "I feel as though I could fly."

It had only been yesterday since Rob Yoder had stolen

into her *Aenti* Beth's barn, and Tabitha could still feel her cheeks warm when she thought of his daring action in seeking her out. She couldn't believe that anyone as handsome and well liked as Rob would want to give her attention.

Tabitha giggled when she finally plopped down on the edge of the feather bed mattress next to the other girl. "*Ach*, Letty, do you think I'm *narrisch*?"

"*Ya*," the other girl replied with a dimpled smile. "Crazy in love."

Tabitha reached to hug her, then fell back on the bed to close her eyes and daydream of Rob's brown, wavy hair and his deep brown eyes. His features were both handsome and endearing, and his white teeth had a tiny gap between the front two that complemented his easy smile.

"How can you be in love with him when you've only just met?" Letty mused, and Tabitha opened her eyes.

"I feel like I've known him forever—like my life was on pause, just waiting for him to come along. I can't really explain it, but I know it's true." Tabitha bit her lip, then laughed out loud as she thought about the secret meeting in the barn. "He held my hand, Letty."

"What?" Her nicely plump friend leaned down on an elbow and raised her brows. "What did you do?"

"I—I allowed it for a few minutes," Tabitha confessed.

"Oooh, Tabby, you must be careful of your sweet reputation. I don't want to say it, but you know that Rob Yoder flirts with many of the girls in the community."

Tabitha nodded, having already thought of this fact. "I know, but I'm sure he's different with me. I know it. His eyes are so warm and tender. He makes me feel like the world is going to stop and then start spinning again only when we're together."

"Is it spinning now?" Letty asked somewhat wryly.

Tabitha knew her friend was only concerned and reached up to take Letty's hand in her own. "Do not worry, Letty. I will not get hurt. He's wonderful!"

Letty squeezed her hand in return. "*Ach*, I hope so, Tabby. I truly do."

"And you, whenever I marry," Tabitha said, "will be my attendant."

Letty's kind face flushed at the suggested honor, but then she giggled. "Unless we both fall off the world when it stops spinning."

Tabitha grinned. "Only then!"

CHAPTER 2

I HAVE A PROBLEM," Rob muttered.

"You don't have to tell me twice," John returned.

"*Nee*, I mean it."

John realized his friend was being serious and slowed his steps as they walked along the dim dirt path that cut through the barren, snow-dusted fields. They were on their way to Rob's house for a late supper.

"Well, what's wrong then?"

"My *mamm* hates Tabby."

"What are you talking about?" John asked, almost coming to a standstill, so that Rob knocked into him and then shoved him away.

John resumed walking, figuring Rob would explain in his own time. But only the sound of the night wind chased through the stray cornstalks. John finally stopped again. "Why would she hate Tabitha? We're not supposed to hate anyone."

"All right, my *mamm* dislikes Tabby. Feel better?"

"*Nee*. Tell me why."

Rob waved a big hand in the gloom in obvious frustration. "I don't know. I brought up the Beilers at lunch today and *Mamm* sort of lost her temper. I couldn't make any sense of what she was talking about, so that's why you're here."

"I'm where?" John asked, not liking the turn the conversation was taking.

"Here," Rob groaned. "Coming to supper. I was hoping you might be able to help me figure out my mother's problem and possibly convince her to—"

John sidestepped his friend and started heading backward along the path.

"Hey!" Rob called, but John ignored him.

After a few moments John heard Rob's boots clumping fast behind him, and he sighed and came to a stop. He turned to face Rob's frustration and held up one long finger.

"Wait! Before you start rambling the way you do when you're about to drag me into some kind of trouble or another with you, I want you to remember one thing."

"What?" Rob cried.

"I won't do it."

John was about to turn when Rob shouldered him hard in the ribs. The blow caught him off guard and he fell, only to reach up and take the hand Rob held out to him. He pulled with his counter weight and felled Rob flat on his face. John leaned back on his elbows and stared up at the fitful sky. He glanced over to see Rob dusting the snow from his face and hair and felt a sting of remorse that he didn't feel especially willing to help his friend out. *But this is the way it always is,* John thought, breathing deeply of the cold. *He pleads and I give in... to my own disadvantage. But still, friends are friends.*

John sat up and turned his head to smile at Rob. "Your *mamm*'s going to wonder if we've been out sledding like *buwes.*"

Rob grinned. "Now that's more like it, John Miller. I deeply appreciate your willingness to help."

John shook his head. "Don't call me willing. Think of it more as resigned."

They both laughed out loud.

～⊙⊙～

The following day Rob decided to take another risk in catching Tabby alone during the very early morning hours when he knew women of his community usually did the baking. He decided to walk the half mile, figuring he'd cause less notice, and fisted his hands into the pockets of his heavy black coat. He knew he'd probably be late to his job at the Millers' wood shop, but it would be more than worth it if he could snatch a few minutes in Tabby's beautiful presence.

He thought back to the previous evening's meal as he walked in the brisk air, frowning a bit in memory. John had indeed been successful in eliciting a response about the Beilers from his mother, but it had not gone as Rob hoped. Although his *mamm* had passed the warm candied sweet potatoes and plate of roast with steady hands, her brown eyes had flashed in suppressed anger and disapproval when John had casually mentioned that Tabitha Beiler was now of courting age.

"Hmmm," she'd muttered. "There are some folks who maybe ought not court, no matter what their age may be."

"*Mamm*," Rob had finally burst out in near desperation. "What do you have against the Beilers anyway?"

His *mamm* had taken a bite of buttered bread before

11

answering. She'd swallowed, then eyed him reflectively. "Some stories are *auld* and best forgotten, *sohn*."

"*Ach*, but I like to hear an *auld* tale now and then," John had chimed in, obviously trying to help.

But Rob's mother had been unmoved.

"Eat more roast beef, John Miller," she'd snapped. "That should satisfy your appetite for food, if not *auld* stories."

Rob had watched John shrug and then return to eating, and he knew the moment was lost. Whatever his *mamm* held against the Beilers was not going to be readily found out. Rob sighed aloud, then realized he was nearing Tabby's house. His thoughts quickly turned to the beauty of the girl's face as he ducked under the barren clothes-lines and headed for the kitchen window.

⌘

Tabitha bent to carefully pull the chocolate cake from the cook stove, having no desire to wake *Aenti* Beth with a stray sound. Her *aenti* had had a restless night and Tabitha had spent much of the wee hours tending to the beloved old woman who'd raised her since she was a young child.

Aenti Beth was bound to a wheelchair due to a childhood case of polio but had been the one who'd taught Tabitha all she knew about cooking and running a home. When Tabitha's parents had both succumbed to influenza, Tabitha might have been absorbed into a cousin's household, but her *daed*'s aged sister had asked for her to come to Paradise. It had been mutually beneficial to both the little girl and the old woman as Tabitha could help care for her *aenti*'s needs but still receive the blessing of a happy home.

Tabitha sighed at her meandering thoughts and was about to bounce a practiced hand off the warmth of the cake when the sound of something hitting the kitchen window caused her to turn.

She was startled when the sound came again, and she saw the curious sight of a pebble bouncing off the glass from the outside. She tried to puzzle it out and then was filled with a glorious surge of joy as she realized that this was the universal Amish signal that a man had come courting. While the pebbles were usually tossed at night, she was more than happy to accept some thrown at daybreak and could only dream that it might be Rob who was calling.

She left the cookstove and hurried to the back door to quietly open it and then to step off the back porch. She rounded the corner of the house only to bump directly into a tall, strong frame. She looked up to find Rob's merry brown eyes gazing down at her and had a heady feeling of exhilaration that he would seek her out.

"Hello, beautiful," he murmured after steadying her on her feet.

She felt herself flush at his words, then swallowed hard. "Would you—like a piece of chocolate cake? It's fresh from the oven. Or I have pie..."

She watched a grin come to his face and noticed a sweet dimple to the right side of his mouth. "Cake is my favorite actually. I've never liked pie all that much."

She nodded, making a mental note about his preference, hugging the scrap of knowledge to herself, and knowing that she'd always have a cake ready whenever Rob might call. She led the way inside and whispered softly over her shoulder. "*Aenti* Beth's still asleep."

He whispered back, "I figured."

Once inside, she hastened to take his dark coat and hat and hang them on the pegs beside the door. She crossed to where the chocolate cake was still cooling. She dusted the top of the cake with a snowfall of powdered sugar and prepared to cut it, even though it was a little hot still.

"Will you eat with me, Tabby?" Rob asked from where he'd seated himself at the table.

"I—um—surely." She stumbled over her words, knowing she'd probably feel self-conscious eating in front of him, especially with something as messy as hot cake.

She moved to take down two simple dessert plates from the cupboard and brought cloth napkins and silverware from a drawer. Then she cut two pieces, setting one in front of Rob. "Cake for breakfast. How wonderful!" he said, his merry eyes charming her all over again.

She smiled and nodded, then took a seat at the table bench, feeling like there were bubbles of lightness flowing through her chest while her heart beat loudly in her ears. To have him in her kitchen in the morning seemed so strange, yet it was lovely at the same time.

"Uh...grace?" she asked quickly when he lifted his fork, and then she was afraid that she must sound like a prude. But he merely lowered the fork with a warm smile.

"You're right...I was—uh—so pleased by the cake that I guess I forgot."

She smiled at the compliment and bowed her head along with him and then opened her eyes instinctively a few moments later to meet his gaze. She watched him as he took his first bite of cake and closed his eyes briefly in appreciation.

"Mmmmm-mmm," he murmured. "Baking this *gut* deserves a gift in return."

Before she knew it, he'd gotten to his feet and bent to gently kiss her cheek. He sat back down, and she sought frantically for something to say. *My first kiss!*

"*Danki*," she finally returned, dropping her gaze.

He reached across the table and caught her right hand in his. "You're quite welcome, sweet Tabby."

She nodded and tried to focus on managing her fork while she was sure her heart pounded in the palm of her hand, which nestled so easily and with such seeming perfection within his own.

CHAPTER 3

YOU MEAN YOU actually kissed her?" John was appalled at Rob's early morning revelation. Kissing was not an idle thing in his world, and although he knew his friend was a genial flirt, he still struggled with the idea of Tabitha Beiler being old enough to be out of school, let alone courting.

"Yep," Rob said smugly. "And I plan on doing it again soon."

John shook his head. "Kissing a girl is no small thing. Do you really think you would marry her? Are you ready for a *frau*? Because I still have my doubts."

Rob gave him a sunny smile. "Think what you like, my friend." He eased backward on a spindle set chair, and John caught him before he tipped too far.

"Stop fooling around, will you?"

John knew when Rob's quicksilver moods changed, and he was suddenly faced with a barrage of questions he didn't feel like answering.

"What's wrong, John? You're sour this morning, and although your personality doesn't exactly shine, you're not usually irritable...so what's up? Will you tell me?"

"No." John turned to some fencing pieces that needed whitewash and grabbed a brush.

"Why?" Rob asked patiently, and John suppressed a

groan. When he wanted to, Rob could weasel a secret out of a situation like nobody's business.

"I—I'm just restless, okay?" John finally said, trying to concentrate on stirring up the white paint.

"You need a wife."

John glared at his best friend and tormentor. "That is the last thing I need in all the world."

◌◌◌

Tabitha whistled cheerfully as she served *Aenti* Beth her breakfast. In truth, the very eggs she'd scrambled seemed as light and fluffy as clouds, and Tabitha fancied the bacon was even crispier and more tasty than usual. Being in love must make the very *weldt* taste better, she thought, then struggled to give attention to her *aenti's* gentle voice.

"Tabby, you look as you did when you were young and just *kumme* in from a run in the rain."

Tabitha knew her face flushed, but she met her *Aenti* Beth's eyes squarely, for courting must be kept a secret at all costs. Rob had seemed particular about that point when he'd left that morning, a piece of cake wrapped snug in his pocket.

"Remember, sweet—ours is a secret courtship. Not for any of the *aulder* folk to know." He'd smiled, and she could not help but nod in agreement. *He must surely have his reasons for stressing the matter.* She pushed the matter aside in her mind and sat up straight at attention when she realized that *Aenti* Beth was speaking again.

"Tabby, I'd like you to run some quilt squares over to *Frau* Miller's across the way. We're piecing a friendship quilt for Laura Mast—the family that's just moved into the district."

Tabitha's breath caught. *If I'm going to the Millers', I might have the chance to see Rob at work in the wood shop.*

"Tabby? Are you attending me at all?" *Aenti* Beth's voice was bemused.

"*Ya, ach, ya*, ma'am. I will go straight after I've cleaned up breakfast."

Her *aenti* sighed. "*Gut*…but the way you're acting, I hope you can remember the direction of the Millers' *haus*."

Tabitha smiled broadly. "How could I forget? It's as easy as pie."

Rob tried to concentrate on his work, but one taste of the chocolate cake he'd secured for a midmorning snack sent him reeling back to the moment his lips had grazed Tabby's smooth cheek. It was a memory to be cherished.

He whistled as he forced himself to focus on a particular piece of balustrade and was surprised to hear the shop door bang open with a sudden vehemence.

He looked up to see his *mamm* standing with her bonnet in disarray, a cloak haphazardly thrown over her shoulders.

He nearly bumped into John as they both moved in one accord toward the door, then John backed away.

"*Mamm*, what's wrong?" Rob asked, never having seen his mother so rattled.

"It's your *grossdaudi*, Rob. There's been a bad accident, and he's asking for you to *kumme*."

"To Ohio? Of course, but what—"

"I'll explain everything on the way home." She grasped his arm."We'll have to make preparations for you to go tomorrow morning. John, will you explain to your *daed* that Rob's not going to be able to work for a bit?"

"Sure...*ya.*"

Rob caught his friend's worried gaze, and a bolt of fear ran through his heart. His paternal grandfather was very dear to him and such an important part of his childhood. *Grossdaudi* had felt the loss of Rob's *fater*, his only son, as much as Rob himself, and as a child Rob had spent a good portion of every summer with his grandparents in Ohio, creating a special bond that his other cousins never shared.

He followed his *mamm* outside and helped her into the family buggy, then noticed the other buggy hitched nearby. He recognized the Beilers' horse, and suddenly Tabby was coming down the front porch steps. Rob made a quick turn and took a half step toward her. Then he remembered his mother's presence and found he could only tip his hat in farewell to the girl he was in love with.

❦

The sleet beat mercilessly upon the weathered roof of the old barn. John and Rob stood in the morning gloom of the interior, both tall and broad-shouldered in their dark Amish coats and hats.

"Will you watch over her?"

John heard the serious intent in his best friend's voice and knew the deep value of the request presented to him.

"*Ya*, I give my word, Rob. You need not worry."

"*Danki*. I know you will do as you say. You know that my *mamm* cannot abide Tabby for some reason, and our feelings for each other must be kept secret." He sighed aloud. "I should be going. The van is supposed to be here at nine."

"I hope your grandfather heals quickly. I will miss you." John spoke with quiet candor.

Rob nodded. "I feel the same, my friend. But you will have little time for missing me in watching over Tabby, I wager." He frowned slightly. "She grows more beautiful each day, and the *buwes* will be swarming this spring since she's old enough to marry." He lifted his gaze to John, vulnerability in his eyes. "I'm in love with her, John. Truly."

John clapped him on the shoulder. "Again, no worries. I'm sure that Tabitha is devoted to you." He felt a slight pang of jealousy, but dismissed it quickly, reminding himself that he didn't want or need the feelings of a girl. But still, Rob didn't know how blessed he was.

They turned in mutual accord as a white van sloshed to a sudden stop outside the open barn door. John stepped forward and caught Rob in a hearty hug, then moved away while Rob shouldered his knapsack. Rob trudged out through the mud puddles and got in.

John returned Rob's brief wave with one of his own and watched the van pull away, but his best friend's words and charge of responsibility echoed in John's mind. Then he told himself that he was being too serious. *After all, beautiful or not, how much trouble could one nineteen-year-old girl be?*

CHAPTER 4

Two Weeks Later

ROB EASED BACK in the hospital bedside chair and tried to concentrate on staying awake. It was late, and he should be heading back to his *grossdaudi*'s house, but the old man was sleeping and still needed to eat his supper, which was growing cold on the tray. Following the amputation of *Da's* right leg, he'd developed a blood clot and an infection—all of which made Rob figure the old man needed all the rest could get.

"I really need to wake him," a soft feminine voice sounded nearby.

Rob glanced up, then straightened abruptly in his chair as he gazed up into the beautiful face of the nurse. His eyes sought her badge and read "KATIE" in bold black print.

"Uh—yeah, sure," he stammered. "I only wanted to let him sleep because he was in so much pain earlier."

The red-headed English nurse blinked lightly made-up green eyes and smiled sympathetically. "I know. I read the chart when I came on at seven. He's due for some pain medicine soon, in fact."

Rob nodded. He'd gotten used to the parade of nurses in the past weeks, some pretty, some not so much, some kind and others apathetic, but this Katie seemed to especially tug on his senses. Then he remembered Tabby and ran a hand across his weary eyes. *I should have written to her by now.*

"You're tired," the young nurse whispered, lightly touching his shoulder for a moment. He wanted to shiver in response but blinked instead, automatically shaking his head in denial.

"*Nee*—I mean, no—I'm fine."

She smiled, a flash of white teeth behind moist, pink lips. "Why not go home, really? I promise I'll keep a close eye on your grandfather tonight."

He swallowed. "I'm sure you will. I—uh—maybe you're right. I could use a bit of rest." He stood up and discovered that the nurse nearly reached his shoulder in her well-fitting blue scrubs. She stepped back, and he bent unself-consciously to brush a kiss on his grandfather's warm forehead. Then he caught up his hat from the bedside table.

"Thank you," he muttered, slipping past her.

"You're quite welcome," she called gently as he left the room.

He walked down the familiar hospital hallway, then paused at the elevators. *I must write Tabby soon,* he decided. *As soon as I feel up to it.*

❧❧❦

Tabitha Beiler gazed with pleasure around the crowded kitchen and open sitting room of *Aenti* Beth's home; all of the youth seemed to be having a *gut* time at the Saturday evening singing. Even *Aenti* Beth, though aged and confined to her wheelchair, looked pleased as she offered a tray piled high with fresh raisin cookies and apple turnovers to the appreciative guests.

"*Ach*, Tabby, the singing goes well."

Tabitha turned to gaze with gratitude at Letty. "It is the first singing since Rob's gone away." She frowned. "February seems like such a long month."

"It's the shortest month of the year." Letty bit into a soft cookie.

"You know that's not what I meant." She sighed. "Still, I am glad for this time of togetherness. It keeps my mind busy. I do miss him so."

Letty reached out her short, plump arms to give Tabitha a hug. "*Ya*, I know it's been hard."

Tabitha cringed at the selfish pang in her heart. While it was difficult for her to be separated from Rob, she knew he had to be struggling, caring for his ill grandfather in Ohio. They were especially close, and Rob had been devastated when the news of his grandfather's accident had reached him.

"Have you heard from him?" Letty asked, before polishing off the rest of the cookie.

With a quick shake of her head, Tabitha replied, "Not yet. But I'm sure I will soon. He needs time to get settled. This isn't easy on him."

"It says much for your man's character that he went to care for him."

That made Tabitha brighten a bit, and not only because Letty had used such personal terms to describe her and Rob's relationship. Rob was loyal to his family and hadn't hesitated to be a help to his grandfather, despite having to take a leave of absence from his job. *And leaving me.* Yet such a man would make a good husband and a wonderful father.

Letty gave Tabitha a quick squeeze, then stepped back and smiled. "But soon, perhaps next winter, you will not have to miss him because you will be married."

Tabitha couldn't help the blush that stained her cheeks or the nerves assaulting her stomach. Courtship, then marriage. The very idea of being the girlfriend, then wife, of the oh-so-handsome and older Rob Yoder filled her with a mixture of anxiety and excitement, though Letty's words made her smile. "Meanwhile, we will find someone for you," she told her friend.

Letty laughed with good humor, making a gesture to her short, stout frame. "Me? I must catch a man through his stomach and then his heart, but you, with your blonde hair and eyes like a summer sky, will make one like Rob a happy man."

Tabitha opened her mouth to protest the compliment when she noticed a single Amish man slip in through the front door. She recognized the tall frame in its heavy black overcoat with dark hat and even darker hair, and thoughts spun in her head. Here was John Miller, Rob's best friend— *Ach, perhaps he's heard from Rob.* She knew that Rob shared everything with John—probably including talk of a romantic relationship with her. Yet John was a gentleman and known in the community as discreet.

But she was still surprised to see John tonight. She'd thought, at twenty-six to Rob's twenty-three, that he was a sworn bachelor, as he now rarely attended youth social events and in the previous year had made the subtle switch to sit with the bearded, married men in church. Yet here he was. Of course, he could have simply stopped by to pick up his younger siblings who were present. He probably bore no message from the one who made her heart beat hard in her throat.

She watched John hang up his coat and hat, then wend his way with easy grace through the welcoming crowd until he reached her *Aenti* Beth. He bent to greet the old woman. Tabitha would have joined them, but she felt a touch on her arm and looked round to see that Letty had disappeared and Henry Lantz, the tallest and one of the most attractive youths in the community, was standing near her.

"Tabby, you look well tonight in blue," he murmured with a smile. "Truth be told, you look well in anything." On the last word of his compliment the tops of his ears turned crimson.

She nodded her thanks as she watched him swallow. The words were nice, but she felt nothing but irritation at being detained. She planned to use the excuse of her hostess duties as an opportunity to greet John—and possibly secure news of Rob.

"It's supposed to snow tonight—*narrisch* weather," Henry went on with haste as if sensing her desire to be gone. "And there's no church service tomorrow. I was wondering if you would like to come with me on a sled ride. Might be one of the last of the season."

Tabitha's heart sank. Sledding was always fun, but she had no desire to give Henry Lantz a reason to think that she liked him. No one but John and Letty knew for sure that Rob and she were courting, but it was only right to keep that a secret.

"Well, I..." she began, only to be cut off by a deep masculine voice that for some strange reason sent a pleasant shiver down her spine.

"*Nee*, I fear she cannot go sledding with you, Henry."

She turned in slow amazement to stare up at John Miller. He had to have been watching her in order to know that Henry was asking her on a date. She continued to look up at him as he regarded her with steady blue eyes. Steady seemed to describe John perfectly.

"Tabitha, your *aenti* Beth, only a moment ago, gave me an invitation to dinner tomorrow. I'm sure she will need your help with the extra cooking and serving."

Tabitha felt the blood throb in her temples as hope grew within her. *Aenti* Beth was known for her hospitable nature, but inviting John for a meal was random, even for her. Had he wangled the invitation in hopes of imparting news about Rob? Personal news? Her heart did a tiny flip at the tantalizing thought. She sought to dismiss Henry as nicely as possible so that she might speak alone with John—she couldn't wait until tomorrow afternoon. She turned to nod at Henry, who, to his credit, looked suddenly like he'd rather be anywhere else. No doubt he was intimidated by John Miller due to John's older age and authoritative stance. She spread her hands helplessly. "I'm sorry, Henry, perhaps another time."

Henry gobbled an affirmative response, then slipped off into the crowd. Tabitha now turned back to John with a ready smile, eager to hear any word about the man she hoped to marry one day soon.

"John Miller, we shall have the pleasure of your company and..." She gathered her courage. "Was there—anything else?" She struggled not to reveal how anxious she was to have a word from Rob.

John kept his dark blue gaze on her, as if he were studying her—or taking her measure? Then he simply shook his head. "*Nee*, Tabitha. There is nothing more than to share a meal with you and your *aenti*."

Tabitha bit her lip in disappointment, and it took all of her composure to give him a demure nod. "Then if you'll excuse me, John, I have the apple cider to serve."

"*Ya*," he murmured. "I will see you tomorrow."

She slipped away, heading for the icebox. No word from Rob? Since he hadn't contacted her, shouldn't he at least have sent word to John? What did that mean for their relationship? Letty already had her married off—but little did her friend know that Tabitha was filled with doubt. Or perhaps this was how relationships worked. She wasn't exactly experienced. She sighed, her heart yearning for the man she loved. *Please, dear* Gott. *Calm my spirit...and whatever Rob is doing, I hope he is thinking of me.*

John watched Tabitha disappear into the crowd at the singing and felt like he'd run a mile in a sodden field. *It's a* gut *thing I came tonight—that Lantz kid could be a problem.*

He decided that he was addled with the burden of his promise to Rob and then realized that he'd lied to Tabitha in an effort to fend off the would-be affections of Henry Lantz. *That gangly upstart of a youth... now I'm going to have to get Beth Beiler to invite me to dinner.* He was confused by exactly how to go about this when a coy feminine voice spoke up behind him.

"John Miller?"

He turned to see Bishop Esch's daughter, Barbara, staring up at him with cool, narrowed, green eyes. She looked like a hawk that never lost its prey, and he had the sudden and sinking realization that coming here to check on Tabitha was also a signal to other single girls that he might be looking for a bride—which he definitely was not doing. He suppressed a groan as he tried to figure out how to extricate himself from Barbara's presence.

She wasn't making it easy. With quick steps she closed the space between them, standing so near he could count the stitches in the fabric of her *kapp.* "I overheard you talking to Tabby and that you plan on attending dinner here tomorrow," she said, her tone resembling a cat who'd finished off a bowl of cream. "But I wondered—I've heard you might have a new cutter sled and I thought, perhaps, if you're free tomorrow afternoon..." She trailed off suggestively.

Ach, how he wanted to run. But then it occurred to him that Barbara Esch might be a temporary useful cover to allow him to watch over Tabitha without things being too obvious. He assumed a cordial expression.

"*Ya,* Barbara, your company would be a pleasure, if the snow lays and if you like sledding."

A mischievous glint appeared in her eyes. "*Ya.* I like sledding very much."

He resisted the urge to cancel his hasty invitation. *This girl will probably eat me alive if I'm not careful, but my promise to Rob is worth the risk.*

"*Danki,* John." Barbara lifted her chin and smiled. "You may pick me up at two."

He nodded with grim satisfaction as she walked away, pausing to give him another cheeky smile over her shoulder. He let out a heavy breath and realized that watching over Tabitha might not be as easy as the proverbial pie. He turned and made his way back to Tabitha's *aenti,* determined to use all his methods of persuasion to successfully angle and secure an invitation to dinner.

❧

Elizabeth Beiler had only been treated to a taste of romance once in her life, but she still recognized when a man was after something. She looked up at John Miller, who had surprisingly—and insistently—invited himself over for dinner. Since the man seemed to want to come over with as much desperation as a working man wanted water, she wouldn't keep him waiting. "Of course we'd be happy to have you join us, John."

"*Danki*," he said, then cleared his throat. "What time should I arrive?"

"Noon will be fine."

He nodded in almost visible relief, then slipped off through the crowd.

Elizabeth smiled to herself as she watched him walk away. Then she glanced at her niece. *Ach*, Tabitha. Her niece was beautiful in both frame and spirit, and John Miller was a fine man, to be sure. She shouldn't be caught off guard that he was interested in Tabby—except his committed bachelor status was well known. What was he up to? She supposed she'd find out tomorrow.

She navigated her chair through the crowd and glanced thoughtfully up at the recipe box on a shelf in the pretty kitchen. She'd made a vow once, to the woman who'd raised her, to only give the secret of the box to a girl in true love with a man of devout character. Would that couple be Tabitha and John? The pairing had never crossed her mind, but God often worked in unexpected ways.

"We will see," she murmured aloud, then reached to fill her tray once more.

CHAPTER 5

MATT, I CAN'T explain. I need the sled—only for a few hours." John struggled to keep his voice down as he pleaded with his younger *bruder*; he had no desire for the rest of the family to hear.

But Matt, usually quiet and passive at twenty years of age, seemed in no mood to bargain. He lounged on his bed with a smug expression and shook his head at everything John tried. "*Nee*, John, that sled is a fine piece of craftsmanship. I've worked on it for months. I might even sell it. But only the truth will get you a ride in it today."

John gritted his teeth but remained silent. The truth…lately it seemed that he'd not been hanging on to that value.

Matt smiled. "Could it be, big *bruder*, that you've finally found a girl worthy of you—because that would be sweet information to know."

"Girl? What *maedel*? Who are you talking about?" Esther Miller appeared in the doorway, her eyes wide with curiosity.

John wanted to knock his head against the door frame. His twenty-two-year-old sister was moody, loud, and extremely nosy. Now there was no escape from either of his siblings. They would pester him until he told them what they wanted to know. But he felt strongly that he could not betray the promise he'd made to Rob, so he'd have to choose another way out of the mess.

"All right," he ground out. "I asked Barbara Esch to go sledding today at two. Are you both happy?"

"*Nee!*" His siblings sounded off in unison. Matt sat up on the bed, and Esther pulled John into the room and closed the door behind them.

"John, are you *narrisch*?" Matt asked. "That girl is a pit viper. She's well and tried to get me to take her sledding already."

"*Ya*, John," Esther echoed worriedly. "Barbara may be the bishop's daughter, but she gossips, chases all the men, tells—"

"Enough," John snapped. He knew better than anyone what Barbara was about. He also knew she was a means to an end. "Can I take the sled or not?"

Matt sighed and shook his head. "Take it. But trust me, you're making a mistake."

John's shoulders relaxed. He'd obtained his goal. But that didn't mean he was happy. Forcing enthusiasm into his voice, he said, "Great, *danki*."

Then he moved past his sister and escaped into the hall before more comments could follow.

Tabitha gave a last glance at the wind-up clock on the frosty kitchen windowsill and adjusted her apron with a discreet pull. For some reason she didn't even want her beloved *aenti* Beth to know how nervous she was about having John come for dinner. She was still trying to decipher why he'd wanted to come over and decided during the night that perhaps John wanted to speak to her about Rob in a more quiet and discreet manner. Which was kind of him, to say the least. If she was wrong and he had nothing to say, she'd also resolved to ask him herself if he had news of Rob. She was growing impatient.

"Might as well mash the potatoes, Tabby. I've never known John Miller to be anything but on time. And I am sure supper will be delicious as always. You are gifted in the kitchen, far more than I am."

Aenti Beth's sweet voice broke into her thoughts, and Tabitha realized once again how grateful she was for her *aenti*'s gentle and encouraging spirit. As usual she had surmised Tabitha's disquiet, and with a few words had settled her nerves, enough that Tabitha could set her hand to mashing the potatoes with butter and milk and salt until her arm ached but the spuds rose light and fluffy in the bowl, with not a lump to be found. And then, right on the hour, John knocked at the front door and entered.

Tabitha watched him step out of his large, snowy boots on the rug beside the door. He removed his coat and hat and hung them on a nearby peg rack. He was wearing an aqua green shirt that went well with his dark hair. When he turned to greet her and *Aenti* Beth, he smiled, a flash of white teeth in his cold-flushed face.

"Ladies, a *gut* afternoon. And thank you both for having me." He came forward and bent to kiss *Aenti* Beth's cheek, then nodded to Tabitha.

She realized that she still held the potato masher. More importantly she realized she'd been staring at him. Quickly she dropped the masher in the sink, too embarrassed and confused to look at him directly. She picked at an imaginary speck of lint on the tablecloth, still averting her gaze. How could she find John Miller attractive when her heart belonged to Rob? The thought confused her.

Flustered, she finally forced herself to look up at him and return his smile. "Dinner's hot and ready," she invited.

Without prompting, John moved to wheel *Aenti* Beth to her place at the table. "Can I help you with anything?" John asked Tabitha.

"*Nee*," Tabitha hurriedly replied, not liking to think of what his proximity might do to her resolve to wait until after dinner to speak with him about Rob. Be patient. Unfortunately patience had never been one of her virtues. She forced herself to focus on serving the meal instead.

As it was, under *Aenti* Beth's approving eyes, she managed to present the stuffed meatloaf, mashed potatoes, gravy, corn off the cob, and cucumber relish with relative ease. She'd save the pumpkin pie to have later with the coffee. She took her place next to *Aenti* Beth at the table, John directly across from her. They all bowed for the traditional twenty-one seconds of silent grace before beginning to eat.

"My compliments, ladies," John smiled after a few moments. "Everything is *wunderbar*."

Tabitha was pleased by his words, but it didn't calm the nerves in her belly. She looked down at her plate; she'd barely touched her own food.

"*Ya*," *Aenti* Beth spoke into the silence. "I am training Tabby so that whoever she marries will not want for *gut* cooking."

Tabitha gave John a swift sidelong glance and decided

she surely must have imagined the tightening of his sculpted jaw at her *aenti*'s mention of a future husband.

"That may be true," he agreed. "But Tabitha, as all girls, must choose wisely and has much time to decide."

"Perhaps I've already decided," Tabitha murmured without thinking, then could have bitten her tongue for the comment. Aenti *Beth doesn't know about Rob...mainly because of his insistence on keeping everything so secret.*

"Do tell," John said with apparent ease.

"*Ya*," *Aenti* Beth said dryly. "Share with us."

"A silly comment," Tabitha returned, reaching for the corn. "I meant—maybe I know the type of man I wish to marry."

"Ahh," John nodded. "I see."

Tabitha sought to turn the attention from herself and smiled at John. "And what of you, John Miller, what type of girl would you marry?"

She was surprised to see a faint flush stain his cheeks as he gripped his glass with long, white-tipped fingers.

"I do not intend to marry."

Aenti Beth clucked sympathetically. "A loss, John Miller, to some woman's life—I'm sure."

Tabitha watched him shrug.

"As it may be."

He asked for the bread and Tabitha handed it to him. "I wondered, John, if I might have a moment of your time after dinner today to talk..." She went on hastily at his raised eyebrow. "There's um—something not quite right with the buggy in the barn."

She knew she'd have to repent later of the fib, but she

wanted to talk to him about Rob so much that she could taste it better than her dinner.

"As it is," John spoke, glancing down at his plate then straight at her with his deep blue eyes. "I'll be escorting Barbara Esch this afternoon in a sledding outing, so I have little time for talking. Perhaps I can come back later to check on the buggy."

Tabitha raised her own brow and sniffed at the polite dismissal. "Determined not to marry yet escorting Barbara Esch—somehow I wonder how the two matters go hand in hand."

"Tabby!" *Aenti* Beth interjected. "John's life is not ours to question."

Her aunt was right, of course. In her disappointment that John had no news of Rob, she'd spoken without thinking. "Excuse me," Tabitha said, then pushed back from the table.

"Tabitha," John said. Did she imagine it, or was his voice touched with a trace of concern?

"I need to get the pumpkin pie." She rushed to the pantry, which fortunately shielded her from John and her aunt's possible searching eyes. Tears burned as she lifted her apron to press hard against them. She missed Rob so much that it hurt.

CHAPTER 6

J OHN SIGHED TO himself as he hitched his horse outside Bishop Esch's house. *It's a wonder the over-eager
Barbara isn't waiting on the porch.* He pushed aside
the uncharitable thought and rallied himself to knock on
the front door. The wood was flung open with enough
verve to make him take an automatic step back, and he
looked down ruefully into Barbara's sparkling green eyes.
Yep, definitely too eager.

Then he assumed a polite smile and slipped his black
hat off. "Barbara, it's a pleasure to see you looking so—
well this afternoon."

The girl visibly preened and widened the door. "John
Miller, *sei se gut kumme* in and say hello to *Mamm* and
Daed."

John hesitated. It might be paranoid on some level, but
he had no desire to appear as though he was formally
meeting her parents, yet he could think of no ready excuse
to decline. He followed her swinging skirt into the cozy
kitchen and nodded to *Frau* Esch and the bishop, unsure
of what exactly to say.

Barbara's rather rotund *mamm* scurried over to put
an arm around her daughter, and John suddenly saw the
innate resemblance between the two women. *Both way too
eager. Great.*

"John Miller, will you have a fresh piece of apple pie?" *Frau* Esch inquired with a faint simper. "Barbara just made it herself."

"*Ach, nee. Danki.* I've just *kumme* from the Beilers and Tabitha made pumpkin—"

Barbara suddenly pulled from her *mamm* to link an insinuating arm through his. "Now, now. Let's not worry over apple pie nor speak of dinners had, *Mamm.* John, don't you want to get going?"

"Uh, certainly. Bishop—a *gut* day to you," John said and received a faintly amused expression back from the community leader.

"I'd wager it's you, John, who'll have to keep an eye out to the goodness of your day," the old man said with dry humor. "My *dochder* can talk a man's ear off when she has a mind to..."

John ignored the frown *Frau* Esch threw her husband and turned with Barbara clinging to him like a limpet. He was glad when they were outside in the cold air, and he hastily assisted her into the sleigh.

Matt's cutter sled was built for a tight twosome fit, and John found himself trapped by the proximity of Barbara Esch and her rather cloying scent of lemon.

"*Ach*, John. What a beautiful day, and you manage the horse so well. What's his name?"

"Hmm? Oh—Tudor." He realized that he wasn't talking enough to be polite, but he couldn't get away from the thought that Tabitha had somehow been upset at the end of dinner. *Maybe I should have delayed meeting Barbara and talked with her...I'll go back later.*

The roads were indeed both snowy and treacherous, but John had driven a cutter sled since the age of nine.

"John, look at the frosted tree limbs. Let's stop for a minute," Barbara whispered.

No, thank you. "*Nee*, Barbara, I think the roads are not as safe as they should be to take a lady driving. I think we'd best head back." *And I will go see what troubles Tabitha— even as to her safety I should guard—and if there's something wrong with the buggy.*

He set Tudor into faster motion, ignoring the poorly contained huff from his companion, and realized that he'd never forgive himself if there was a buggy accident that he might have prevented. *What* en der weldt *would I say to Rob?*

⚬⚬⚬

Rob entered the hospital room in the bright afternoon to find his grandfather's bed empty. He turned to go to the nurse's station to ask where the old man was, trying to ignore the faint feeling of unease that he had. *Suppose something has happened worse to Da?*

He exited the room with determination, only to run smack into a tall female form. He caught her before she could fall and set her easily on her feet. Then he looked down into Katie Girton's sparkling green eyes. "Where is my grandfather?" he asked, trying to keep a calm tone.

Katie gave him a reassuring pat on the arm. "He's all right, Rob. They've taken him down for a CAT scan."

"He's making progress, then?"

The sparkle in her eyes dimmed a bit. "Yes. Some. A

little slower than we had anticipated." Then she smiled again. "But progress is progress."

Rob sank down on the edge of the bed, relieved. Earlier this morning *Da* had opened his eyes and tried to speak. But the words were garbled, and he'd drifted back to sleep. *Da* was in his late seventies, but Rob wasn't ready to lose him. He *couldn't* lose him.

He looked up at Katie and blinked. "I'm—uh—surprised to see you here. I thought you were only on at night."

The truth was that he was glad she was here. The other nurses were kind and did their job well. But there was something special about Katie. They had a connection, but not a romantic one, which was new territory for him. He'd never had a girl that he thought of as a friend. Girls were desirable to flirt with and date, and in Tabby's case, court, but never anything platonic. Yet since he'd spent so much time at his grandfather's bedside, he'd appreciated Katie's professional and compassionate nature. *Not to mention she is quite pretty.* All of this ran through his mind in a second, and he thought with faint remorse of Tabby Beiler. He'd dashed a card off to John, wondering if he should mention Katie. Then he decided against it. They were only friends—actually more like friendly acquaintances. Thus he said nothing about the nurse he looked forward to seeing each night.

"I had to take a different shift. My daughter was sick. Your grandfather is just down the hall for some tests."

"*Ach*, okay. Your daughter? I mean..." He swallowed hard. "I didn't know you were married."

She gave him a visibly determined smile and shook her

head. "I'm not. My husband died in a car accident a year ago."

A rush of emotion welled up in Rob as he realized how hard it must be to be a single mother and working full-time. At least with the Amish, the community usually helped out. "I'm sorry," he said, feeling inadequate to the moment.

"So am I. But we're carrying on. We don't have a choice." Katie smiled at him again. "Do you want a chocolate pudding or a turkey sandwich? The lunch cart had extras."

He tried to mentally shift gears to the mundane talk of food and felt off balance inside. "Um, yeah, sure. Pudding will be fine. Chocolate pudding, please."

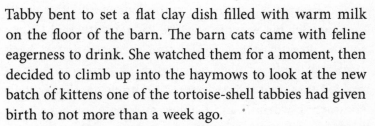

Tabby bent to set a flat clay dish filled with warm milk on the floor of the barn. The barn cats came with feline eagerness to drink. She watched them for a moment, then decided to climb up into the haymows to look at the new batch of kittens one of the tortoise-shell tabbies had given birth to not more than a week ago.

She had her foot on the second rung of the ladder when the barn door slid open and John Miller stood there.

She kept on climbing, deciding that he probably had no word from Rob and had come to inspect the buggy instead. Either that, or perhaps Barbara needed another buggy rug to warm her.

"Tabitha?" His deep voice halted her near the top, and she glanced down as he strode forward across the hay-strewn floor, sidestepping the purring cats.

"What is it, John? I thought you were sledding with Barbara."

"I was, but then I recalled your mention of the buggy. I saw Barbara home and had some time, so if you'd care to show me…"

Tabitha took a quick breath and hung her head, then lifted it a moment later. *I'd best tell him the truth.* "Do you want to see the new kittens?" She gained the loft floor and took a slight step back to turn and stare down at him in the half light of the open barn door.

"*Nee.* I came back because I thought you might be unsafe…you or your *aenti* Beth." He sounded faintly exasperated, and she turned toward the hay mows, walking out of his line of vision and searching for the words to tell him the truth.

She heard his footsteps on the ladder and the wood creak under his weight, and she sought with rapid steps for the litter of kittens. She found them, in the far back corner, a nestling, mewling mass of pink, rough tongues, padded toes, and pointy ears. She put her hand over their comforting warmth and listened as John approached, his boots crunching through the hay.

"Tabitha, what are you about?" he asked.

She cuddled closer to the kittens thinking of the warmth of Rob's hand on hers and sighed. "I miss him so much, and I had hoped…" Her voice shook a bit. "I had hoped that you might have some word from Rob to give me, so I lied about the buggy. There…hate me or tell Rob he's courting a liar." She looked over her shoulder in defiance but realized that she must sound an utter child to him. But to her surprise,

John moved in the gloom above her, then sank down on his haunches on the other side of the kittens.

He sighed, and she could faintly see him reach a hand to rub at the back of his neck, as if he had a headache—that she'd given him.

⤳⤳

John took his time responding to her. He admired her courage in admitting to the lie, and he also understood her wanting to hear from Rob. Finally he said softly, "I think a liar is someone who cannot speak the truth, which you did. I did have a postcard from Rob but no mention of you...I'm sorry, but I'm sure he's fully occupied with his grandfather."

John tried to push aside the vivid memory of the tersely written post card he'd had from Rob not more than two days before. *Surely he should have written to Tabitha as well. Perhaps her card was lost in the mail.* He idly reached down to stroke the kittens, and his fingers came in contact with Tabitha's. He jerked his hand back as if he'd touched hot coals, then rose to his feet.

"I'm glad there's nothing wrong with the buggy. Let me know if I can help you out anytime with that sort of thing. And I will keep you posted about Rob." He started to walk away, unsure of why he'd reacted the way he did when her warm fingers met his but not willing to dwell on the matter—even though his hand strangely tingled as if a jolt of electricity had passed through them.

He'd reached the ladder when he heard her faint sob, and he froze.

"Tabitha?" he said her name tentatively, hoping he was mistaken in what he heard. *Maybe one of the kittens had a big mouth.*

But then it came again—a faint, womanly sob and a sure sniff. He sighed and turned back to walk across the hay.

"Tabitha?"

"Please—*sei se gut, geh*, John. I'm fine. Only missing Rob, as I'm sure you can understand." Her voice was strained.

He stuffed his hands in his pockets. "I do miss Rob, sure to say. We—well, we've been friends since we were *kinner.* I actually remember helping him learn to walk, I was six to his three. *Derr Herr* has truly blessed me with Rob's friendship. He is a *gut* man." *A gut man who's gotten me in a tangled position between the truth and a pile of lies, but then, Rob's always had the tendency to get into a bit of trouble and try to drag me into it with him. Maybe this time, he's succeeded.*

He broke from his thoughts, relieved to hear that she had ceased sobbing and must have taken comfort in his words.

"*Ya,*" she agreed softly, dreamily. "A very *gut* man."

John turned to go once more when she whispered his name.

"John?"

"*Ya?*"

"*Danki*...for speaking of Rob."

"You are most welcome."

John felt like he'd handled the situation as best he could and determined he'd write to Rob and perhaps tell him how much Tabitha missed him, though he didn't want to burden his friend when he was helping his ailing grandfather. *Perhaps best to say nothing at all.*

Decided, he climbed down the loft ladder and let the now sated cats twine about his legs for a moment before heading to the barn door and sliding it closed.

CHAPTER 7

OR *AENTI* BETH silence was of infinite value, as it was to many of the Old Order Amish of Paradise. But this evening Tabitha chafed under the restriction of a silent half hour during prayer time. Instead she felt as though she wanted to sing with memories of Rob's curling hair, brown eyes, and *ach*, his merry deep laugh. She couldn't help smiling at the thought, and even when *Aenti* Beth cleared her throat to signal the end of silent reflection, Tabitha kept her head bowed while she smiled in fond recollection.

"Tabby?" her *aenti* said gently, and Tabitha nearly jumped in her chair.

"*Ach*, sorry, *Aenti* Beth."

"Do your thoughts wander far afield tonight?"

"*Ya*, you might say so."

"Hmmm...I noticed John Miller back here this afternoon. Was everything as it should be?"

At the mention of John Miller and the thought of her brazen admittance to lying, Tabitha felt her cheeks flush. "Y—*ya, aenti*, all is well. He just came back to check on the buggy, as I'd asked him to."

"That's *gut*. John Miller deserves for things to *geh* well in his life. He may well do himself a blessing to court the bishop's daughter, after what happened with Phoebe Graber."

Tabitha nodded, barely listening, then something

intuitively pricked her consciousness and she sat up straighter in her chair. "Why? What happened with Phoebe Graber?"

"Hmmm?" *Aenti* Beth raised a gray brow. "*Ach*, never mind, it reflects poorly on me to speak of the past and to gossip at that." She stretched to pat Tabitha's hand. "Let us allow the past its silence, as we should, Tabby. Will you *kumme* and help me get ready for bed?"

Tabitha nodded obediently and rose to push her *aenti*'s wheelchair into the master bedroom on the ground floor. It was a room of sweetness and light, having a bright pink and green Christmas Roses quilt on the double bed and *Aenti* Beth's Bible and her book of martyrs carefully placed on an oaken stand near her bedside, within easy reach. Then a bone-white bowl and pitcher stood on a dresser, not for water, but so that Tabitha might roam far to bring her lame *aenti* samplings from the flowers and plants of the field, during all the seasons. This evening there were sprigs of evergreen and the last of the winter holly berries. She couldn't wait to replace them in the spring with yellow daffodils, which she always carefully bolstered up in the pitcher with wet moss. Still, the evergreen gave off a spicy-sweet scent that *Aenti* Beth enjoyed.

Tabitha helped her into bed, then bent to receive the kiss and hug she'd been given for as long as she could remember, the dear elderly arms stretching to encompass her.

"*Gut nacht*, child," *Aenti* Beth murmured, and Tabitha softly returned the words and then drifted out of the room, closing the door behind her.

⮑◉⮐

Elizabeth reached for her Bible, then simply closed her eyes in prayer. Her legs, a gift from *Derr Herr* since her birth, ached a bit, though she knew it was mere phantom pain and not proof that they wouldn't support her small frame. She sighed aloud, knowing that Tabby seemed burdened, and then she herself had nearly told of John Miller's past with the beautiful and reckless Phoebe Graber. Elizabeth could remember the errant girl's face and the times she'd noticed during supervising various youth activities that Phoebe had flirted with John.

Ach, Gott, *perhaps I should have spoken to her about it then*—she broke off the direction of her thoughts and refocused on Tabby—*when I die, Gott, you know this* haus *must go to my* bruder *and he—with his meanness—is hardly likely to provide her a happy home. Ach, please let me be able to share the secret with her before I pass from this life*—

She continued to pray softly until she felt the pull of sleep wash over her in gentle, soothing waves.

⮑◉⮐

Tabitha normally would have sought her own bed on the second floor after prayers, but tonight she felt keyed up and restless. She wandered out onto the front porch and gazed up at the star-strewn night sky. It brought some comfort to know that Rob was under the same celestial blanket as she, no matter how far away he was. Then she began to pray softly, her heart aching.

"Dear *Gott*, have mercy on Rob and on his *grossdaudi*, and I ask that You would give me grace to wait patiently for word from him. *Ach, Fater, sei se gut,* help him to know that I long for his presence, and may all things work out for Your glory."

She felt peace with the last of her words and slipped back inside to seek her humble bed.

⌘

Later that night, after he'd sat with his grandfather until the man had fallen asleep, Rob returned to an empty house. His grandmother had died several years ago, and his grandfather had refused to move from his childhood home to live with any of his daughters. The man was as stubborn as an oak tree root, but Rob wouldn't have him any other way.

Days and evenings spent at the hospital were taking a toll, and Rob sat down wearily at the desk in his grandfather's bedroom and quickly wrote a few bland sentences on a generic postcard to Tabby Beiler. It was all he could muster tonight. After the brief missive was complete, he did something he rarely found himself doing. He started to pray—for his grandfather, for peace, for wisdom, and then, sweetly unbidden, for Katie Girton that her life would be easier and for blessings on her daughter.

His eyes flew open, and he found himself not sitting but with his cheek resting against Tabby's card. At some point during his prayers he'd fallen asleep. He lifted his head, pulled the card that was stuck on his face, and tossed it on the desk. He'd address it in the morning. Right now, all he wanted to do was go upstairs and get some sleep.

❧❧❧

John sat in his room at his desk and tried to concentrate on a rather difficult verse from his Bible—"Behold, I make all things new..." *It's something to consider given the fact that there is no way things with Phoebe Graber could ever be made new.*

He sighed aloud at his thoughts, unsure why the idea of Phoebe had come up—it had been long ago, when he'd been nineteen—the same age as Tabitha.

He half startled as his door burst open and Matt barged in to make himself comfortable on John's bed.

"So, how'd it go?"

"What?" John asked, tiredly rubbing his eyes and closing his Bible as he glanced sideways at Matt.

"The sledding...I take it you survived without having any marriage banns called?"

John frowned at his younger *bruder* and spoke with a determined stiffness. "Barbara is..."

"Is what?" Matt's brow lifted curiously.

"She, uh, has—beautiful eyes."

"*Ya*, like a cobra's—mesmerizing." Matt grinned.

John suppressed the smile that came to his own lips when there was a knock on his door and Esther slipped inside.

"I'm sorry to intrude, John, but I had to know how it went."

"Barbara has beautiful eyes," Matt mimicked and John shook his head.

"I said that, *ya*, but..."

"*Ach*, John." Esther sat down next to Matt. "You don't really plan to marry her, do you?"

"Marriage?" John twisted in his desk chair. "Who said anything about marriage? One sled ride and I'm marrying her, why..." He broke off and realized he'd almost revealed his reason for staying close to Barbara Esch, but he did not want to betray Rob under any circumstances. He knew the reason Rob was so intent on such secrecy about his relationship with Tabby and the fact that it had to do with his disapproving mother. In fact, he thought on impulse, perhaps he could help Rob's mother to see the value of Tabitha and help Rob out a bit while he was gone.

Matt groaned. "Now you're thinking. Have mercy. I could not abide Barbara Esch as my sister-in-law."

"Everyone has value in *Gott*'s sight, whether you can abide them or not," John chided. "And right now, I'd value some sleep. So out you two."

He watched his siblings reluctantly leave, and then he sought the comfort of his narrow bed, meditating on *Gott*'s Word and His promise to "make all things new," until he fell into a deep, restless sleep.

CHAPTER 8

As MARCH FINALLY made its appearance, Tabitha rejoiced in an early morning walk. The snow was melting fast, and it wouldn't be long before she would see her white, yellow, and purple crocuses springing up from the slushy ground. She clasped her hands together in thankfulness and looked out over the area that was to be her and *Aenti* Beth's kitchen garden. Then she looked back to the ground and dug the toe of her sensibly soled shoe into the ground and felt it give. Not enough to plant, but in a couple of weeks she should be able to put the first of the cold-weather crops into the ground.

Making a mental list of her spring chores helped keep her from fretting over not hearing from Rob. *I'm really getting to the point of frustration with Rob, even though I am so in love with him. But I simply cannot understand why he hasn't at least written.* She spun round, putting aside her thoughts, and ran into the house, careful to slip her muddy shoes off first.

"*Aenti* Beth, I'm going to finish planning the kitchen garden today." Tabitha swooped to press a kiss on her *aenti*'s rose petal-like cheek, then went to the desk and snatched up a rudimentary drawing she and *Aenti* Beth had done some weeks past when they'd been looking through seed catalogs and planning the garden. She had some final touches to add to the sketch. She spent the next few minutes modifying the drawing.

"Does this look all right?" She handed her *aenti* the paper and waited with suppressed excitement while the older woman studied the neat drawing.

"*Ya*, Tabby, it will do—but mind you're gentle with the deer tongue and oak leaf salad greens as always, child."

Tabitha nodded. "I will be." She grabbed her coat from the peg near the kitchen door.

"Where are you off to now?"

"To the green*haus*."

Her *aenti* smiled. "Have a *gut* time."

Tabitha went to the rather long greenhouse that she kept up during the winter and began to survey the plants, organizing the stoutest ones and adding a little fertilizer and water to the ones that had struggled to grow during the winter. She went to the work shed and gathered a shovel and trowel, put them in her pull wagon, and dragged it over the slushy snow back to the greenhouse. It was busy-work, and something she could have done when planting time actually arrived, but she had to keep herself occupied.

Then she went to the garden. Right now it was covered with damp snow, but she could visualize what it would look like by the end of the month. She could practically feel the cold dirt beneath the soles of her boots, remembering how refreshing it was to go barefoot after the long winter. She surveyed the garden plot. She would plant the salad greens first, mindful of her *aenti*'s instructions, then add bibb and ruby leaf lettuces. After that she would focus on green onions and radish plants.

Perhaps Rob could help her with the planting this year.

Her mood dimmed, and she went back to the greenhouse. He was never far from her thoughts, which intensified her impatience. She tried to focus on the section of the greenhouse that held the plants she would put in once the danger of frost had completely passed—or as *Aenti* Beth liked to time it, "Once the last killing frost follows the last full moon in May." Tabitha wasn't sure how much her *aenti* believed in traditional wisdom, but it did seem to make sense and have accord with how *Derr Herr* conducted the weather. At this point she wondered if Rob would even be back in May.

She silently chastised herself. He was taking care of his grandfather. A noble cause to be sure. Here she was, healthy and with very little care in the world, save for her yearning for Rob. Her thoughts were pitiful and childish.

Taking a deep breath, she calmed herself and gently stroked the bell pepper plant leaves stretching toward the morning sun coming in through the plastic roof. Suddenly she felt a brief peace in her heart. Her only memory of her *mamm* and *daed* was centered around budding plants—she must have barely been three, but she could remember her *mamm*'s gentle fingers showing her a plant and her *fater*'s deep laugh somewhere in the background. Soon after, they had both succumbed to the influenza, leaving Tabitha homeless but for the gentle love and kindness of *Aenti* Beth.

Tabitha sighed aloud as she stopped before the old crackle painted dresser where she kept her seeds. No matter how long ago it had been, every so often she missed her parents. She pushed her sad thoughts away and concentrated on the packets of heirloom seeds: tomatoes, green beans, zucchini, sweet corn, and melons. Ach, Gott *has given us so much to be thankful for.* She grew more cheerful, and she went on to organize the seed packets with grateful fingers.

⤫

As she watched Tabitha bustle about the yard and greenhouse, busying herself with the early spring chores, Elizabeth longed for the time when she was young and her *grossmuder* had allowed her out of her chair to pull herself along the fresh earth to help with the planting. No one thought it odd or called her strange as the mud seeped through the front of her work dress, and it gave Elizabeth the fun privilege of feeling like she was an especial part of *Gott's* nature, like a worm or a caterpillar.

She remembered the clean, fresh smell of the ground, the sight of the tips of burgeoning baby grass, and the sound of the blue swallows as they swooped past, looking for a stray seed. But Elizabeth was always careful, especially with pumpkin seeds, to see that each was planted tip down in its little mound of earth. Later she was allowed to elbow among the growing, scratchy vines and leaves, careful to study and treat each green bulb with careful reverence as she explored the baby pumpkins.

Now she smiled to herself as she thought of being an old woman and what neighbors might think if she took to dragging herself along the ground, but the activity had taught her both exuberance and humility, and she was glad to share the love of the garden with her niece.

She pushed aside the nudging thoughts of what might happen to Tabby in the future with Fram, Beth's *bruder*, due to inherit the small place. Then she sighed and concentrated on the sweetness of the moment, knowing *Gott* would have His will.

⚜

John headed out to the family woodworking shop soon after breakfast. His *daed*, Dan, was already there, polishing a burled elm veneer for a piano that an *Englisch* customer wanted.

"Sleeping in, *sohn*?" his *fater* teased in his normal, jovial way.

John smiled in return, knowing the *gut* humor of the big, barrel-chested man who had such a light hand with woodworking and a light heart along with it.

"*Ya*, though I did hear Matt snoring…"

They both laughed, each knowing Matthew's penchant to work far into the early hours of the morning and then stagger out to the shop with only a few hours' sleep.

John picked up a small lathe and ran a practiced finger down its edge. "Do you want me to start those spindle-back chairs, *Daed*, or—" He broke off as a red sports car wheeled into the slushy, muddy driveway, its tires spewing the wet earth everywhere. "Looks like we have an early customer," John murmured with a faint frown. It wasn't that he minded *Englisch* customers—in truth, the shop would not flourish as it did without them. But John didn't appreciate the sometimes high-handed attitude that some of the younger *Englischers* seemed to possess, and the young man who got out of the car looked like such a fellow.

Still, John followed his *fater*'s actions and walked forward with a smile, even if it was a bit forced.

"What can we do for *ya*?" His *daed* asked pleasantly of the lanky youth who had long dirty blond hair and a sullen expression.

"You got any plants started yet? My mother sent me out—she's more than a pain since she's gotten older, you know what I mean?"

"No," John said flatly, ignoring the warning wink his *daed* gave him.

"Well, we're a woodworking outfit, but if you go down the road a mile on the right and ask real nice for Tabby Beiler, she's likely to have something growing in her greenhouse. Although it is early to start planting."

The young man shrugged. "I just do what she tells me."

He'd started back to his car when John was struck by the sudden image of Tabitha being enticed into taking a ride in the red car—*I can just see her, kapp off, long, blonde hair flying in the wind like lit sunlight, and Rob would absolutely never forgive me if she actually—* "Ah, Daed…I mean, hey—buddy—I'll ride down the road with you if you'd like," John called. "Might be that she'll give you a better deal if a neighbor was along."

The blond youth shrugged. "Whatever. But don't muddy up the car any more than you have to."

John put down the lathe and glanced briefly at his *daed*.

"Being kind to strangers, John? Hmmm…I'll have to tell your *mamm*; she'll be pleased."

"Right," John mumbled, then hurried off to slide into the passenger side of the red car. He'd barely gained his seat when the kid took off at breakneck speed.

"You might want to slow down at bit," John said laconically. "There's a cow crossing ahead."

"What?" The brakes were applied with fervor, and John caught the dashboard with one hand. "Dude," the *Englischer* exclaimed. "How can you stand to live out here?"

"I manage. Turn here." John indicated the narrow dirt road and the Beilers' weather-beaten mailbox. *I'll have to do something about that mailbox post—I'm sure Rob would if he were here.*

The *Englisch* kid let out a low whistle of appreciation as they came in sight of the house and clotheslines. John saw that Tabitha was stretching out a clothesline between two oak trees. He noticed her trim form was complemented by her pinned apron.

"That's a fine-looking Amish girl, dude. Maybe it wouldn't be so bad to live out here after all." He turned to grin at John, who frowned faintly, confused by the surge of anger that pulsed through him.

John was not given to temper, nor was physical violence the way of his people. But right now he felt he could easily wring the kid's neck and take pleasure in the doing.

"I'd calm down—er, dude," John said. "If you expect to get any plants."

"You dating her?"

"No," John snapped, appalled.

"All right, calm down. I thought you Aim-ish were supposed to be all Zen-like and not flip out."

John's frown deepened as Tabitha began to cross to the car. "I am not flipping out."

"Whatever." The young man opened the car door, and John quickly followed suit, in time to see Tabitha smile shyly in greeting.

Why is she smiling at some Englisch *kid when she should*

be missing Rob? John broke off in his thoughts when he saw the circles beneath her blue eyes and realized she was smiling for show and nothing more.

⤳⦶⦵

Tabitha tried to contain her enthusiasm at seeing John; she simply knew he must have word of Rob by now. She gave a brief, absent nod to the *Englisch* youth, then turned to gaze up into John's blue eyes. But his dark brows were furrowed and he made a slight motion with his head, as if warning her off. She stopped, confused, until she realized he must be waiting to speak with her in private.

"Hiya, sweetheart."

She looked up at the *Englischer*, suppressing a feeling of distaste when the young man took out a cigarette pack with his free hand. She glanced at John, who crossed his arms over his chest and gave her a faint shrug.

"There's no smoking on this farm," she said quickly, in pleasant tones. "It's too dangerous with all of the baby grasses."

"Aw—right."

"Can I—help you both with something?" she asked, looking briefly once more in John's direction.

John sighed and heaved his big frame off the car where he'd been leaning. "Uh, Tabitha, our friend here would like to buy some early seedlings for his mother—that is, if you have any ready."

"Tony," the *Englischer* supplied his name, making an awkward sidestep when Tabitha headed directly past him for the greenhouse.

"Do you know what your mother would like?" Tabitha asked. The two men had followed her into the greenhouse and now stood surveying the rows of tiny budding plants.

"I dunno. Some vegetables, I suppose. And flowers too. She was sick this winter and didn't have time to raise them from seed like she usually does."

"I'm sorry to hear that," Tabitha murmured politely. "Most of these plants are for our own garden, but I can spare two trays—a variety of vegetables and a few hardy flowers like marigolds and geraniums."

"Fine," the *Englischer* said. She could feel his gaze burning into her as she began filling brown box lids with plants. "There." She turned with a bright smile and held the boxes out to Tony.

"Well, that was fast. I thought maybe we could have some time to get to know each other better."

Tabitha suppressed a giggle as John now put his arm around the *Englischer's* shoulders. "Nope. No time for that. Got to get the plants home to your dear mother," John said heartily.

"Hey, let me at least pay the chick." The boy looked all of his seventeen-some years, full of false bravado. Tabitha couldn't help but contrast his boisterous immaturity with John's measured and thoughtful regard. She began to suspect that he'd come along with the boy just to protect her from his *narrisch* flirting.

"The—uh—chick says the plants are at a discount. Five dollars." Tabitha grinned. "Please give my compliments to your *mamm*."

The *Englischer* passed her a bill, and John opened the

car door with a flourish, deposited the plants, and waved Tony inside.

"Don't you need a ride back, dude?"

Tabitha watched John shake his head. "The dude will walk."

"Whatever."

Tabitha waited until the red car had torn back up the lane, spewing mud and clumps of dirty snow from beneath its wheels, then turned to John. "Thank you for coming with him. I'm sure I could have handled him on my own, but it wouldn't have been pleasant."

"I dare say," John said, his dry tone implying that this was the understatement of the year. He gestured at her muddy boots. "You've begun spring planting so soon?"

For some reason she blushed as she pulled one foot behind the other, as if to hide them. "Not yet. But I can't wait to dig into the ground as soon as my *aenti* says the time is right."

"She should know. My *daed* said once that she always had a great love for gardening."

Tabitha nodded, and a moment of respectful silence fell. She appreciated his concern for *Aenti*; it spoke of a kind and thoughtful heart. Still, she had a more pressing matter to discuss with him—Rob, and whether he'd heard from his good friend. How should she raise the topic? In a roundabout way? Casually? Or straight out?

John made a move as if to leave, and all her calculations flew out the door. She reached for his arm, stopping him. She found herself asking, baldly and boldly, "Do you have a message from Rob for me?"

CHAPTER 9

JOHN STARED DOWN into her sky blue eyes and couldn't find it within himself to disappoint her, yet the vestiges of his dream lingered hauntingly in the back of his mind, and the Bible commanded that one should not lie. *But that's all I've been doing since I made this promise to Rob... lying... and it doesn't feel good.* He took a step backward and shook his head, sighing faintly as her blue eyes welled with tears. He balled his hands into fists and stuffed them into the pockets of his black coat.

"Tabitha, Rob's *grossdaudi* is still very ill. Rob probably doesn't have that much time, and he's never been much of a writer. In school he was always good with figures, but he hated reading and writing." John broke off, unable to continue. Why should he be defending Rob, when clearly his friend wasn't treating his intended as he should? Tabitha kept staring at him, as if hoping he would explain away something inexplicable to both of them.

Unable to bear Tabitha's hurt gaze, he ducked his head and scratched behind his ear, searching for another way to soothe her feelings. Then he was struck by an impulsive thought. "Tabitha, I'll tell you what, while you're waiting for Rob to write, why not let me help you become more acquainted with his mother, *Frau* Yoder, and perhaps improve her liking of you."

Her eyes grew round, despite her tears. "Improve... her...liking of me?"

John felt a sick sinking in his stomach. Was it possible that Tabitha did not realize that Mrs. Yoder didn't care for her?

"I mean...*ach*...improve...in the way that all future *dochder*-in-laws must do with their new *mamm*s and..." Another lie.

She took two staggered steps from him, then sank down onto a nearby tree stump. The stump was low to the ground, and her skirt dragged in the snowy mud surrounding it. "I've always wondered why Rob's *mamm* avoided me." Her pretty voice was flat, and John wanted to kick himself, but he wanted to kick Rob too. The girl deserved the truth.

He moved forward and hunched down next to her. "Tabitha, I didn't mean..."

"You said it; you meant it. I've never known you to be anything but honest, John Miller, and I don't suppose you'd change now." She swiped at her rosy cheek with her hand, and he pulled a clean handkerchief from his back pocket.

"Here."

She took the snowy white cloth and blew her small nose prodigiously, only to begin crying anew.

"Perhaps Rob is using this opportune distance to let me know that because his mother doesn't like me much that maybe he thinks he shouldn't court me." She glanced at him, and John shook his head.

"*Nee*, don't think that way, please, Tabitha, *sei se gut.*" He reached out and lightly touched her dark blue sleeve, then drew away sharply when he realized that he was thumbing the fabric in soothing motions. For a moment he felt tempted to tell Tabitha of how Rob had charged him to keep an eye on her while he was gone. He knew that information would help reassure her that Rob cared for her, but for some strange reason he found himself unable to tell her. *It's that it would make your job more difficult*, he told himself, but he wasn't sure that he might not be lying to himself.

He got to his feet. "Tabitha, you can either buck up or keep wallowing. You should keep your thoughts focused on *Derr Herr*, who walks beside us and before us— perhaps not worrying so much about Rob." He knew he was speaking more harshly than he intended, but he was uncomfortable with the way he felt when she was near.

Without offering her his hand, he glanced down at her and then away. "I'm going to fix your mailbox. *Kumme*, Tabitha. I will fetch some tools from the barn. You *geh* inside before you catch a chill." He sighed in silent relief when she scrambled to her feet and walked away from him.

He waited until he heard the creak of the screen door before he turned toward the barn, intent on repairing what he could.

Tabitha swiped at her face with John's handkerchief, then stopped short inside the kitchen door, realizing that the hem of her dress was dripping with watery mud.

"Tabby, was *en der weldt* are you doing?" *Aenti* Beth

called from the kitchen, holding a carrot and peeler poised in midair.

Tabitha swallowed hard; she had no desire for her beloved *aenti* to know she had bawled like a calf in front of John Miller or that Rob's *mamm* didn't like her over-much. She had to stave off fresh tears at the thought, then slipped out of her boots.

"An *Englischer* came wanting some seedlings for his mother, and John Miller showed him the way. I also got a little muddy." She felt ridiculous for stating the obvious, but her thoughts were jumbled. "I'll run and change quickly and then clean up the floor."

Aenti Beth frowned. "Well, where is John Miller now? I hope you asked him in."

Tabitha paused in peeling off her damp wool sock. "Um...I did; I mean, I will—he's fixing the mailbox post."

"Why?"

"It's a bit off kilter. I'll be right back down, then I'll go and fetch him." She hurried across the hardwood floors and took to the stairs, trying to avoid her *aenti*'s curious gaze.

Once she'd gained her room, she hastily changed her wet and dirty clothing and balled it up into a wicker basket, along with John's handkerchief, to take downstairs for washing a bit later. John's piece of linen was a keen reminder of what he'd said about Rob's *mamm*, and Tabitha wondered how it could be that Rob hadn't told her about his mother's feelings. *And yet I'm not telling* Aenti *Elizabeth the truth.* At the thought, she felt fresh tears threaten and drew a deep breath.

Then she resolutely went back down to the first floor, knowing she'd have to face John again to ask him in for at least a cup of tea—*Aenti* Beth was an excellent hostess and would settle for nothing less. But first, there was the mud to clean up and a fresh rag rug to place before the back door.

"Mercy, Tabby." Her *aenti* smiled as she reentered the kitchen. "That was fast."

"I didn't want the mud to have a chance to dry," Tabitha said, going to the pantry for the old tin wash bucket and scrub brush. Soon the kitchen smelled of fresh pine soap and was in its normal pristine order. Putting the cleaning supplies away, Tabitha took a quick glance out the kitchen window and saw John's black coat and hat as he worked at the mail post up the lane.

"John Miller is still about, child?" her *aenti* asked.

"*Ya*. I'll go up and invite him in for a cup of something hot, but I'm sure he'll need to get back to his *daed*'s to work."

Aenti Beth glanced at her sharply. "That almost sounds like wishful thinking on your part, Tabby."

"Hmm?" Tabitha wrapped a light blue shawl round her head and put her boots back on. "*Nee*... of course not. I'll be right back."

She shivered as she walked, wishing more than anything that it was Rob's tall frame that was intent upon the mailbox post and not John Miller's, but this seemed mean-spirited somehow and she pushed her thoughts aside and concentrated instead on avoiding the muddier patches of the lane.

Elizabeth sighed to herself as she continued with the preparations of a macaroni salad to go with lunch. She had to admit that she hoped John Miller would come in for a bit. It was pleasant to have a man about, and John's dark hair and blue eyes reminded her in poignant flashes of the *buwe* who'd long ago professed that he loved her, wheelchair and all.

"And that worked out well," she muttered grimly at her thoughts. Then she bit her lip.

What right do I have to say to Derr Herr *what is or isn't gut for my life? Perhaps Nathan's love was real for me for a time, and certainly I became stronger because of the pain. Still, it's better to learn lessons without such discipline.*

She ran the peeler down the carrot she held and smiled softly to herself.

John swung the mallet with precision, working up a sweat as he straightened the post into the hard earth. It would have been easier to fix the mailbox when the ground was warmer and softer, but he'd given Tabitha his word that he would repair it. He was bent placing stones around the base when he saw Tabitha approaching. He got to his feet slowly and waited until she'd drawn near.

"*Aenti* Beth wanted to ask you in for a cup of tea," she said. He watched her glance at him briefly, then look away.

He took off his hat and wiped his brow with the back of his hand. "And what do you want me to do, Tabitha?" The words were out of his mouth before he could stop, and he frowned heavily, annoyed with himself for some reason. He slammed his hat back on his head.

She looked at him straight on then, her fine brows

arching in confusion. "What do I want? Why does it matter?"

He shook his head. "It doesn't."

She sighed. "You're strange, John Miller, but no stranger than I am, weeping and lolling about because Rob's *mamm* doesn't... won't—"

John put a hand on the mailbox. "Look, I shouldn't have said that, all right." *But Rob should have told you.*

"But you did, and I'm willing to accept any help you might give me in the cause of winning *Frau* Yoder's heart to me. I want a family badly... I mean, *Aenti* Beth is, but she may pass sometime, and I mean, we're an oddity I suppose among the Amish, with so few relatives..." She trailed off, and he set his mouth in a grim line.

Idiot. You've got her all worked up, and she has enough to worry about. He absently ran a thumb over the rusted edge of the metal box and blinked when she gave a small cry.

"*Ach*, you're bleeding. Hold still."

She'd taken his hand into hers before he could say a word, and once again he felt a disconcerting tingle pass through him as she took the edge of her shawl and bound it round his thumb.

He stood frozen for a moment, connected to her by homespun threads and blood and fingertips, and he wondered why the sudden image of a hearth and two bent-wood rockers suddenly burned into his brain.

He pulled away roughly, ignoring her frown, his blood clearly visible on the cloth. "*Danki*, Tabitha, but it's nothing, and now you'll have to wash your shawl."

She shrugged indifferently, then a sudden brightness

came over her face. "How shall you help me win Rob's mother's heart?"

He stared down at her, resigned to his promise to Rob. *And now to making Tabitha happy.* He smiled slowly. "Pie."

CHAPTER 10

PIE? WHAT DO you—" Tabitha broke off as the mail truck pulled to a stop alongside them on the road.

"Letter for Miss Elizabeth Beiler and postcard for Miss Tabitha Beiler," announced Freddy Bann, the friendly but rather nosy *Englisch* mailman. "It's from Rob Yoder, out there in O-hi-o. Says everything's goin' okay. All right...gotta get movin'." He tipped his hat and spun away, leaving Tabitha holding the card and longing to savor its words.

John cleared his throat. "I'd better be headed back home. I'll take that tea some other time. Give my regards to your *aenti*." He turned and started off down the side of the road and Tabitha barely glanced at his retreating back.

She studied the photo of the bright field on the front of the card then turned it over, wishing for a brief second that Rob might have chosen to write a letter instead for more privacy. But then she began to read.

> Dear Tabby,
>   All is going well here. *Grossdaudi* needs regular care at the hospital and is working to regain some strength. I expect I'll be here some time. It's not

the same as Paradise, but it's interesting here and people are friendly. I hope this card finds you well.

Best,

Rob

Tabitha read it again and then again, seeking some cryptic language that might remind her how much he loved her. Instead she wondered who "people" were and if that included Amish girls—then she shook her head. *I'm not jealous by nature, and I won't start now. And surely Rob was wise to write a simple postcard with no obvious remarks.*

She hugged the postcard to her chest and smiled to herself as she headed back down the lane, all mention of *Frau* Yoder and John's pie comment forgotten for the time. Then she wandered down the road to the house, keeping her own postcard snug and hidden within her shawl.

She found her aunt in the kitchen. "There's a letter for you," she said.

Aenti Beth wheeled around to face Tabitha. With a surprised lift of her brow she said, "A letter?"

"*Ya.*" Tabitha handed it to her. "No return address, though."

Her aunt studied the letter, and after a few seconds passed, her normally vibrant cheeks turned gray. Alarmed, Tabitha went to her. "What's wrong?"

Placing the letter on her lap, *Aenti* Beth smiled. "Nothing. I'm sure it's... nothing."

But her aunt's words did little to stem Tabitha's dismay. The smile didn't reach *Aenti* Beth's eyes, and her pallor continued. Yet when her aunt wheeled back to the counter and began stirring the macaroni salad, Tabitha knew not to press her. Perhaps her aunt was correct, and whatever was in the letter was nothing.

☙◖◗❧

After Tabitha left the kitchen, Elizabeth sighed softly to herself. She set the spoon next to the macaroni salad and wheeled herself to the table. She looked at the letter again. She'd recognized her *bruder* Fram's scrawled handwriting instantly. She eased her chair to the table and reluctantly opened the envelope, feeling as though the contents might come tearing out to bite her when she considered her brother's bad temper.

The wording was brief:

> Beth,
>   Will arrive soon for a visit to take a look at the land and *haus*.
>
>   Fram Beiler

"Well," she muttered aloud to herself, "at least he had the courtesy to say he was coming." Elizabeth set the letter on the table and wheeled over to the sink. She glanced out the window as she automatically began to peel potatoes that would be added to a thick stew for supper tonight. There was no mistaking the fact that Fram's letter had disturbed her in both mind and spirit. She discerned the true message behind Fram's simple words.

Elizabeth had inherited, from her beloved grandmother, the small house and lands as well as a sum of money sufficient to meet her meager needs for a lifetime. Then, when Tabby had come to live with her, there'd been an amount of money saved by the little girl's parents, which had then been given to Beth by the bishop's charge for Tabby's care. All of this added up to resentment on Fram's part, for her *bruder* loved money. He'd always considered himself the true owner of the property. That their grandmother had bucked tradition and passed the inheritance to Beth, who was not only a cripple but also a woman, had angered him profoundly. Who knew what legal measures he'd taken to make sure Tabitha didn't receive her inheritance? She wouldn't put it past her brother to seek out legal counsel, even though it wasn't often done among their people.

Beth stopped the scraping of the potato she held and felt its damp sturdiness against her hand. *Surely the* Gott *who brings fruit from the soil is substantial enough to meet all of my needs—and to take care of all of my worries.* She bent her head and began to pray.

❦

John had barely a quarter mile's walk to home from the Beilers' when a buggy pulled abreast of him. He slowed his steps to a stop, and Barbara Esch smiled at him with determined charm from where she sat, practically reaching over her *mamm*'s lap to wave in greeting.

Great, John thought. *Just great.*

But *Frau* Esch smiled at him also with slightly faded green eyes that held all the calculation of her daughter's. "John, the bishop and I were wanting some new flower boxes for spring. Barbara and I are driving to your *daed*'s shop to put in our order, but perhaps you might take on the job yourself?"

John held out his hands. He wasn't about to turn down the bishop and his wife, even though it would surely mean more unwanted contact with Barbara. "Sure. I'm headed to the shop now."

He heard Barbara suck in her breath as she leaned even further across her *mamm*. "*Ach*, John, you're bleeding!"

He longed to roll his eyes; instead he shook his head, glancing at the thumb Tabitha had already tended. "A simple cut—nothing more."

Frau Esch spoke firmly. "It's only a bit of a ways back to our *haus*, John. I insist that you let Bar...I mean *us* tend to your wound, and then you can use our tools to measure for the flower boxes. Barbara can drive you home after."

John met the older woman's quelling gaze. If he had any intention of being close to Tabitha at youth events, he needed Barbara, despite her pursuing him like a bass chasing a worm, which was definitely getting on his nerves. He drew a sharp breath as he stepped toward the buggy and realized that "needing" Barbara also meant using her—and that was not something he was comfortable doing for long.

In any case *Frau* Esch promptly handed him the reins, hauled her not inconsiderable bulk into the back of the buggy, and seemed disinterested when Barbara opened a lap robe and sat near him.

John found her cloying behavior started to give him the beginnings of a headache and wondered briefly why all girls couldn't have Tabitha's unself-conscious charm. Then he concentrated on turning the horse and headed reluctantly for the Esch home.

❧❦

Tabitha felt slightly guilty hiding Rob's postcard between her mattress and box spring. She realized that she'd taken to a lot of secrecy lately, and it wasn't normal between her and *Aenti* Elizabeth. But Tabitha wanted to keep this first writing a secret to herself alone—despite the fact that the postman and John knew about it.

She suddenly recalled John's mention of pie as the mysterious means to Rob's *mamm*'s heart and decided she needed to brush up on her pie-making skills. Her pumpkin was all right but sometimes failed to set perfectly. Perhaps blueberry would be a safer choice.

She scampered down the stairs, wondering if she could get *Aenti* Beth to give her a few pie-baking tips.

"Lattice-top crust blueberry pie?" *Aenti* Beth peered up at her through delicate spectacles. Tabitha was glad to see the color had returned to her aunt's face, meaning that the letter must have been of little importance.

"Do you have the time?" *Aenti* Beth asked as she slid cut potatoes into a large cooking pot. "Isn't it wash day, Tabby?"

"*Ach*, I could do both. Surely when I marry, I'll have to be able to keep the wash going and make a pie for supper." Tabitha bit her lip at the thought of what it might be like to cook and keep house for Rob, then had to refocus her attention when she realized that *Aenti* Beth had repeated herself.

"Um...what did you say?"

"I wonder where your mind is these days, Tabby," her *aenti* said with a slight smile. "Could it be that you have thoughts of a certain man?"

Tabitha flinched. Her *Aenti* Beth knew her so well, and yet she'd so far succeeded in keeping knowledge of Rob from her beloved relative, and she had no desire to begin revelations now. Her relationship with Rob felt too new and uncertain to subject to the scrutiny of her *aenti*.

"*Nee, Aenti* Beth, only thinking that I must improve on things—especially pie, since it seems to be a favorite of everyone."

"Mmm-hmmm," her *aenti* murmured. "Well, go and fetch the ingredients. I think there's a few jars of blueberry pie filling left in the pantry. We'll have to put some more up this summer."

Tabitha bent and gave her a quick kiss on the cheek, then hurried to gather the things she needed.

An hour later she was torn between thoughts of pie, Rob, and his distant *mamm*.

"You're not concentrating, child," *Aenti* Beth gently admonished, and Tabitha suppressed a sigh and rerolled the pie dough that she was using to practice.

"And," her *aenti* warned kindly, "if you work the dough too much, your crust will lose its flakiness."

Tabitha frowned and abandoned the dough ball, exchanging it for a fresh one from the large yellow mixing bowl with a chipped edge that had been part of the kitchen for as long as she could remember. Yet still, even with the comfortable familiarity of the flour on her hands, her thoughts drifted.

Knowing now that Ann Yoder did not approve of her, Tabitha wondered why Rob had never said anything about it. *Perhaps Rob meant not to hurt me and was hoping his mother would come around.*

"That's salt, not sugar," her *aenti* said pointedly.

Tabitha moved her hand with haste and decided to take an impulsive risk. She glanced down at her *aenti* and tried to sound as casual as possible. "*Aenti* Beth, how well do you know Ann Yoder?"

Elizabeth looked up at her niece, not missing for one moment the fact that the child was seeking information— and about Ann Yoder. Rob Yoder's handsome face suddenly filled Elizabeth's consciousness, and she knew instinctively what Tabby's seemingly innocent question meant. The child was in love with Rob Yoder, and Ann, given the history of Tabby's family, was probably fit to be tied.

Yet a selfish part of her was glad for the distraction. The moment Tabitha had entered the kitchen and asked for help making blueberry pie, Beth had been able to put aside Fram's letter and focus on helping her niece. Now it seemed her niece needed more than mere cooking tips.

"Well, I know her," Beth said. "As we each know each other in community, of course."

Tabby shrugged. "*Ach*, I thought maybe you might have been friends at one time or another when you were girls, although I know you're older."

"*Ya*...Ann and I were never too close, but your *mamm*..." Elizabeth paused cautiously. "Your *mamm* was her friend at one time."

Tabby slapped down the lump of dough and dropped into a chair. "Really? Can you tell me about it?"

Elizabeth gazed into the eager blue eyes before her and wondered how she could begin.

⌘

John drew the reins at the Esches' farm and set the brake. He saw the bishop stepping off the front porch, and yet he noticed Barbara made no effort to conceal her giggling pleasure at having John move to help her down.

"Hiram," *Frau* Esch called as she ignored John's hand and clambered down out of the buggy. "I told you to take down that wash before we got home. Now John Miller is here and our underthings are out to dry."

John shifted his weight from one foot to the other. Then he met kind Bishop Esch's mild brown eyes and suppressed a laugh.

"It's all right, my dear," the bishop spoke lightly. "I would imagine John recognizes underclothes when he sees them."

"Not Barbara's," the erstwhile mother hissed, and once again John had to try not to laugh. He wondered idly if the woman threw her *dochder* at every man or just the ones that seemed older and more unsuspecting.

"John's hurt, *Fater*," Barbara simpered. "I must tend to him."

"Really?" the bishop smiled at John and stroked his long grey beard. "You seem well enough to me, *sohn*."

"A cut," John explained, indicating his hand. "It's nothing—but your family was kind enough to um…bring me back here for a quick bandaging."

"And flower boxes," *Frau* Esch reminded him in an imperious tone.

"Right," John nodded. "I'll have to borrow a measuring stick, sir."

The bishop nodded. "Certainly. I'll go and fetch it. Miriam, perhaps you might get started on the laundry while Barbara...uh...tends to John."

John found himself rustled into the three-story brick farmhouse and seated at the kitchen table while Barbara rushed about, tearing cloths and bringing a basin of water to him.

She took his injured hand and plopped it in the water; John wiped his eye.

"There's a singing on Friday at Henry Lantz's *haus*," Barbara said invitingly.

Ach, *how I hope Rob comes back soon—or maybe Tabitha will stay home, though I doubt it.*

He nearly jumped when she yanked the bandage too tightly, then found himself having to squirm down the bench as she tried to move an inch closer.

"Uh, Barbara, look, I..."

"*Ya*, John?" Her green eyes were like cold marbles and he blinked.

"I—um better check about those flower boxes for your *mamm*, but I'll—I'll see you at the singing on Friday." He slid off the end of the bench, got to his feet, then turned away, ignoring his would-be nursemaid's obvious pout.

CHAPTER 11

As it happened, the bishop said he had a local errand that he wanted Barbara to attend to, so John was left to walk home in peace, despite leaving behind a disgruntled Barbara Esch.

He arrived in time to discover his family nearly finishing the midday meal.

"The long-lost *sohn* returns," Matt crowed with a smile. "I sure hope you weren't with...I mean..." Matt's face reddened under John's glare.

"What were you going to say, Matthew?" John's *mamm* asked with quiet curiosity.

John suppressed a groan. His mother was the most gentle of souls but was as tenacious as a bulldog when it came to the idea of John having a girl to court.

Matt snatched up his plate and quickly dumped it into the sink so that it shattered, whether by accident or design, John wasn't sure, but he nevertheless cast his younger *bruder* a grateful glance at the distraction.

"Matthew, be more careful," his *mamm* scolded, then hurried to bring John a warmed plate of roast beef, potatoes, carrots, and onions.

"Where have you been, *sohn*?" his *daed* asked after John had slipped onto the bench and bent his head for a few moments of silent prayer. "I would have thought that *Englisch* lad would have easily found plants from the Beilers."

John shot a discreet warning look at Esther, before she might say something about worrying he was with Barbara, then swallowed a forkful of food. "*Ya, Daed,* surely. But I noticed their post box pole needed some fixing and then the Esches passed by as I was walking home. They're wanting some new flower boxes." He fished in his pants' pocket for a scrap of paper. "Here's the measurements. I can get them made up in a day or so."

"And I'll deliver them," Matt volunteered with alacrity. John could have laughed at his *bruder's* obvious attempt to save him from Barbara's clutches, but he genuinely appreciated the offer at the same time.

"Hmmm..." John's *daed* unfolded his copy of *The Budget* and shook it out to straighten the pages. "It occurs to me that, as neighbors, we might do a bit more to help Beth Beiler and little Tabby."

"She's not little, *Daed*," John said idly. "Nineteen this past winter."

"*Ach*, and I'm still seeing her running about the fields," his *daed* smiled. "Chasin' the baby bunnies for a pet."

John stared down at his plate, struck by sudden thoughts of a young Tabitha wading in the creek when he and some other older *buwes* had passed by. She'd fallen with a splash on a slippery rock, and he'd been the only one to go and help her up while the others had laughed. *Had Rob been there then? Why hadn't he pulled the soaking scrap of a girl from the creek water?* Ach, *I'm thinking too much.*

He pushed away his food, no longer hungry, and was

glad to soon join his *fater* back out in the familiar comfort of the wood shop.

Tabitha tossed and turned in her bed that night, unable to get the conversation she'd had with her *aenti* during their pie making out of her mind.

They'd both abandoned the dough as *Aenti* Beth began to tell the story of a time that seemed to Tabitha to be long, long ago.

"Actually, Tabby, it was both your *mamm* and *daed* that were *gut* friends with Ann Yoder, and now that your parents are gone, I almost feel it's better to leave *auld* tales behind."

"*Sei se gut, Aenti* Beth..." Tabitha had pleaded.

Her *aenti* had reached tender, aged hands to touch Tabitha's cheeks. "Why do you want to know so badly, my child? What is Ann Yoder to you?"

Tabitha tightened her toes beneath her bed sheets as she recalled trying to meet her *aenti*'s penetrating gaze. "I—I only thought that...a pie might cheer her in particular."

Aenti Beth had dropped her hands and reached to idly finger through the flour on the table near her chair. "I see," she'd said finally. "All right, then I will tell you what I know, but truly, I think, it is mostly Ann's story to give. I will pray that perhaps, someday, she is moved to tell you what you ask for."

Tabitha had nodded, waiting, wondering, as her *aenti* sighed and sat back in her wheelchair.

"There was a time when folks expected my *bruder*,

your dear *fater*, to marry Ann, but there was some sort of falling out—I'm not sure why—and then your *mamm* caught your *daed*'s heart. I don't think Ann ever forgot that she felt betrayed by a friend, and she didn't attend the wedding. Even years later, after she'd married herself and had Rob, she was always sort of stiff toward me."

"*Ach*," Tabitha had murmured, wondering if Rob had ever been touched by the bitterness of his *mamm* during his growing-up years.

"Of course," *Aenti* Beth mused with a sad smile, "after your parents were lost, Ann came over with some poppy seed bread."

Tabitha had swallowed. "Did she—did she go to the funeral?"

Aenti Beth shook her head and murmured softly. "*Nee*."

Tabitha turned restlessly in her bed, recalling her *aenti*'s negative answer. It all seemed so wrong, that Rob's *mamm* would choose to harbor anger rather than give in to forgiveness as *Derr Herr* would surely desire.

A hoot owl called outside her open screened-in window, and Tabitha closed her eyes. She wished she might write to Rob himself, but what would she say? His postcard had not given her much to respond to. She drifted off in a cloud of gloom and wondered whether Rob missed her as much as she did him.

On Friday afternoon John stared down in consternation at the letter from Rob and found himself praying silently that Tabitha had received one as well. Rob's words were glib, despite his grandfather's illness, yet John knew that Rob often hid things close to his heart—like his love for Tabitha.

Still, it bothered John that his best friend seemed to make no mention or give any hint as to wondering how things were going with Tabitha and any would-be suitors. *Perhaps he cannot even bring himself to think on it,* John mused as the missive came to a close.

John pulled a writing pad and pen from his desk. His hand hovered over the page as he prepared to respond, but then a sudden image of Tabitha's blue eyes soaked with tears swam before him, and he felt an odd pull in his heart. Against his will he recalled the touch of her small hands against his as she tended his cut, and he knew instinctively that she'd make a kind and loving wife and mother. *Rob's a lucky man*—nee, *not lucky, blessed by* Derr Herr. Still, his seeming lack of devotion to Tabitha through words was troublesome. Surely Rob knew of the great blessing that Tabitha could be to him.

John tightened his jaw as his thoughts drifted. He'd once felt himself blessed as well, when Phoebe had been willing to let him kiss her—indeed, she'd been eager and he thought he'd found real love.

"And why am I thinking of that?" he asked himself aloud in irritation, then shook his head and began to write to his best friend.

He looked up a few moments later when a knock sounded at his bedroom door. "*Kumme* in," he called absently.

He half-turned to see Esther slip inside, a dish towel in one hand. "John?"

"Mmm-hmmm?"

"There's a singing tonight." She perched near his desk on the edge of his bed.

"And?"

"You're not going, are you?"

He put his pen down with a frown and gave her his full attention. "Why do you ask?"

"You're too *auld*," she blurted.

"What?" he bristled, feeling a little put out. "I'm not that *auld*."

Esther nodded. "Barbara Esch is nineteen—the same age as Tabby Beiler. Now I know *auld*er men sometimes marry younger girls, but you wouldn't consider yourself young enough to court Tabby now, would you?"

"*Nee*," he snapped and then was horrified into silence when somewhere within him, a refrain echoed with enough intensity to make him feel sick. *Would I? Would I?*

Esther was still talking, but she sounded far away as John drew a ragged breath. *Am I attracted to Tabitha? To my best friend's girl? What* en der weldt *is wrong with me?*

"John!" Esther's exclamation cut through his dark thoughts, and he looked at his sister blankly.

"What?" He swallowed.

"Are you even listening to me? I can't believe that you're so focused on Barbara Esch that you cannot even pay attention to me...now, do you agree or not?"

He eyed her cautiously. "To what?"

She flapped her dishcloth and got up. "Ohhh, you— never mind. Clearly you're so lovestruck that you cannot even think straight." She marched to the door and exited with a disapproving click while John looked with a frantic gaze to the floor, wishing the aged hardwoods could open wide and swallow him whole.

CHAPTER 12

ARE YOU SURE, child?" Elizabeth asked her niece as the child stood balancing the blueberry lattice-crust pie in her hands. The pie had been carefully wrapped in tinfoil against the light spring rain, and Elizabeth recognized the look of determination on Tabby's face.

"This is my third and best attempt yet, *Aenti* Beth, and after what you told me about my *mamm* and *daed* and Ann Yoder, I really want to take her a pie."

Elizabeth nodded. "All right, Tabby, but you know you could pile me into the buggy and I could go with you."

"I have to do this alone." Tabby dropped her gaze, and Elizabeth had to suppress a feeling of pride at her niece's determination. *But Rob Yoder? I hadn't dwelt on it much before because I never suspected they were courting—but what would it be to have Tabby marry Rob? Why, I remember him as a naughty little* buwe *who stole fried chicken during Sunday dinner prayer time…yet a man can change, I suppose.*

"*Aenti* Beth? I'm going now."

Elizabeth sighed. "Very well, but take an umbrella to get from the house to the buggy and so forth."

"All right." Tabby threw her a bright smile and slipped out the front porch door.

❧❧❧

The buggy ride to the Yoders' was accomplished in less than fifteen minutes, but Tabitha deliberately slowed Swopes, the horse, when she turned onto the lane before the small white farmhouse. She knew, from Rob, that his *fater* had passed away when Rob had been only eight years old and that his *mamm* was consequently a bit overworried at times about her only *sohn*. *But I surely mean him no harm,* Tabitha thought as her grip tightened on the reins. She considered what it would be to do "Rob *gut* and not evil all of his days" and felt her heart begin to pound a bit with nervousness. *What if John had meant something else besides actual pie as a means to* Frau *Yoder's heart and I'm here on a wild goose chase?*

Finally she had spun out the last bit of the drive and the winding of her thoughts as long as she could, and she pulled up before the hitching post. She set the brake, then slid down, balancing the pie. She dodged puddles, the rain making a tinkling sound on the tinfoil, until she stepped up to the covered front porch. She knocked hastily, before she could lose her resolve, but no one answered.

Perhaps she's on the back porch. Now that spring was edging closer and the weather had been unseasonably warm since March arrived, Tabitha remembered that Rob's *mamm* made and sold fragrant soaps to both English and Amish alike to augment the income that Rob brought in working at the Millers' wood shop—and she did so from the back of the house. Tabitha was about to make her way round when the door was *y*anked open and Ann Yoder stared up at her with a fierce frown on her face.

"Tabitha Beiler. *Ya*, what is it?" the older woman asked in obvious irritation.

Tabitha drew forth her most winning smile and plastered it on her face. "A blueberry lattice-crust pie, *Frau* Yoder, for you."

A long moment passed, then Ann Yoder reached from her short height to suspiciously poke at the tin foil. "Hmmm? Pie, you say?"

A surge of relief coursed through Tabitha. "*Ya*, blueberry. Will—will you take it?"

The other woman's frown deepened, but there was appetite in her dark eyes, which reminded Tabitha of Rob's own. "*Ya*, I suppose, but then I want nothing more from you. Do you understand?"

The pie was snatched from Tabitha's hands and the white door slammed in her face so fast she barely had time to catch a breath. She stared at the closed portal for a moment, then slowly turned and walked off the porch and back to the buggy. There was a time that she would have been completely daunted by such a reaction, but now she found a strengthening in her spirit that she knew must surely come from *Derr Herr.* "Well, Swopes," she clucked finally to the disinterested horse. "We've made a start, and I plan to get past her obvious dislike of me, no matter how many pies it takes."

❧❧

A light rain was falling, and John threw himself into work that afternoon, reasoning with himself that his earlier troubling thoughts would surely be dispelled once he saw Tabitha again that night at the singing.

"Are you all right, *sohn*?" his *fater* asked in concern after Matt had left with a delivery.

"Me? *Ya, Daed...*" *Except that I'm probably a man of the lowest sort and I—*

"John?"

"*Ya, Daed*?"

"That's the fifth time you've sanded that veneer. I fear there won't be much left to the burl if you were to continue."

John dropped the sandpaper sheepishly and blew away the dust on the piece of burled elm. "I'm sorry."

His father came near the worktable and patted him on the arm. "You've worked hard all afternoon, *sohn*. Maybe the shellac is getting to you..."

John smiled at the old joke. "Maybe."

"Well, in any case, I was thinking of doing more for our neighbors and took the liberty of making some extra flower boxes for the Beilers—I eyeballed their front window sizes, and I think the new boxes are a nice fit. Elizabeth and Tabitha do love their flowers. Will you take them over for me? The fresh air will probably do you *gut*."

John felt uncomfortable at the thought of seeing Tabitha on the heels of his morning thoughts but knew there was no help for it. *I can hardly watch over the girl and avoid her at the same time.*

As he loaded the wooden boxes in the small wagon, he reasoned with himself and decided that he was probably blowing any notions of fancying Tabitha far out of proportion. He waved to his *daed* and set off on the short drive, letting the rhythmic drumming of Tudor's hooves on the pavement soothe him as usual.

When he turned into the lane that led to the Beilers, he noticed a visiting buggy and debated about stopping, but then he decided that he might as well not delay and drew rein beside the other horse. He recognized the big brown gelding belonging to Letty Mast's family and felt happy that he'd most likely be able to install the flower boxes without much pulling on his emotions while Tabitha visited with her friend.

John went to the back porch door to ask Beth Beiler's permission to put up the new boxes. Presently the door was eased open as Beth wheeled her chair backward a bit to allow him to enter.

He did so reluctantly, glancing over Beth's gray, capped head to see Tabitha and Letty deep in conversation at the kitchen table concerning what seemed to be pie dough. But Tabitha looked up and caught his eye, then gave him a pleasant smile. She dusted her hands on her apron and came forward.

"John, what a nice surprise."

Her blue eyes shone up at him, and he nodded in return, knowing that she was hoping for some word of Rob, which was why her eyes looked like twin jewels. "Tabitha...ladies. I—uh brought some flower boxes over for your front windows. My *daed* made them, and I thought I might put them up for you."

"How nice." Beth Beiler smiled up at him. "Tell your *daed danki*, and please go right ahead and put them up before it starts to rain any harder."

"I'll go and hold an umbrella for you," Tabitha offered. "I'll be right back, Letty."

"A man doesn't need an umbrella with a *gut* hat on," Beth Beiler admonished gently. "Let him work in peace, Tabby."

John watched Tabitha's face flush a delicate pink but knew he couldn't embarrass her further by suggesting that he'd accept the proffered shelter from the rain. He half-turned to take his leave when Beth called after him.

"John, but what a man can use is a *gut* piece of pie. The girls have been experimenting with a peach streusel today. Would you care for a piece when you're through?"

"*Ya,*" he smiled, his eyes roaming once over Tabitha's face. "I surely would."

Tabitha glanced at her friend as they scraped flour from the wooden tabletop. *Aenti* Beth had gone into her room for a few minutes.

"Why the sigh, Letty?" Tabitha asked, putting the cap back on the cinnamon jar.

"*Ach,*" the other girl smiled. "John Miller is so handsome."

Tabitha grinned. "You think nearly every unmarried man is handsome."

"*Nee,* but there's something fine about John—in the way he talks and moves. He's a gentleman."

"I suppose so," Tabitha mused then lowered her voice. "And he is Rob's best friend."

"Have you heard from Rob?"

"*Ya,* a postcard."

"That's all?"

Tabitha frowned as her friend echoed her own thoughts. "He's busy with his *grossdaudi*."

"I know," Letty soothed. "I'm sorry. I'd like him to have written more for your sake. I bet he writes to John."

Tabitha's hand slowed on the dishcloth she was circling about the table. *Suppose Rob had written again to John? Wouldn't John have told me?*

She glanced up when there was a brief knock at the door and John entered, looking big and dark and suddenly very capable of keeping many secrets.

❧

Elizabeth retreated to her bedroom for a brief moment when she felt the familiar pain in her head. *It's nothing*, she told herself as she gripped her chair handles with damp palms. As quickly as it came, the pain was gone, and she drew a deep breath of thanksgiving. She'd been having the inconvenience of these little attacks for a while now and decided she'd soon have to seek the advice of the local healer, *Frau* Ebersol, if things did not improve. But, as it was, she was glad for the respite from the kitchen. It was increasingly hard to see John Miller and not be reminded of Nathan, the love of her youth. Lately her past had been chasing her with gaining speed—first the letter from Fram, then having to tell Tabitha about her parents and Ann Yoder. Now Nathan's image had returned to her with such clarity as if she had seen him only a few minutes ago.

She wheeled her chair to the low dresser where she wound her gray hair into its complicated braid each morning and remembered when the gray was a shining mouse color—not that she'd been overly vain. But Nathan had praised her for the shine of her hair, and it was difficult to forget sweet words even when time had its inexorable way. She glanced in the mirror and straightened her *kapp* a bit, then remembered the moment when Nathan had suggested that he ask permission to court her. She'd been seventeen and had wanted to leap out of her chair when he'd tenderly knelt beside her and caught her hand in both of his.

She sighed aloud and decided such ruminating could not be *gut*, so she turned from the mirror and wheeled herself back to the doorway, prepared to greet John Miller, no matter what he stirred up of the past.

❧❦❧

John slipped off his wet things and went to sit at the kitchen table while Letty fluttered about, getting him tea and silverware. But Tabitha seemed preoccupied, and he realized that it was as easy for him to perceive her feelings as it was to understand the movements of a doe in the forest, and the thought unnerved him. *It's because I take seriously my pledge to Rob; that's all.*

"How much do you want?"

He drew a scalding sip of tea too fast and nearly choked when he realized Tabitha had settled on the bench next to him, her fine-boned hand holding a pie cutter.

"Uh…whatever you think, I—"

"*Ach*, John Miller, a fine strapping man like yourself

surely needs a large piece," Letty laughed. "Besides, I made the crumble on top."

He watched Tabitha cut him a slice that was nearly quarter of the pie, and he knew her mind was elsewhere.

"*Danki*," he said, accepting the plate she slid his way.

"How is it, John?" Beth asked as she wheeled up to her place at the table.

He swallowed the heady concoction of peaches, brown sugar, and vanilla, but barely tasted what he ate, his thoughts so consumed with what might be bothering Tabitha.

"Uh, great...*wunderbar*. Really." He swallowed another bite and saw Letty glance at the wind-up kitchen clock.

"*Ach*, Tabby. It's time I was going. I promised to help *mamm* with the butter, but we haven't yet done the dishes."

"That's all right, Letty," Tabitha smiled. "I'll see you tonight at the singing."

She slid from the bench to see her friend out, and John caught the scent of her soap, fresh mint and rose. He felt his head swim. *What is wrong with me?*

"It's a strange thing, isn't it?" Beth asked low beside him.

"What's that?"

"Love," she said simply.

He coughed, and she swatted his back with a firm hand.

"I—don't know—I mean, what?" he murmured, glancing over his shoulder in time to see Tabitha closing the door as Letty left.

Beth Beiler laughed. "Never mind, John. Simply the ramblings of an old woman. Easily said. Easily forgotten." She glanced up. "Tabitha, while John's here, why not let him help you take some dirt round to the new boxes. It should only take a bit, if you have the time, John?"

He was back on relative level footing and nodded. "Surely."

"*Gut*," Beth smiled. "Very *gut.*"

But John had the uneasy feeling that not everything at the Beiler house was as easy as pie.

CHAPTER 13

HAS ROB WRITTEN to you again?" Tabitha struggled to sound casual, but her fingers curled with nervous tension in the fresh earth.

The rain had given way to filtered sunlight, and John's dark blue eyes flashed in her direction as he shoveled a mix of cold, wet dirt and potting soil into the long planter box. "Why do you ask?"

"Then he has," she mumbled dolefully, knowing for some reason that he was trying to stall.

John sighed aloud and she lifted her chin. "How many times?"

"What difference does it make? Rob loves you. That's all that matters." He moved to begin filling the second box, and Tabitha followed slowly. "You sound so sure."

"And you're not? Shouldn't you..." He broke off as an *Englischer* in an old pickup truck roared down the lane that ran parallel to the farm on the opposite side.

Tabitha blinked in surprise as John dropped the shovel and caught her hand. "*Kumme* on. I recognize that truck. That guy drives over here once every—"

"What? Where are we going?" she asked bewildered as she followed hastily by his side.

"To Stehley's Pond down the lane. We've got to hurry and be quiet."

She ran with him, respecting the quiet note of determination in his voice. Clearly something was wrong, but the time for asking questions was not now.

They hitched up beside some tall shrubbery in time to see the grizzled *Englischer* fling a large, brown cloth sack far out into the pond where it landed with a deep splash, then sank slowly. The man got back in his truck and pulled away to rattle back up the lane without looking back. Then John dropped her hand, and for a brief moment, she felt dizzily like she'd lost her sense of direction in the world, but she didn't have time to process the flash of feeling. She realized that he'd pulled off his coat and hat and was dashing for the murky pond water.

"John...what ...?"

"There are puppies in that bag," he said over his shoulder, then dove into the water.

Tabitha gave a small gasp of horror, then did the only thing she knew to help the situation. She kicked off her boots and followed John head first into the pond.

The water was shockingly cold. Tabitha swallowed a mouthful of the water, then came up choking. She saw John's broad back break the surface about three feet from her and swam rapidly in his direction before diving under again. Visibility was like looking through green stained glass, and she found herself kicking toward the bottom, feeling for the sack, and realizing that time was running out.

Then her fingertips grazed human flesh and she realized she was touching John's hand. She felt desperately below his fingers and suddenly grasped the fabric of the sack. She began to pull with John on the seemingly heavy bag until they'd broken the surface of the pond once more.

Then she swam beside him while John managed to touch bottom and hold the sack above his head.

They gained the bank of the pond and she listened desperately for any sound from inside the fabric, but all she heard was John's harsh breathing and the best of her own heart. She watched his long fingers work in desperation at the knot on the bag, and then he'd managed to open it. Still, there was silence.

"We're too late," she breathed.

"*Nee,*" John said firmly, his dark hair dripping like a raven's wing after a storm. He reached into the bag and pulled out a sodden ball of gray and white fur, rubbing it gently between his hands. The scrap stirred, and Tabitha's heart jumped.

"Here, try and keep it as warm as you can in your lap." John handed her the little creature and she leaned over it, blowing out air onto its dampened fur.

Out of the corner of her eye, she watched John withdraw a second puppy, but this time there seemed to be no response to the brisk motions of his hands. He turned the creature onto its back and bent to gently put his mouth over the little black muzzle, blowing warm air into its nostrils and mouth.

Tabitha felt her throat tighten with tears at John's kindness and wondered vaguely if Rob would do such a thing. She chided herself for making such a comparison. Then the pup gave a choking gasp as John pulled away and turned it onto its side to expel a baby bellyful of pond water.

"*Ach,*" Tabitha half sobbed. "He's breathing."

John nodded, handing her the puppy. Then she watched him stare down at the bag, a stillness coming over his handsome face. He laid his hands on the soaking black fabric covering his thighs and sighed aloud.

Tabitha stared down at the unmoving lump in the bag and swallowed hard as he reached inside the sack. She wanted to look away but she couldn't, and then she saw John's face light up. He turned blazing blue eyes to her and pulled a single heavy rock from the bag.

Tabitha choked on a happy cry and had to stop herself from flinging her arms around his neck in joy. Instead, she reached out for his hand, and he caught her fingers in a warm grip.

"*Ach*, John…you saved them. You were *wunderbar*."

He smiled faintly, and she noticed his fine cheekbones flush with color, but then he shook his head. "*Nee*, and I've missed many a litter to the bottom of that pond." He half glanced over his shoulder at the water, and she frowned.

"What do you mean? How do you know?"

"That guy runs a puppy mill outside of town. He drowns the runts. I went to his farm once, and he bragged about it almost. It was by *Derr Herr*'s blessing that we saw him today." He looked at her suddenly and reached to pull a long piece of pond grass from her *kapp*. "And you were the one who was wonderful. I don't know another *maedel* who'd dive headfirst into a messy pond to save an animal."

She smiled at his praise, feeling her eyes well again with tears as her gaze locked with his. She was aware that his blue eyes had darkened and his grip on her fingers tightened. She felt warm and flustered and confused. Then he dropped her hand and half turned away, staring straight ahead at the grassy bank.

"John?"

"What will you name them?" he asked almost bleakly.

She frowned, then an idea came to her. "You mean what will we name them? We'll each have one, and I'll never forget how you—"

He stood abruptly. "*Kumme.* You must be freezing."

Then she had to struggle in her sodden skirts to keep up with his long legs as he headed back toward the farm while she carried the pups.

❧❧

"I send you to install flower boxes, and you *kumme* home with a *hund*," John's *fater* joked lightly as he stroked the black ball of fur in John's outstretched hands.

"I've got the box of flannels ready," his *mamm* declared, hastily coming across the kitchen to take the puppy and nestle it in a warm cocoon. "Now, *geh* upstairs and change, or you'll be sick for sure."

John left the room with a lingering touch on the pup's head and headed to his bedroom. He only realized that his big body was shivering when he'd stripped off his shirt and went to wash in the large bowl and pitcher on the strapped wood dresser. He caught a glimpse of his pale face in the small mirror on the wall and met his own eyes in the glass with reluctance. *When I knew she'd jumped in that water with me, when she reached for my hand, there was such a connection...I saw her heart in her eyes for a moment.*

He splashed cold water on his face, then gripped the edge of the dresser with rigid force. He bowed his head and began to pray. *Derr Herr, help me through this. Rob is my best friend, and I made a promise to him. Please have Your way in my life and guide me.*

He hurried into clean clothing, then noticed that the afternoon sun was fading. He closed his eyes against the thought of going to the singing that night but knew he had no choice.

CHAPTER 14

TABITHA WET HER lips and tried to concentrate on what Letty was saying beside her in the warm kitchen of the Lantz house. She'd been distracted all afternoon by the experience of rescuing the puppies and the strange feeling she'd had when she and John had touched hands. *It wasn't like when Rob and I held hands—but, ach, how I miss him! That must be the reason for the awkwardness with John—I miss his best friend so much.*

She looked up in time to see Matt and Esther Miller enter and then John. He slipped off his hat and coat. Barbara Esch made her way through the crowd with obvious grace and took his belongings from him to hang them on the pegs near the door. Then Tabitha watched as the other girl brushed beside John's tall frame and he bent his dark head to listen to something she'd said. Tabitha was about to look away when John glanced up and their eyes locked across the busy room.

Tabitha had the same disorienting feeling she'd experienced at the pond and hastily decided that it was too warm in the kitchen. She stepped nearer to Letty, finally breaking eye contact with John, and suggested they go and help *Frau* Lantz with the refreshments.

Still, even as she passed around snowball cookies, delicate mounds of powdered sugar and diced almonds,

Tabitha felt nervous for some reason. She wanted to both avoid John and ask him how the puppy was doing at the same time. Then the singing began; youths calling out song titles that all knew—some in High German and then relaxing later in the hour into English. Tabitha concentrated on the words, not letting her gaze roam around the room. She desperately wished to speak to Rob, to have a mooring for her anxious thoughts.

Then someone suggested that they play "Hide and Seek." Tabitha wished Rob was here, the idea of kissing him giving her a small thrill, and her heart ached at his absence. So she ignored Letty's encouragement to get outside and decided to help *Frau* Lantz wash up.

"*Kumme*, Tabby." Letty nudged her. "Don't you want to play?"

Tabitha shook her head and noticed Barbara Esch stretching on tiptoe to whisper in John's ear.

"*Nee*, Letty, *geh* ahead. Have fun," Tabitha insisted.

Letty reluctantly gave in and turned to fetch her wrap.

But *Frau* Lantz, Henry Lantz's *mamm*, must have overheard and quickly came to Tabitha's side. "Tabby, *sei se gut*, all must participate in the fun. Besides"—she indicated her *sohn*, standing across the room, with a gesture of her hand—"I'm making Henry play too."

"But..." Tabitha began.

"*Nee*, I insist as hostess," *Frau* Lantz smiled. "*Geh* outside."

Tabitha was too polite to disagree and found herself swept along with the crowd outside to disperse in the dark, hoping desperately that she could hide herself from Henry.

Sometimes in this game boys sought out girls they liked, and she had no desire to be alone with him.

She remembered that there was a tangle of raspberry bushes on the backside of the Lantz kitchen garden, and once she was free from the mellow light of the open kitchen door, she took off at a run to get to the spot, aided by the moonless night.

She found the bushes after a few missteps, then sank down into a ball on the ground, putting her head on her knees and longing for Rob.

∽◯◯∽

John ignored the whispered instructions that Barbara had given him to meet her near the left side of the horse barn. *Yeah, like that is gonna happen.* Instead, he trained his keen eyes on Tabitha as she fled the slender fall of light from the door and saw that she was headed for the kitchen garden. She was also moving fast, obviously in an effort to avoid being alone with anyone.

John didn't know the Lantz property well, but basically kitchen gardens and orchards were laid out about the same. He found himself among some low apple trees when he heard the first outraged squeak and then a firm, feminine "*nee*" somewhere in the near distance.

He sighed and turned around, hastily treading the dips between rows, so he wouldn't crush any plants. Then he reached out and felt the scratch of new raspberry bushes against his skin and paused as Tabitha's outraged whisper came to him in the dark.

"Henry!"

"I'm sorry. I didn't realize you were right there. It's so dark out tonight."

"That's it," John said sternly, taking a step nearer the voices. "Get going, Lantz."

"*Ach*, John," Tabitha breathed in obvious relief. Then he felt her small frame bump into his side, and he automatically put his arm around her and felt her shiver.

I'd like to pound the kid.

Surprisingly Henry's voice lowered to a sneer. "So that's how things lie, is it? Don't you think you're a bit *auld* for her, John Miller?"

John thought fast—*here, perhaps is the best answer for watching over Tabitha, to pretend that I'm intent on courting her. I could explain to Rob.* The words were out of his mouth before he could think further.

"*Ya*, Lantz. So you know. Now *geh*." John ignored Tabitha's gasp and pulled her a bit closer. He listened as Henry stomped off through the plants, probably to seek some other girl, and minimally, to let it be known that Tabitha was unavailable.

"He'll spread the news like wildfire," John said softly, bending so that his chin brushed the top of her *kapp*. "There may be a benefit to Amish gossip after all."

Tabitha opened her mouth to speak and found herself at a loss for words. Finally she asked upward in the dark. "But what about…Rob?" Was it her imagination, or did her love's name come out sounding rather thin?

"What about him? He'll think this is perfect." John

steered her deeper into the raspberry patch when a giggle sounded fairly close nearby. "*Kumme*, let's hunch down here. They'll bring out the lanterns soon, signaling that the game is over."

Tabitha sank to the ground with him and sought for a diversion of some kind to speak of. Was John really asking to court her? The thought brought on a strange mix of emotions deep in her belly, and she swallowed hard.

"All will work out well, Tabitha," John whispered. "In truth, Rob asked me to watch over you, and this will be the best way. We can pretend to be courting until Rob returns and then create some sort of believable breakup."

"*Ach*," Tabitha murmured, telling herself that it wasn't disappointment that she felt at John's explanation. Instead she focused on the fact that Rob loved her enough to want someone to watch over her. "Rob—he really asked that of you? He—he must care so much."

"*Ya*," John's voice sounded tight. "*Ya*, he does. So, do you agree?"

"I—*ya*; I do." But even as she spoke the words, she felt lost somehow but wasn't sure why. She blinked in the darkness and wondered what else to say.

"They're taking a long time with the lanterns," John commented, and she heard him shift his position.

"Won't Barbara Esch be wondering where you are?" As soon as the words were out of her mouth, she regretted them and reached out, coming in contact for a brief moment with his sleeve. "I'm sorry, John. It's none of my business."

He laughed low, a deep throaty sound that seemed to

reverberate down her spine. She ignored the feeling and focused on his words.

"Barbara will find some other...victim, I have no doubt."

"But you said you took her sledding?"

"So I did," he whispered. "But only as an excuse to rejoin the youth, and frankly, to be closer to you." He cleared his throat. "Because of Rob, you see."

She nodded. Because of Rob. That's how it should be. Yet she was keenly aware of John beside her, and the loneliness she had felt earlier at Rob's absence had disappeared. John was a good friend, to both of them. Certainly that's all she was feeling at this moment—deep, abiding friendship.

Specks of lantern light appeared from the house, signaling the end of the game. Tabitha thought she heard John expel a long, relieved breath as he rose. She followed him as they emerged from the bushes.

"Stay close," he bent down to whisper. "Remember, we have to make this convincing."

She nodded, moving to stand at John's side. At that moment Barbara appeared, her face illumined by approaching lantern light. When Barbara took a step toward them, Tabitha felt John's hand slip into hers.

Barbara's gaze dropped to their clasped hands. Then she looked up at John, her eyes cold and bitter. "It seems you have been keeping secrets, John Miller."

John nodded, but didn't say anything, only squeezed Tabitha's hand tighter.

"And secrets are little more than lies in the dark." Barbara cast a black look at Tabitha before whirling around.

As soon as everyone started for the house, John released

Tabitha's hand. He glanced down at her. "I'm sorry. I may have overstepped my bounds."

"But it's for *gut* reason," Tabitha said quickly. "Because of Rob."

John hesitated before he spoke. "Because of Rob."

As Tabitha followed John back to the house, she knew she'd do good to remember to whom her heart truly belonged.

❧

Rob knew it would probably shock his *da* to further distress if he could see him as he was dressed now. The English clothes—blue jeans, white button-down shirt, no hat—and Rob was anxious, a completely foreign feeling to him. He'd promised to meet Katie and her daughter at a local pizza place and had decided abruptly that he wanted to wear the different clothes. *Almost as if I wished I fit into the English world—Katie's world.*

He knew his *Da* was supposed to move to the rehab therapy location the next day, and Rob's time of stolen minutes in Katie's company at the hospital would end. He felt lost somehow. Yet he knew in his heart that he had to find a life that he could share with Katie. She had been his anchor during *Da*'s recovery. When he'd had a relapse, he had sought comfort from her. Now *Da* was doing better, and Rob could relax his vigil a bit. *Da* had even told him to go home, that he would be fine by himself, as the community would take over his care once he returned home. But Rob couldn't allow that. He couldn't leave his *da*, and it was becoming clearer to him that he couldn't leave Katie, either—even if it cost him being Amish.

CHAPTER 15

ELIZABETH GLANCED AT the clock and realized that the evening had gone by quickly with the tender puppy in her lap for company while Tabby was at the singing. Beth had soaked the rolled edge of a scrap of flannel in warm milk and the small creature had used nearly all of its energy to suck at the nourishment. Now the gray and white ball cuddled with cozy ease beneath Beth's hands, bringing a smile to her aged lips.

She looked up as the door opened and Tabitha slipped inside, her fair cheeks flushed and her blue eyes bright. "You look troubled, child. Did the singing go well?"

"The singing...um, *ya*. Surely." The girl crossed the room to kneel at Elizabeth's side, putting out a gentle finger to stroke the puppy.

Elizabeth eyed her niece's bent-down, kapped head. "And was John Miller there this evening?"

Tabitha lifted her head quickly. "*Ya*, but why do you ask?"

"*Ach*, it seems we've been seeing a bit more of him lately...I simply wondered if his pup was faring as well as this one." Elizabeth wondered at the flash of relief she saw in Tabby's wide blue eyes but chose to ignore it for the moment. "What do you plan on naming the *hund*, child?"

"Rough." Tabby swallowed. "I'm going to call him Rough since he survived and his fur has that edge to it."

"A *gut* name. It was surely *Derr Herr's* will that John recognized that *Englischer* and his truck. I cannot understand such cruelty as trying to drown a bag of puppies."

"*Ya*," Tabby agreed softly. "Do you want me to take him up to my room for the *nacht* after I help you get ready for bed?"

"Would you think me a selfish *auld* woman if I asked you to share Rough with me? I find him comforting."

Elizabeth cherished the soft young lips that were quickly pressed to her cheek. "Of course not, *Aenti* Beth. *Sei se gut* have him every *nacht*. *Kumme*, I'll help you get settled together."

Elizabeth caught Tabby's hand and held it for a long moment. "Tabby, I wanted to tell you that I've had word that your uncle Fram is coming for a visit." She paused and then swallowed. "He wants to—look over the property."

"What?" Tabby's voice rose a bit. "Why, he's so nasty, *Aenti* Bath, even if he is your younger *bruder*. And 'look over the property'? What right does he have to *kumme* and—"

"Shhh," Elizabeth soothed quietly. "You know as well as I do that if anything happens to me, Fram will likely inherit the *haus*. It is what he wants, after all."

"But nothing is going to happen to you," Tabby protested with the calm assurance of youth.

Elizabeth smiled. "*Nee*, but we must still work to make him welcome. Will you try, child?"

Tabby gave a great sigh, then nodded with visible

reluctance. "*Ya, Aenti* Beth, I will try. Anything for you." The girl seemed about to say something else but then was silent.

"*Kumme* then," Elizabeth patted the arm of the wheel-chair. "Let's get ready for bed."

∾

"Tabitha Beiler, hmmm?" Matthew gave a low whistle of approval from where he perched on the kitchen table munching an oatmeal raisin cookie.

John cast his *bruder* a sour look. "Look, be quiet, will you? *Mamm* and *Daed* might not be sleeping yet."

Esther clasped her hands together and looked sweet and distinctly happy for once. "*Ach*, John, I'm so glad that it's not Barbara Esch. I tell you she was fit to be tied tonight when word got round about you and Tabby. You didn't even let *Mamm* and *Fater* know."

John sighed and took a deep swallow of cold milk while running a gentle hand over the huddled puppy in the box. *This is going to turn into a circus faster than I can control it—I have to not panic, that's all . . . and I have to write to Rob tonight. I can only imagine what he would think if he heard somehow that I—but still, this is all Rob's doing— his asking for secrecy, for lies.*

"John," Matt hissed.

"What?"

"Esther, *geh* upstairs," Matt suddenly insisted. "I want to talk to John about—manly things."

"*Ach*, pooh," Esther frowned, then flounced to the stairs. "I am only going up so that I can think of the proper flowers we might use to decorate. You know that November rolls around fast, John."

November—the time most weddings took place in the community…suppose Rob wasn't back in six months? Then what?

John put his cup in the sink and started to automatically wash it, trying not to think too hard. Then Matt cleared his throat.

"What?" John snapped.

"So are you courting her?"

"Maybe." John felt himself flush against his will, and Matt chortled.

"At last." He slapped John on the back. "When did you decide you liked her?"

"I don't talk of such things," John quipped. "Besides, who do you have your eye on these days?"

Matt scowled. "Never mind."

John couldn't resist a smile at his *bruder*'s morose expression. "Don't worry. You're find the right woman some day."

"But it looks like she's hiding. I'm seeking and I'm not finding." Matt admitted reluctantly. "In fact, last night all I found was a clothesline. Almost choked myself."

John laughed and took his turn giving a pat on the back. "You'll get over it. After all, he who seeks finds!"

Matt's good humor returned, and he grinned. "Yeah, but not for you, big *bruder*. You're done seeking. Congratulations."

John nodded, tightening his jaw. The enormity of the deception he was about to perpetrate with Tabitha hit him hard. *People might get hurt…and all of this for Rob.*

But he nodded just the same at his *bruder*. "*Danki*, Matt. Thank you."

❧❧

Tabitha undressed slowly and started to pray even before she sought her bed. She had realized downstairs that her plan with John would ultimately fool *Aenti* Beth and possibly hurt her when she discovered the truth.

Tabitha sat on the edge of her bed and lowered her face into her hands. *How can I do such a thing? It's a massive lie...but Rob wanted this—for me to be watched over. And it can't be for long...Rob has got to come home soon. He's got to.*

She rationalized that it would only be a brief deception and could be kept very casual and quiet. In addition she knew that, although the youth might gossip to desperation among themselves, there was an unspoken code among them not to mention anything to older folks at home. Courtship was to be kept a secret so that no one would be hurt should the relationship not work out.

She lay down and thought idly of what John's strong hands would look like in the mellow fall of melting wax, then jerked her consciousness up in a sharp mental pull. *Why am I thinking about John? It's probably because he's so close to Rob too and misses him dearly.* She comforted herself with the thought, then began to pray again.

CHAPTER 16

TABITHA WOKE BEFORE daybreak with the determination in mind to bake another pie for Rob's *mamm*. She hoped it would assuage some of the churned-up feelings she was having and started to get out ingredients with quiet purpose. *Aenti* Beth was still sleeping, and Tabitha hoped to present her *aenti* with a warm piece of lemon meringue pie for breakfast.

She grated the lemon rind and carefully measured sugar and cracked eggs. The problem she had, as usual, was getting the meringue to brown nicely without burning in the fussy old oven. She double-checked the recipe with the lard-stained card *Aenti* Beth kept in the antique recipe box, then added everything to her already made pie crust. When she was through, she made a second pie, deciding to take the best-looking one to Rob's *mamm*.

She'd carefully placed the second pie in the oven when there was a loud pounding at the back door. She hurried to open it, not wanting *Aenti* Beth to wake, as she glanced at the barely pink sky out of the kitchen window. She wondered who it might be at this time of the day and for a brief moment felt her heart stop at the thought that it might be Rob coming home.

She pulled on the doorknob only to step back as a tall,

scowling man grunted hello at her. *Ach, nee,* she thought, feeling her heart drop.

"*Onkel* Fram." She found her voice after a moment. "We didn't expect you for a few more days."

"*Ya,* well," the old man bristled. "It's to be my home. I expect I can *kumme* as I please."

Tabitha fought back an angry retort at his brashness, then remembered her promise to *Aenti* Beth—to make Fram feel welcome and hopefully soften his heart with kindness. "*Sei se gut, kumme* in," Tabitha said finally, widening the door.

She glanced with some dismay at the two old heavy-looking suitcases he carried in and dropped on the kitchen floor.

"Uh, *Onkel* Fram, I've got a pie in the oven and *Aenti* Beth is still asleep."

"And?"

And I'm going to go against Amish tradition and bop you in the head if you mutter one more rude thing. "Would—would you like a piece of lemon meringue? It should be cool enough..." She trailed off as he gave a disdainful sniff.

"I'll have eggs—scrambled, bacon, fried green tomatoes, and grilled cornbread. And you'd best hurry. I'm stiff from that van ride half the *nacht* and twice as hungry."

Tabitha simply stared at him in mute fascination until he gave a loud clap of his hands. "Go on, girl. Are you short of hearing?"

She couldn't fathom what she might have said if another knock hadn't sounded at the door, this one low but purposeful. Tabitha stepped past her uncle to open the door and stare up in surprise at John's handsome face.

"Uh—I know it's early, Tabitha, but I had to talk to you and—"

"Who's this now?" *Onkel* Fram demanded. "Some lame-brained suitor *kumme* courting at daybreak instead of at *nacht*?"

Tabitha gritted her teeth and forced a tight smile to her lips, remembering silently the morning that Rob had come courting. "John Miller, you might know *Aenti* Beth's *bruder*, Fram Beiler?"

John gave a brief nod to the older man, then caught Tabitha's hand in his. "Excuse us, sir," Tabitha was amazed to hear John say, as he ignored her uncle's rudeness and pulled her out the door at the same time. "We'll only be a moment."

❧❧

John leaned wearily against the wooden banister of the Beilers' back porch and stared down at Tabitha's expectant face. He was exhausted, having been up all night writing to Rob and wrestling with the deception he was creating.

"What is it, John?" Tabitha asked softly. "You don't look so well."

"I didn't sleep. Look, I was thinking that we'd might be doing Rob better service if we did try to cultivate a relationship with his *mamm*..." He trailed off cautiously, not wanting to upset her again.

But to his surprise, Tabitha clapped her hands like a

little girl and smiled brightly. "We must be of one mind. I've got a pie in the oven for *Frau* Yoder right now."

"Is it meringue?" John asked. "Because I think it might be burning."

"*Ach, nee!*" She spun from him and fled back into the house, leaving the door ajar. John sighed and followed wearily.

The kitchen was filling with smoke, and he hurried to open the window. He turned and saw Tabitha open the oven door, causing a fresh wave of smoke to billow forth.

"Here." He caught her slender wrist. "I'll get it out. You might burn yourself." He grabbed the oven mitts she held and slid the ruined pie out and into the sink in one deft motion. The meringue was a steaming, blackened mess as he pumped water onto it, conscious of Tabitha flailing a dishcloth about at the smoke.

"Now this is a fine welcome," Fram Beiler spoke in a subdued roar. "I want my breakfast."

John looked over his shoulder at the angry man and shook his head. "You won't be eating this, sir."

"I know that," Fram blustered. "If this worthless girl knew how to cook, I'd be—"

John's temper gave in a fine snap and he spoke up. "Sir, I would like you to know I am courting Tabitha, and I happen to know she is a very fine cook." *And now it means that I'm coming out with the idea of courting to a man—who might likely tell other folks—not merely the youth. Ach... what a mess.*

"John, never mind," Tabby murmured, still flapping her dish towel.

Fram looked smug. "Well, then she can cook for me while she's still unattached.

John's mood shifted and he stepped away, pleased that Tabitha could rout the old man herself with feminine accuracy. "You'll have to get your own breakfast. Tabitha needs to get her *aenti* up, and then she and I have something to do with our early morning. And don't"— John's voice was level as Fram Beiler stepped toward the remaining lemon meringue—"lay a finger on that pie. It's already promised."

John had to suppress a grin when Fram froze in mid-stride then slowly backed away.

"I'll make my own gosh darn eggs," the old man growled.

"*Gut*," John said evenly. "Very *gut*."

⸎

Elizabeth had to smother a laugh in her pillow even as she cuddled Rough close to her chest. She'd heard nearly the whole of the exchange in the kitchen and felt especially giddy at the bold pronouncement John had made that he was courting Tabitha. Of course, Elizabeth couldn't let on that she knew, but it thrilled her heart just the same. Ach, *maybe now I can give the secret of the recipe box, for John is a fine man, but I must be sure of Tabitha*—

She remembered the day her *grossmuder* had given her the seemingly simple box and the charge that went with it. It had been raining and high summer. She could still smell the wafting scent of earth and grass coming in through the open kitchen window, and there was something indelibly sweet and cleansing about those moments that still resonated in her soul. She wanted that for Tabitha, wanted the understanding of the secret for her.

Elizabeth looked up as Tabitha came into the room. The girl's cheeks were flushed a pretty pink, and one golden tendril had worked loose from her *kapp*. *Ach*, what a beautiful sight she was, and what a handsome couple she and John Miller would make.

"I'm sorry, *Aenti* Beth. I burnt the meringue on a pie." Her pleasant voice lowered. "And *Onkel* Fram is here."

"*Ach*, well, we must deal with things as they *kumme*." Elizabeth smiled.

"*Ya*," Tabby hesitated visibly. "John Miller is here as well— he—uh—felt as I do about ministering to Ann Yoder. He suggested we take her the pie that survived...together."

"A charming idea," Elizabeth said, holding on to the strong young arms that helped her into a sitting position. "And so nice and early in the morning too. She might have a bite for breakfast."

"*Ya*." Tabby's response was quiet, and Elizabeth struggled to hold her peace about the courtship. But then they set about the business of dressing and Beth focused on going out to meet her *bruder*—an unpleasant task, she knew, but still one that she prayed might be turned for *Gott*'s greater blessing in time.

CHAPTER 17

JOHN HANDLED THE reins with ease, but his head ached with tiredness and he told himself that was the reason the faint nearness of Tabitha was sending his mind spinning. He glanced at her sideways, out of the corner of his eye, and noticed her slender fingers were pressed white against the rim of the foil-covered pie dish.

"Don't be nervous," he said gently.

"*Ach*, how did you know?" She turned her blue eyes full in his direction, and he pulled his hat down a bit, focusing hard on the road.

He shrugged and clicked to Tudor to pick up the pace. "I just know." He thought his words sounded odd, so he added hastily. "I suppose it's from having a sister."

Tabitha sighed. "Rob's always been an only child, but I'd like to think he knows me well."

John ignored the strange feeling he had in the pit of his stomach at her wistful words. "Of course he knows you," he said more roughly than he intended. He was about to apologize when an oncoming red minivan suddenly swerved dangerously close to Tudor. The horse reared as the van sped past, and John struggled to maintain control of the buggy.

He heard Tabitha's faint cry as the wheel teetered on the edge of the roadside and the grass, and then Tudor reared again and came down in the field adjacent to the road. John's heartbeat thrummed in his ears as the buggy came to an upright stop.

He turned to look at Tabitha, and something moved within his spirit. He knew in that moment, as sure as he knew his own name, that he loved her beyond a shadow of a doubt. Part of him wanted to laugh at the absurdity of it and the other part wanted to sob—so much so that he felt tears swell at the back of his throat. He had to choke out words of normalcy. "Are you okay?"

She nodded, her lashes damp with her own tears, and she sniffed. He kept the reins in one hand and reached in his pocket for his clean handkerchief. She took it with a broken laugh.

"I'm going to have a collection of your linen soon."

"It's all right."

It's all right... it's all right. The refrain echoed in his mind, and he bent his head in misery. *But it isn't all right and never will be again.*

⁓☙☜⁓

Tabitha reached shaky hands down to lift the pie from the floorboards near her feet. She lifted the tinfoil and stared at the meringue, which had stuck to the covering in the tumult of the near accident.

"*Ach*, John, it could have been so awful," she whispered.

She glanced at him, his hat blown off, and his black hair clinging to his high-boned face; he looked as shaken as she felt. She reached out almost instinctively and touched the strong bones of his hand where he held the reins.

He didn't move but spoke hoarsely. "*Derr Herr* was watching over us. It is by His mercies that we are safe."

"*Ya*," she agreed, then withdrew her fingers from his and gave an impulsive swipe at the underside of the tinfoil, longing to break the somberness she felt emanating from his big frame.

She popped her finger in her mouth and tasted the meringue, then offered the tinfoil to him. "Have a taste. It's not bad."

He turned with visible reluctance, then put out a long finger to catch a piece of meringue. He held it poised over the foil.

"Go on," she said, striving to keep her tone light. "Taste it."

She watched him obey, putting his finger to his lips, and then giving a brief suck. His throat worked, and he gave her a rather sad smile. "It's *gut*," he said low.

"*Gut*," she said briskly. "So will you take me home since I have no pie for Rob's *mamm*?"

He stretched his arms out and gathered the reins tighter. "*Nee*. We're going to have our visit as promised. Ann Yoder needs to know what a jewel she's getting as a future *dochder*-in-law."

She drank in his words as he scooped his hat up from the floorboards, then eased Tudor back onto the road. She spoke softly. "*Danki*, John. I—it means a lot to know you think well of me."

"Why?"

"Why?" She paused, feeling nervous, then latched on to the most sensible reason she could come up with. "Because you're Rob's best friend, of course."

"Of course."

She looked at his profile. He appeared stricken for some reason and decidedly grim. She decided not to speak again until they turned down the lane to the Yoder homestead.

"Maybe she's not home," she ventured.

"At this time of the morning? She's home." His voice seemed to have regained its normal strength of tone, and she felt better inside, not stopping to examine why.

"She's home," he continued. "And apparently still in her *nacht* clothes." She watched him gesture with his chin and Tabitha saw *Frau* Yoder bolt from the clothesline around the back of the house. Her arms were filled with sheets and she was wearing a shockingly pink nightgown that trailed against the ground.

"*Ach*, we need to leave, John."

"And have her thinking you saw her and might gossip about her—uh—penchant for vibrant color? *Nee*. We'll give her a few minutes, then knock at the door like everything is perfectly normal." He pulled the buggy up to the hitching post and set the brake. Then he climbed down and came round to help her down. But first he calmly took the pie dish and walked it up front to Tudor.

"John!" she exclaimed, knowing what he was about to do.

"What? Old Tudor had a bad scare too. He deserves a bit of the spoils."

Tabitha crossed her arms over her chest and listened to the slurping sounds of the great horse as he sucked down the lemon and remaining meringue. John came back with a pie plate licked clean. "Here you go, madam. I'd wager you don't really even need to wash it."

She caught the wicked glimmer in his dark blue eyes

and couldn't resist the laughter that bubbled to her lips as she accepted the dish. "You're a bad man."

"You have no idea."

She put the plate on the seat, then stretched out a hand to be helped down, but he caught her around the waist instead, swinging her down to the ground with ease. She ignored the strange thrill she felt as she found her feet and concentrated on John's broad back as he mounted the steps with apparent familiarity to knock on the front door.

Hasty footsteps from inside shook the floorboards of the old porch, and Ann Yoder soon opened the door. Tabitha half hid behind John, expecting the same reception she'd received when she'd brought the last pie.

But, to her surprise, a hastily dressed *Frau* Yoder, with her *kapp* slightly askew, answered the door and smiled up at John.

"Where have you been lately, John Miller?" she asked. "I was beginning to think that you forgot about me."

"Never that," John said bending his broad back to embrace the woman. Then he caught hold of Tabitha's wrist and pulled her forward. "And here's Tabitha Beiler. She was intent on bringing you a lemon meringue pie, but we—had a bit of a tussle and the horse got the best of it."

Tabitha's toes curled inside her sensible shoes as Ann Yoder peered up at her.

"Hmmm...brought me a blueberry pie not long ago—wasn't half bad, though the girl's family is...well...not my favorite in the community. And that's being honest, it is."

Tabitha glanced down at the floorboards of the old porch with sadness. *Would this woman ever accept her, especially as someone who was courting with Rob?*

And then John spoke with quiet seriousness. "You can always do the right thing in life, *Frau* Ann...it's never too late for that, no matter the past. You can choose to change your feelings of not favorite or favorite."

Tabitha blinked as Ann Yoder seemed to consider the weighty words and finally gave a faint nod. "Fair enough, John, but admit that I know you, have known you since you was a *boppli*—and you mean something more than just me and pies and this girl."

Tabitha looked up at John and noticed the grim set of his handsome profile and could only wonder what was churning in his powerful mind.

CHAPTER 18

JOHN ENTERED THE home of his childhood friend and breathed in the familiar smells of soap scents and baking bread. His bleak gaze swept the neat living room, looking for an anchor of sorts for his thoughts about Tabitha, but he could find nothing but seeming condemnation in the casual indications that this was Rob's home—a straw hat, a carved bear he'd whittled when he was twelve, and the family desk littered with Rob's distinctive scrawl.

"Well, you both might as well sit down," Ann Yoder muttered, breaking into his thoughts. "I've just been writing to Rob at my *fater*-in-law's. The *buwe*'s been a big help, so I've heard."

"That's *gut* indeed," John said, struggling to make his tone cheerful as he took a place on the quilt-backed couch and Tabitha sat down beside him. "When is Rob coming back, do you think?" *Soon...soon, soon, soon. Let it be, Derr Herr, so that I do not dishonor our friendship by feeling this way.*

Ann sniffed. "Hard to say. He's still helping his *da* quite a bit."

"John says you like pie," Tabitha spoke up suddenly.

John watched the older woman swing her gaze in

Tabitha's direction and tried to remember that he was here to build Tabitha up for Rob's sake.

"So I do, missy. But I'd imagine that I'd like some help with my soaps and oils a bit more right now since Rob's not about to lift the kettles out back."

Tabitha rose immediately, and John followed.

"Aw, sit down, the both of you do-gooders," Ann bawled. "I don't mean today. I haven't got anything on the boil right now, but if you wanted to swing by, say next week sometime, that might be *gut*."

John watched Tabitha bend to perch back on the edge of the couch and reluctantly did the same. Ann Yoder got up and crossed to the writing desk.

"Here, John, it's Rob's phone number should you ever want to sneak off to the shed and give him a call. There's a few younger cousins running about who'd get him to the phone. I know you must miss talking with him."

She went back to her chair, and John fingered the slip of paper between his thumb and forefinger. He knew, without looking at her, that Tabitha was desperately trying to see and memorize the numbers even if she never called. He passed her the paper when Ann Yoder was distracted by an apparent itch on her calf, then half closed his eyes when Tabitha's fine fingertips brushed his hand in accepting the paper.

Ann looked up, and John felt the weight of her sharp gaze. "So, are you two courting, or what?"

∽∾

Elizabeth held her younger *bruder*'s gaze as he poked a disinterested finger at the old recipe box on the table. He'd cooked his own breakfast and was making no bones about it, even though he'd left the kitchen in an uproar that she supposed he'd expect her to straighten.

"Lizzie, you haven't changed a bit. Always willing to settle—for this tiny *haus*, barely three acres of land, and a tart miss of a niece who can't bake worth a lick."

Beth arched a brow and watched Fram squirm a bit. "Yet I think you'd be all too happy to have the *haus*, land, and a pie... or two."

He pulled from the table to turn his back on her, and she suppressed a sigh. She was five years older than Fram and could remember, even when they were young, trying to help occupy him from her chair. He'd always been naughty as a child and later, as a teen, dissatisfied and cynical. Still, in memory of her mother, she loved him, though they'd both been raised by their *grossmuder* when their own mother had given up on Amish life and run away when their *fater* had died. Perhaps Fram had a reason or two to be angry, but no more than she. She wondered vaguely when he might be leaving even when he'd just come through the door.

"Are you planning on cooking anything else, Fram?" she gently plied his rude back.

He turned with a faint sneer. "Not very hospitable, are you, Lizzie? You can well and *gut* clean up this lot while I look over the outbuildings."

"That's fine," she said, intent on keeping a serene tone.

She watched him pause halfway across the kitchen. "That kid who was here a bit ago—John Miller? It's funny, but he reminded me in looks of the fool who once proposed to you…what was his name? Nathan something or another?"

Elizabeth felt her lips tighten. "Black. His name was Nathan Black."

"Right," Fram agreed. "Well, you can't deny he dodged a bullet that time, huh, *auld* Lizzie?"

Elizabeth watched him cross to the door and close it with a distinct click behind him. Only then did she bow her head and allow the hot tears to spring up that seemingly had come from nowhere. Ach, *to have such a* bruder. She bit her lip, blew her nose in the handkerchief she'd drawn from her sleeve, and then began to pray with determination.

⟨◎⟩

"How do you think she knew—er—suspected that you, that we…" Tabitha fumbled to a stop, watching Tudor's backside jog in time to the movements of his powerful legs.

She glanced at John and watched him sigh. "Ann Yoder's as sharp as a hawk. And she's known me for—" He broke off suddenly, and Tabitha wondered what he'd been going to say.

He cleared his throat. "I'm glad you've got the phone number of where to reach Rob. Maybe you should try calling him."

"Why?" she asked, surprised as the word popped out of

her mouth. *I should want to call Rob, be dying to hear his voice, shouldn't I?*

"Why?" John repeated in almost irritation. "Well, why not?"

She flashed him a look, feeling angry all of a sudden and with no idea why. "I don't know," she snapped.

"Well, don't ask me," he fired back.

"Are we fighting, John?" she asked, somehow bereft, all anger drained from her.

She watched his broad shoulders sag almost wearily. "I don't know," he muttered.

She sought to alleviate the moment and began to remark on the blooming roadside flowers and the white clouds in the blue sky. But all she got in return was a noncommittal grunt. Then he lifted his head.

"I've got to *kumme* over tonight and court you." He said the words with abrupt surprise, and she looked at him, feeling wide-eyed and jittery.

"You do?"

"We've got to keep up appearances to make people believe our—intentions." He was back to being gloomy again.

"Well, don't sound so happy about it, John Miller. We certainly can call off the whole thing if only for Rob and…"

"Do you want to?" he asked.

"What?"

"Call it off?"

She felt her throat tighten with banked emotion and shook her head. "*Nee—nee.*"

"*Gut,*" he nodded. "Neither do I. It's the best thing—for Rob's sake."

"*Ya,*" she agreed, though she knew a disquiet in her heart that belied the peace of the beautiful day.

❧

Rob tucked his hands into the front pocket of his jeans and then came to a dead stop outside his grandfather's room. *I forgot to change*, he thought blankly. He'd been running the gambit between English and Amish worlds, and today was the day that he was supposed to pick his *da* up to go to the rehab facility so that he could learn to use his prosthetic leg in a more capable manner.

Rob was about to turn from the door when his *gross-daudi* hailed him from inside the room.

"Rob?" the old man growl in a voice as gruff as a bear's growl.

"*Ya?*" Rob replied automatically.

"*Kumme* in…I knew it was you standing out there. What'cha waiting for, *buwe*?" Rob sighed and reluctantly entered the room, denim jeans and flannel shirt to boot.

His *da* looked him up and down through minute spectacles, the same way he used to do when Rob had done something interesting as a child. Even now, Rob felt like squirming under the piercing gaze.

"You gone English, *buwe*?"

Rob sighed. It would be so easy to lie—to keep lying—to this man he loved. But then how could he share Katie and Clara, her daughter, with *Da*? He swallowed hard and suddenly thought of John—always stalwart, true, not given to lies. *Yeah, all I have to do is be like John.*

John was in the barn, running expert hands over Tudor, when Matt entered, whistling cheerfully.

"What's up with Tudor?"

"We had a near miss with a minivan this morning. Tudor kept his feet, but I want to make sure he didn't pull anything."

"Who's we?" Matt asked, moving to the other side of the horse with a brush.

John didn't want to answer the question. It would only send off the train of thoughts again that made him feel like he was swimming upstream through molasses, and he didn't like the accompanying painful pull on his heart.

"Tabitha and I," he bit out.

Matt laughed. "Don't you have your courting hours messed up, big *bruder*?"

"*Nee.*" John threw him a sour look over Tudor's back. "We were paying a visit to Ann Yoder's—I expect she's been lonesome since Rob's been gone."

"But you haven't been," Matt quipped.

John splayed his hands across Tudor's back and gave his *bruder* a grim stare. "Look, Matt, I—"

"You what? Want to be with her all the time? Feel lost when she's not around? Can't stop thinking about her when—"

"That's enough. How did you become such an expert on—love—anyway?"

Matt handed him the brush and turned to go. "I read."

"*Ya*, well, it better be the Bible that you're reading."

Matt grinned over his shoulder. "Haven't you ever heard of the Song of Solomon, *bruder*?"

John snorted then turned back to the horse when the barn slid closed. "Song of Solomon," he muttered to himself aloud. "*Ya*, so I need to read my Bible more…"

Tudor gave a low snicker, and John frowned as he began to gently brush the animal. But soon the soothing motion set his mind wandering. *Suppose this is just what I did wrong with Phoebe Graber all over again… another misjudgment, and this time, it could hurt my best friend… and Tabitha herself.*

The horse rumbled a sound of protest when John paused in his brushing.

"And I don't need any comments from you."

CHAPTER 19

I WANT TO KNOW what there is to this rumor about you and John Miller." Letty's voice trembled a bit, and Tabitha glanced with sympathy at her best friend. She knew that Letty was thinking she'd kept things from her, and that hurt, especially since they'd shared so much over the years. Tabitha longed to tell her the truth but couldn't bring the words out of her mouth.

They were outside together in the chicken pen, feeding the birds—the Leghorns, Anconas, and Minorcas, all of which fought and pecked for the handfuls of grain and grit. Letty had come over for the express purpose of speaking her mind—Tabitha recognized the rare set look on her friend's sweetly rounded face, and she didn't know if she was prepared to face that quiet confrontation. She'd told Letty everything for as long as she could remember, and to change that now seemed foreign and uncomfortable.

Tabitha sighed aloud over the noise of the hungry clucking. "Letty, I didn't mean to hurt you. In fact, it all happened so suddenly that—well, it's hardly been a day, and I—"

"What about Rob?" Letty interrupted, her voice sober and confused. "How have you told him?"

"I—haven't."

"*Ach*, but don't you think that he deserves to know and understand before he comes home to his best friend...and you. I don't understand, Tabby."

Tabitha was about to try and explain when *Onkel* Fram came stomping past the coop area.

"Your friend had best head out," the old man snapped, pausing outside the wire. "It'll be time to cook lunch soon, and I'll be quite hungry."

Tabitha longed to roll her eyes. *Did the man think of nothing but food?* "Letty only arrived a few minutes ago, *Onkel* Fram."

"Now don't you try your fussin' on me, girl. It might work with Lizzie, but I'll not have it. Besides, you already had your courting fellow by this morning, and you don't need to be discussing it with your friend here. Now, *kumme*."

Tabitha longed to sink into the ground at her uncle's revelation of John's early morning visit.

Letty turned to her in disbelief. "John was here already this morning? You—you must be moving fast together. I feel as though I don't know you anymore, Tabby. I—I guess I'd better *geh*." Letty dropped the feed pan, and Tabitha heard her soft sob as she struggled with the wire latch.

"Letty," Tabitha cried, ignoring *Onkel* Fram. "*Sei se gut*, wait. I'll explain."

But Letty had managed to open the gate and fled across the yard to her buggy, leaving Tabitha standing with tears in her own eyes.

She heard *Onkel* Fram clear his throat. "So...what'll we be having for lunch?"

❧❧

Elizabeth handed Tabby the cookie sheet that was covered with the crumbs of the fresh corn bread they had to accompany their lunch of corn and bacon chowder. Fram had pushed back from the table, declared his tepid satisfaction with the meal, and gone outside with a loud burp. Beth was thankful for the ensuing silence as her head was starting to hurt again.

But Tabitha distracted her by turning from the washing up and looking down with a wistful expression.

"What is it, child?"

"*Ach, Aenti* Beth, have you—have you ever been in love?"

Elizabeth felt her eyes fill with tears for the second time that day. "*Ach*, Tabby, *ya*, but it was a lifetime ago."

Her niece bent and caught her hands with her own young, soapy ones. "*Aenti* Beth, tell me, *sei se gut*. What was it like? And what happened to him? I mean…where…"

Beth squeezed Tabby's hands in her own and smiled despite her tears. "*Ach*, Tabby, it was indeed long ago, but I can still remember the feelings. His name was Nathan, Nathan Black, and oddly enough, John Miller has reminded me of him often in looks."

Tabitha dropped her earnest gaze, then grabbed a dish towel, quickly drying her hands and then Elizabeth's. "*Ach*, will you tell me more?"

"*Ya*, child, let's go over to the table and have a cup of tea while we talk," Beth said.

While Tabby got the teacups, Beth had time to compose herself and found thankfully that her headache had gone.

"So, Nathan looked like...John?" Tabitha asked, pouring the rose tea.

"*Ya*, but looks are only one part of love, child. I didn't know the difference of that then with Nathan, though. I thought that being in love was the same as loving someone."

Tabitha appeared puzzled for a moment. "What do you mean exactly, *Aenti* Beth?"

Elizabeth smiled faintly. "Being in love one day can often mean that you are out of love the next, as if it's a baseball diamond with boundaries that are easily marked and moved. Loving someone...*ach*, that's something else entirely—it's not simply a feeling but a decision, a decision to endure together and meet life together as *Derr Herr* would will—not as you would will for yourselves."

"And did you—love Nathan like that?" Tabitha asked softly.

Elizabeth sighed mournfully. "*Ya*, child. I did, but he— he was simply in love with me for a time even though he asked to court me, to marry me actually."

"*Ach, Aenti* Beth," Tabitha cried, reaching out to grasp her hand.

"Now, now, child, as I say, it was long ago."

"What—what happened to Nathan?"

Elizabeth swallowed hard. "He married another and left the area. I heard two years after that he was killed in a buggy accident. I cried for a week...but I had to go on."

Elizabeth watched slow tears seep down Tabby's face. "And now, tell me, what of you, child? Is there someone whom you love truly?"

"I—I—"

Elizabeth held her breath as Tabby stumbled over her

answer. Just then Fram barged back into the kitchen with a snap of his suspenders.

"You women should have things cleaned up already and started thinking about supper," he said loudly.

Elizabeth knew the moment was lost as Tabitha looked away, but she still hoped that her words had made an impression on the dear child and that she could realize the truth of love—mature, enduring love—in her own young life.

John wielded the axe with ruthless precision, hacking up the pine knots that would be used as fire starters in the fall.

He jumped when his *fater* spoke from behind him.

"Are you upset about something, *sohn*?"

"*Daed*, be careful, or I'll end up taking an ear off somebody—you nearly scared me to death."

"Sorry, but the way you're going after those knots tells me that something is up. I brought a jug of your *mamm*'s iced tea—do you want to have a bit of a talk?"

Nee...nee, *I do not want to talk about why I've been running around all day like I'm* narrisch *because I love my best friend's girl.* He dropped the axe. "Sure, *Daed*."

They sat on some stumps near the wood pile, and John took a long, grateful pull from the iced tea jug before meeting his *fater*'s eyes.

"I—I haven't been sleeping well," John admitted at last. "Trying to tire myself out, I guess."

"Mmm-hmmm," his *daed* agreed but then went on.

"Let's see—you did some plowing for your *mamm*, installed bookshelves for Matt, helped Esther lay out the kitchen garden plants, and now you've been at this wood for two hours. You're soaked with sweat and bound to catch a chill I say, but surely, you might sleep well tonight."

"Might?" John asked with a wry smile.

"*Sohn*, I've known you forever, and since you were a *buwe*, you've liked to work when something's been bothering you. So, what is it? Your *mamm*'s worried—"

"It's nothing, *Daed*, really." *And now I'm lying to my fater.*

His father took a drink of the iced tea, then murmured reflectively. "I haven't seen you this stirred up since you were nineteen."

"*Daed*..."

"A woman'll do that to you sometimes."

John had to laugh, though it came out a bitter sound. "That's probably true."

"But the right woman, now she might stir you up for a bit, but then she'll bring you peace. Peace in your mind and spirit and heart. And that's something worth having, and it doesn't *kumme* around too often and only as *Gott* wills."

John couldn't respond. He felt his throat work and stared at the wood chips on the ground instead.

His *fater* got to his feet after a few moments. "Well, I'll leave you the iced tea, *sohn*."

John found his voice. "Hey, *Daed*?"

"What?"

"You're a great man, do you know that?"

His father shook his head and gave a low laugh. "*Danki,* John," he said softly. "That means *der weldt* to me."

John watched him leave the clearing, then got slowly to his feet. He bent to pick up the axe but found that he didn't have the heart for abusing the pine knots any longer; his *fater*'s presence had given him peace for the moment.

CHAPTER 20

TABITHA LOOKED UP from where she was sitting on the edge of her bed when the small splatter of pebbles hit her bedroom window. She rose hurriedly and tiptoed passed the guest room where Fram was snoring like some deranged woodchuck. Then she headed downstairs, her heart beating feverishly.

Though some other communities frowned on the practice, courting was done in secret and at night in her community. When the elders of the household had gone to sleep, the *buwe* would typically come over at a prearranged time, signal the girl to let him in, and she would. Typically they would sit together in the living room and talk and perhaps hold hands. But Tabitha had no idea what to expect from a "pretend" courting with John. It made her queasy in her stomach, and she swallowed as she hurried across the dark living room to open the door.

"*Kumme* in," she whispered softly to his tall frame.

"*Danki*," he whispered back in what seemed a somber tone.

She took his coat and hat. As she hung them up, she noticed that he was wearing a burgundy shirt that went well with his dark hair. She pulled herself up smartly, telling herself that she shouldn't be noticing how he looked in the first place.

"Please, sit down," she invited, indicating a small chair. She told herself that she had no desire to offer him the couch as she had with Rob.

He obligingly took the chair. After lighting a lamp, she perched anxiously on the chair's mate, noticing that his seat creaked alarmingly under his weight and he had to apparently struggle to get comfortable.

"So, I'm glad Rough isn't *auld* enough to bark yet. He's in with *Aenti* Elizabeth," she said after a moment.

"Rough?" he asked.

"*Ach*, the puppy we rescued. I guess I forgot to tell you what I named him."

He smiled at her, and she caught her breath. "What is it?"

He shook his head. "Nothing really. Only that I named our girl pup, Tumble...so we've got Rough and Tumble."

Tabitha smiled. "That's a happy coincidence."

"Yep." He sighed and ran a hand through his dark hair. "So, you've done this with Rob?"

"*Ya...*"

He nodded, and Tabitha scrambled for something to say as he shifted on the chair again. She was horrified when she blurted out her next question. "Who was Phoebe Graber?"

She popped a hand over her mouth when he pinned her to her chair with his penetrating, dark blue gaze. "What?"

"Nothing...I was just—"

"How do you know about Phoebe?"

Tabitha shrugged, wishing she might sink into the floorboards beneath her sensible shoes.

John got up and paced a bit, his big frame casting long

shadows on the opposite wall. Tabitha waited, wondering what he might say and what she had gotten herself into.

"I was nineteen," he said, stopping to stand in front of her. "Like you...and like you, I fancied myself in love— with Phoebe."

"John, you really don't have to—"

He broke through her words; his gaze above her head, lost somewhere in years and memories. "If you only knew," he laughed bitterly. "We courted. But she ended up rejecting me."

He paused, and Tabitha felt her heart fill with compassion. "Perhaps she was not the right person?" she ventured.

He glared at her. "It was my fault, my doing."

"And is that why you think you don't deserve to ever love again?" *Now where did I* kumme *up with that?*

"And where did you come up with that?" he asked in an angry whisper.

"Well," she said with a calmness she wasn't feeling. "You stopped coming to the youth outings, started sitting with the older men, and you certainly didn't say anything to Rob about a girl that I know of."

He bent near her chair. "Did you ever stop and think that maybe Rob doesn't tell you everything?"

"So there is a girl?"

He straightened and backed away. "*Nee*," he said.

She folded her hands in her lap. "What happened to Phoebe?"

"You don't give up, do you?"

"Usually I do, but tonight, well, we are supposed to be courting, so I may as well know the truth about your past."

He blew out a frustrated breath. "All right then—I'll tell you what few know."

And then she wasn't too sure she wanted to know.

⌍⊚⊙⌌

John threw himself down on the old sofa, where he sat staring at Tabitha for a few moments. Somehow, she'd managed to get his heart beating and his dander stirred up in a way that not even Phoebe Graber had been able to do. Nee, *with Tabitha there's something deeper in my spirit involved, and even sitting here is probably a bad idea.* But he'd promised the truth and was determined to tell it no matter what the memories cost him.

"Phoebe left the Amish community," he said, watching Tabitha to gauge her reaction.

To his surprise, she simply nodded.

"She gave up our way of life and ran away with an *Englischer.*"

"That is so sad." Tabitha's soft voice was moving the ice out on the river of his heart, sliding away old hurts and turning over the things that he'd hidden away. He leaned forward and lowered his head in his hands, trying to think.

Then he felt a soft, feminine presence beside him on the couch. He looked sideways at Tabitha, then lifted his head.

She reached out and tentatively brushed his hair out of his eyes, and he winced away. She immediately dropped her hand, her blue eyes filling with tears. "I'm sorry, John. I didn't mean to be forward or to repulse you... I just... I wanted to say it's all right and—" She sniffed as a single tear fell and slid down the creamy warmth of her cheek in the mellow light.

Without thinking, he turned to her, reaching to catch her tear with his callused thumb, then holding her face gently in his hands for a long moment. "Repulse me?" he managed. "*Nee*, never that."

He bent his head closer and could feel her sweet breath on his face. It would be so easy to kiss her, right here, right now, and forget the consequences.

She wavered then leaned closer to him, her eyes limpid pools. Then he abruptly remembered Rob and dropped his hands, scrambling to a standing position.

"John, what—"

"I have to *geh*," he bit out, striding across the room and snatching up his jacket and hat.

"But..." Tabitha had gotten to her own feet and spread her hands in confusion.

John stole one more glance at her. "I'll see you at church tomorrow. *Gut nacht*."

He closed the door behind him and then paused to lean against the wood, sucking in deep gulps of the cool night air and suddenly knowing in his heart what he must do.

CHAPTER 21

ELIZABETH NOTICED FROM her vantage point with the elderly women that Tabby did not sit in her regular place next to Letty at church service the following morning. She wondered what was wrong between the two girls, then let her thoughts drift back over the morning with an inward sigh.

Fram had been cantankerous, of course, insisting on hotcakes and ham slices even as they were hurrying to get ready for the twice-monthly church service. Today it was being held in the Masts' barn, and it always took some doing on Tabitha's part to get Elizabeth situated in the buggy and then at the meeting.

"Fram, really," Elizabeth had half-scolded. "Tabitha cannot go down to the cellar for root beer in her Sunday dress. Drink milk."

"It's all right," Tabitha had confided by her *aenti*'s side. "I'll go."

Elizabeth had caught her niece's hand for a moment. "Tabby, are you well this morning? You look tired."

"No more tired than you." The child's glance at her *onkel* had made Elizabeth smile.

Now, sitting in the airy barn in her wheelchair, Elizabeth smiled again at the subtle reference Tabby had made, though Beth was sure it was not the proper attitude for church. Still, her *bruder* was enough to drive anyone *narrisch*, and a little humor might provide some relief to his visit.

Elizabeth looked up as someone took the end seat on the backless bench near her chair. She was surprised to see Ann Yoder, who normally sat frowning on the far side of the older women.

"Why, Ann—it's a pleasure to see you this morning," Elizabeth said in a genial voice.

"Hmmm, I suppose so. Tell me, Elizabeth Beiler, why that niece of yours knows my liking for pies, and do you know she's courting with John Miller?"

Elizabeth blinked and then regained her composure. She was about to answer these pointed remarks when a stray starling flew overhead and unfortunately deposited droppings on Ann's bonnet, which slid unpleasantly down the side of her frowning face.

"*Ach*, Ann," Elizabeth whispered, hastily reaching into her blue church bag for a handkerchief, but Ann Yoder had already risen to her feet in a dignified fashion and brushed past the wheelchair with her speckled white face held high.

"Elizabeth, *sei se gut*, excuse me. I will *geh* to the pump outside."

Beth watched her leave and struggled with a sudden bout of helpless mirth. *It takes all kinds to make a world*, she thought. Then she forced herself to focus as the service began.

The traditional singing had finished, and Bishop Esch rose to begin to speak on the text for the day. He repeated it, his kind voice carrying over the crowd and soothing Tabitha's fraught nerves with its calm familiarity.

She hadn't slept a wink and felt worse than ever when Letty chose a place to sit, far away and amazingly near Barbara Esch. *Why have I not gone to Letty's haus? Told her the truth about everything? Why am I lying to everyone I love just for the sake of Rob Yoder—his very name now unsettles me.* Tabitha could also see John nearer the front, his handsome head bare, his profile stern. I have no idea what to even say to him, she thought miserably. And I really need to talk to Rob and tell him that we cannot go on lying like this. Then the bishop's voice claimed her thoughts once more and she became lost in the wisdom of his words.

"As the psalmist writes, 'Keep me as the apple of your eye; hide me in the shadow of your wings.'" Bishop Esch paused, then gazed out at the community, clasping his hands behind his back and beginning to pace, as he so frequently did when he was speaking at a Sunday meeting. "It's no doubt a time-honored expression—'the apple of your eye.' I've heard many of you say it of a first grand-child, a new *frau*, or someone beloved to you in a special way. Few of you may know that such a saying comes from *Gott*, and even fewer of you may embrace this characteristic of *Derr Herr* in the way He yearns for you to do. Many of you have moments when you feel lost, comfortless, and alone—even with the gift of community. But God sees each one of us as the apple of His almighty eye.

You are cherished and loved, wherever you are—whatever you've done."

Tabitha drank in the words, then noticed John out of the corner of her eye. His head was bent, his eyes closed, and she wondered what troubled his heart.

John chafed under the bishop's words, struggling to ignore the question Tabitha had so accurately posed the night before. *Do I really believe that I deserve love? Not only from a woman but also from* Gott? *What if everything that happened with Phoebe really has affected me in ways that I don't even realize?*

But then he pushed away the potentially healing thoughts and crossed his arms over his chest. The three-hour service wound to a slow close, and Matt had to elbow him in the side when it was done. The young men started to get up and head outside for the lavish Sunday meal.

"Daydreaming about someone, big *bruder*?" Matt asked with a wink.

"*Nee*." John's tone was sour.

"*Ya*, well, I suppose you don't have to dream when she's right here. Hiya, Tabitha."

John nearly tripped over his own feet as the cheerful crush of community members brought him in a surge right near Tabitha. She was looking beautiful as always in a fresh, light blue dress, but he saw the hesitancy in her smile, her pearly teeth biting anxiously down on her soft lower lip for a moment.

John had to look away.

But the moment steeled his resolve for what he was planning.

"Is everything all right, John?" Tabitha murmured low when Matt had drifted off into the crowd. "You left so suddenly last *nacht*."

He looked at her then and nodded, thinking of Rob, of his promise, of the honor involved in friendship, *even if a friend makes an unreasonable request... watch over her.*

"*Ya*, it's all right now." He paused. "Will you talk with me, Tabitha—before we eat? There's something I have to tell you."

He saw the flash of worry in her eyes but ignored it; he had to ignore it.

She nodded. "Of course."

John shouldered a path for them out into the sunshine where women were already hurriedly moving, spreading white table cloths on picnic tables and bringing covered dishes from inside the house. The rich smells of ham and roast beef began to waft in the air along with a myriad of other delicious scents. But John had no appetite today.

He led Tabitha away from the barn and up a small hill. The fields around them still lay bare and muddy under the warming March sunshine.

"What is it, John?" she asked when he didn't speak.

He fisted his hands and stuffed them in his pants pockets, knowing he'd be tempted to touch her if he didn't. He faced her then and wet his lips. "Tabitha—I—I'm going away. I'm leaving Paradise."

"What?" Clear disbelief shone on her face as it drained of color.

He pushed on in haste, wanting to get the words out before she could say something that might stop him.

"My uncle Samuel has a woodworking outfit up in the Allegheny Mountains. He always needs crew, and I think it'll be a *gut* experience for me—"

"What have I done?" she asked in confusion.

"Nothing. It's me. I feel...led to move away."

"But what about Rob and your promise to him—to watch over me?" Her voice rose a fraction, and he swallowed hard.

"You heard the bishop this morning, Tabitha," he said low, moving closer to her. "*Derr Herr* will watch over you, for you are surely the apple of His eye."

She shook her head. "Something's wrong—you're not saying what it is."

"*Nee*, this will make everything all right. You will see." He brushed past her and went down the hill without looking back.

❧◉❧

Tabitha watched him go and suddenly knew in her heart with a surety what the difference was between being in love and loving someone. She swatted at a stray tear as it slipped down her face and almost laughed at the absurd situation. She'd been in love with Rob, but she now loved John Miller with her whole heart. It took all the spirit and self-possession she had not to run after his broad retreating back and tell him so.

CHAPTER 22

WHERE ARE YOU off to this morning, child?" Elizabeth asked in the early morning light. "You've barely picked at your food."

It was Monday morning, and Beth had not missed the fact that Tabby had gone to her room as soon as evening chores were finished. Nor did she miss her niece's swollen eyes and bright pink nose.

"I'm fine, *Aenti* Beth," Tabitha murmured. "I wanted to rebuild the worm box today before it gets warm outside." "That's men's work," Fram muttered, pointing with his fork.

Elizabeth smiled wryly. "Does that mean that you plan to help Tabby?"

Her *bruder* looked taken aback. "Me? *Nee*...planned on fishing. I will need some bait worms though."

Elizabeth was surprised when Tabby rose from the table and spoke tartly. "Well, you'll have to dig them yourself, *Onkel* Fram. I've already got mine and plan on using their castings as kitchen garden fertilizer."

"Sassy *maedel*," Fram grunted.

Elizabeth hid a smile but still could not suppress her worry for Tabby as the girl washed the dishes in silence and then went outside.

"You should have taken a firmer hand with her over the years, Lizzie," Fram commented, draining his coffee cup.

"Tabby is a *wunderbar* young woman, Fram."

He snorted. "A wonderful young woman would share her worms."

Elizabeth sighed, feeling the beginnings of a headache come on as she wheeled away from the table.

❦

Tabitha dug her hands into the moist layers of shredded newspaper, peat moss, manure, and leaves. She knew the environment that would grow chubby worms, which meant richer castings after the worms ate the kitchen scraps from two nights a week. She tried hard to focus on the mundane subject of worm food because it was so far from any thought of John Miller, but still, his handsome face danced behind her eyes.

Whatever would he think of me if he knew I loved him? He can never know, of course, because he'd see it as a betrayal of Rob—and it is. But I cannot help my heart... ach, Gott, *what should I do?*

And then, like a heart echo, *Gott* seemed to speak to her. She rose from her earthy job to go to the pump and wash her hands with the lye soap that was there. She would go and see Rob's *mamm* because that was what *Derr Herr* told her to do, and she understood His voice well enough to know to obey.

⊚⊛⊚

John forced his breakfast down, then spoke up as his *mamm* prepared to rise to clear the table.

"Uh, *Mamm*, a moment, *sei se gut*...I would speak with you all."

His mother sank back onto the bench, her blue eyes wide with expectancy.

John glanced at his *daed*, then down the table to Matthew and Esther. *How can I leave them? How can I leave...her?*

"John," Matt snapped. "I'm falling asleep here."

"Right. Okay, well—I've decided that I'm going to go up to the mountains to work with *Onkel* Samuel."

The silence was as thick as butter, and then everyone burst out talking at once.

"Are you *narrisch*?" Matt demanded.

"But, John," his *mamm* wailed. "I thought you were going to tell us about some girl at last!"

"What is wrong with you?" Esther shrilled above the din.

"*Sohn*, are you sure?" His *daed* laid a hand on John's sleeve.

John hung his head for a moment, then got to his feet slowly. Everyone quieted.

"I have to do this. I—I'll miss all of you, of course, but I feel called to *geh*." He swallowed hard. "Please accept this. I could use your support."

His *daed* nodded slowly. "*Ya, sohn*, if you must...we will support your decision."

When his *fater* spoke in low, measured tones, everyone

ceased their protests. John could feel the change in the atmosphere and was grateful for it.

He left the now quiet kitchen and went upstairs to his bedroom. He had the sudden urge to hold the puppy, Tumble, and withdrew it gently from its comfortable box near his bed.

He stroked the puppy with a gentle hand. "I suppose Esther will have you when I'm gone, little one."

"Esther'll have to fight *Mamm* for that dog," Matt said from the doorway.

John half turned with a faint smile. "*Kumme* in."

Matthew entered, closing the door behind him, and took a seat at the desk. John raised an eyebrow in question. "Have you been sent to talk me out of going?"

"*Nee*, that'll be Esther later. I came to ask something a bit more personal."

"And?" John asked.

"Are you leaving because something happened between you and Tabby? I mean—you just started courting, and now you're on the go...what went wrong?"

John looked down at the puppy and shook his head. "Nothing. I—we—thought it would be a *gut* experience."

"Because you both plan on leaving Paradise for the wild woods someday?"

"Look, Matt—"

His younger *bruder* held up a hand. "I know—it's none of my business. But if it were me—"

"And it is not you," John pointed out evenly.

"*Nee*...but if it were, I wouldn't leave as fine a *maedel* as Tabby Beiler left on her own for long. Someone else is bound to want to court her."

Dear Gott, *let Rob* kumme *home soon.* The prayer beat like an echoing refrain round John's brain until he almost dizzily put the puppy back in her box.

"*Danki* for the advice, little *bruder.*" John got to his feet. "I'd better start packing."

Matt gave him a good-natured grin. "Fair enough—the least I can do is help a bit. When are you planning on leaving?"

"Tomorrow morning, I guess."

The words came simply enough to John's lips, but he felt a heaviness in his heart that had all the weight of an old ship's bell. With deep reluctance he turned to his dresser to begin sorting clothes to pack.

"I don't have a pie, *Frau* Yoder, but I felt led by *Derr Herr* to come and see you this morning." Tabitha waited anxiously for the older woman's response, wondering if she had heard *Gott* correctly.

"Well, best to *kumme* in then. You can help me scent a couple batches of soap I've got going." Ann Yoder widened the door, and Tabitha stepped inside. She realized that the usual feelings she had in relation to Rob were absent—there was no heart pounding or drinking in of each random object with her eyes. It was almost like she had wakened from an enchanted dream but to a much stronger and beautiful reality.

She would always care for Rob, she knew, but only as a friend. *And somehow, I must find the strength in* Gott *to tell him so when he returns. And at all costs, John must never know of how I really feel or it would break his and Rob's friendship for sure.*

"Are you paying attention to me?" Ann Yoder's tart voice demanded an answer, and Tabitha came back to the present moment.

"*Ya*, ma'am. Sorry."

"All right then."

Tabitha followed Ann through the small house to the back porch, which was actually a wide room filled with bubbling sounds and a myriad of delicious scents.

"*Ach*, this is lovely," Tabitha exclaimed, reaching a finger toward a small brown bottle labeled Petigrain. She got her hand slapped for her trouble, and Ann frowned up at her.

"No touching unless I tell you to. The wrong scent or oil can ruin a batch of soap. Take Petigrain, for example, that's for refreshment and relaxation, but if you're wanting something more—potent—like Neroli, for skin healing, you'd not be doing yourself a favor."

"How did you learn all of this?" Tabitha lifted a cautious hand to gesture at the bottles and large pots.

"My *mamm* taught me as her *mamm* taught her. And I'll tell you that my *buwe*, Rob, knows a bit more than he'd like to admit about the soap-making business."

Tabitha smiled politely, but her thoughts drifted back to John. *How am I going to stand it when he's gone?*

But she was soon absorbed in the task of shaving and molding soaps, and hours passed without her even realizing it.

"There's a storm coming up," Ann Yoder observed. "Looks like a bad one."

Tabitha glanced out the porch window and saw that

the fluffy clouds of the morning had fled in the face of an ominous blackness.

"I'd better get home," she said, thinking of her *Aenti* Beth.

"Well, I can't say I didn't appreciate your help. By the way, once this storm clears out, I'm due to make a phone call to Rob. I'll be glad to tell him about you and John Miller."

Tabitha dropped the rose mold she was holding. *I cannot let* Frau *Yoder speak to Rob first—I have to talk to Rob, explain something... that it was a just a story... not true love—*

She thought fast. She'd memorized the number to Rob's *grossdaudi*'s phone shack, and now she was determined as to what she should do. She bid a hasty farewell to Ann Yoder and ran out onto the porch. It was a half mile across newly planted fields to get to the phone shack, and it had begun to rain, heavy, soaking drops that pelted at her as she made her way down the stairs.

Soon she was slipping through the field, jumping between rows, which were fast turning into muddy puddles dotted with sharp balls of spring hail.

Tabitha finally gained the phone shack and flung open the small door only to stop in sudden surprise.

John stood inside the wooden shack, his dark hair and shirt plastered wetly to his big body. He held the phone receiver in his hand and he stared at her for only a second before speaking hoarsely.

"I'm calling for an ambulance. My *daed*'s had a heart attack."

CHAPTER 23

THE AFTERNOON HAD begun much as usual in the woodworking shop. Matt had gone out on a delivery, and John was helping his *daed* with the biscuit joinery on an oak desk that an English woman had requested to match her primitive kitchen.

It was quiet but for the turn of a lathe here and there, and John knew his *fater* was thinking of his leaving the next day.

John wanted to say something, to explain somehow, but no words would come. Then his *daed* said softly, "A true pleasure it's been working with you, *sohn*, all of these years."

John felt emotion choke his throat. "*Danki, Daed.* I feel the same."

"But Samuel will give you a truly authentic experience with the wood that I cannot. Lumbering is tough business, but you've got the back for it and..."

John looked up from his work to see a strange expression on his *fater*'s face.

"*Daed*, what is it?"

"My—chest," his *fater* breathed, dropping his tool and suddenly sinking to his knees.

John thrust the desk out of the way and slowly eased his *daed* back on the wood shavings of the ground.

"It's going to be all right, *Daed*," he soothed, opening a few buttons of his *fater*'s shirt. "I'll let *Mamm* know and go get help."

"Don't—don't upset your mother," his *daed* managed to say, and John decided to make the run for the phone shack without wasting time stopping inside the house. He prayed as he ran, knowing that the Holy Spirit made intercession for him as he could barely concentrate beyond a few words.

It was then that the storm had begun in earnest, and he was soaked by the time he reached the shack and grabbed the dark green rotary phone receiver. He dialed 911 with trembling fingers and connected to the dispatcher. He hardly recognized the voice that came out of him as he explained the situation and named the address.

At that moment Tabitha had opened the door.

His heart leapt even more into a tumult as he gazed into her blue eyes, but now the dispatcher was telling him an ambulance was on its way.

"I've got to get back," he gasped, hanging up the phone.

"I'll run with you," Tabitha said. "He's going to be all right, John."

He nodded and took her outstretched hand, and then they ran together back over the sodden field.

They got to the workshop just as the wails of a siren could be heard in the distance. John dropped to the ground near his *fater*, relieved and deeply thankful to see that he was still breathing. Tabitha ran into the house and now brought his *mamm* and Esther as the ambulance swung into the lane and jostled to a stop, spewing mud.

And then John watched as his *fater* was loaded onto a

stretcher and carried to the ambulance. His *mamm* and Esther insisted on traveling with the crew to the hospital.

"I'll stay here and tell Matt, and then I'll get a van ride in," John called as the rear doors closed on his *mamm's* anxious face. Then he stood, aware of Tabitha next to him in the pelting downpour, feeling as though the sky itself was weeping with him as he prayed.

❦

"Child!" Elizabeth exclaimed. "Where have you been?"

Tabby had come shivering in through the back door just as Beth was getting supper on the table.

"Runnin' around with that Miller *buwe*, no doubt," Fram growled.

Elizabeth wheeled herself over to Tabby and caught one of the girl's cold hands in both of her own.

"Daniel Miller had a heart attack. They took him by ambulance to Lancaster General Hospital."

"*Ach*, the poor family! We must pray—"

"Not before supper," Fram called.

Elizabeth ignored her *bruder* and bent her head, praying on the spot for the Miller family. When she was through, Tabby leaned down to kiss her cheek.

"*Danki, Aenti* Beth."

"Of course, my dear. You'll see…everything will be as *Derr Herr* wills. Now, run and change out of those wet things and I'll keep a plate warm for you. It's chicken pot pie and fresh brown bread."

Elizabeth watched her niece nod and walk quickly to the stairs.

"I need my supper," Fram insisted, tapping his knife and fork handles on the surface of the wooden table like a petulant child.

Elizabeth sighed and wheeled round and into the kitchen to begin serving the meal.

She took her own serving once Fram was settled and began to eat, still praying inside for the Miller family.

"You know, Lizzie, it beats me how you can cook so *gut* but never caught yourself a husband. Though I suppose that chair would be a burden to any man."

Beth continued to chew, opting for "a quiet answer turning away wrath" as her defense.

But Fram rambled on. "'Course it could be that you're always willing to settle for someone else to have what you might...take when *grossmuder* died—sure, you got the house and land, but what is it really worth? And that *auld* recipe box...remember how she treated that like a treasure? She said you had to pick who it goes to before you die...imagine, a recipe box! You might as well bury it with you, Lizzie, 'cause I'll have no use for it, truth to tell."

Elizabeth looked up from her plate, longing inside to lob a piece of brown bread at her *bruder*'s gray head, but then she composed herself. "It's good, Fram, that you enjoy my cooking. I'll miss your—uh—compliments when you go back to Ohio."

"Well, as to that, I thought I'd stay on for a while."

Beth closed her eyes for a moment, listening to him chew like a jackrabbit, then looked at him squarely.

"That will be fine, Fram. Just fine."

❧❧

Tabitha knelt by her bed in her wet clothes and prayed for John's *fater*. She had never seen someone look so poorly, so awfully pale, and it scared her inside. She was afraid Daniel Miller might die.

She'd had experiences with death in her young life but had never gazed upon someone so sick. It gave her a consciousness of the brevity of life and the preciousness of every moment. She longed to share this with John, tell him that she loved him. But she knew she could not, especially not now with his father so ill.

"*Derr Herr*, please show me how to minister to John, to share my love with him without a word. *Sei se gut*, please *Fater*..." She bowed her head for a moment, and then the spark of an idea came to her, bright and light as a flame. And she knew what she would do.

❧❧

The English surgeon looked grave as he approached John and his family in the waiting room of the hospital.

"You're the Miller family?" the man asked.

"*Ya*...yes," John answered, standing for a moment to shake hands with the other man.

"I'm Dr. Caulder. I operated on your father, but it was a bit tricky. His aortic vessel is displaced, probably a congenital defect and—"

"I'm sorry, Doctor Caulder," John interrupted, seeing the confusion on his family's faces. "But could you speak—uh—English, please? We don't understand..."

The doctor smiled. "I'm sorry. I get carried away.

Basically, your husband, your father, will need to spend some more time in the hospital. We'll need to run more tests, see if another surgery is possible, and then he'll have rehabilitation or services that will build up his strength to get him back home."

"How long?" John's *mamm* asked timidly.

"I don't know...several weeks perhaps—perhaps less. He's a strong man, and I expect he'll do well. Thank you all."

Dr. Caulder left in his light blue surgeon's clothes, leaving John with an impression of how weak man's power was compared to the glory and strength of *Derr Herr*. He turned to his family.

"*Daed* will be well to bring glory to *Derr Herr*," he said with quiet strength.

But his *mamm* shook her head. "But you cannot know for sure, John, You must think as *Derr Herr* wills."

John smiled and lifted his head. "But we must have faith as well, *Mamm*. And I will use my faith, as we all should, to believe that *Gott* will heal *Daed*."

His mother nodded slowly. "*Ya*, perhaps you are right, John, and I will do as you say."

"Excuse me." An English woman in a light pink skirt and top approached them. John noticed she was wearing a hospital badge. "Are you the Miller family?"

John rose once more to make introductions.

The woman smiled warmly. "I'd like you all to know that the hospital has a hospitality suite—free rooms to stay overnight while your husband is here. It would make it much easier on you than traveling, I think."

"*Ach...*" John's *mamm* breathed a sigh of relief. "What

a blessing. I would want to stay, and John, what do you think of Esther staying with me?"

John smiled and nodded. "Of course." He knew what a comfort Esther was to his *mamm*. "Matt and I can batch it for a while. It'll improve our cooking skills."

He put an arm around his mother and looked deep into her eyes. "It will be well, *Mamm*. I know.

She rested her head briefly on his chest, and he met Esther's worried eyes over the top of his *mamm*'s head.

"All right," he murmured again, and Esther nodded.

Then the pleasant hospital worker led them through a myriad of halls to a comfortable suite where John felt reassured at leaving his family in peace.

CHAPTER 24

WORD CIRCULATED RAPIDLY through the community grapevine that Dan Miller was in the hospital. It was common of Amish communities to not have traditional insurance but rather to have a fund, managed by the bishop, that would help pay hospital bills and the like. Besides the community fund, many of the women would help out if there was work to be done around the house, and the Miller family was no exception to these versatile aids in funding and support.

In fact, John was awakened the morning following his *daed*'s admission to the hospital by the smell of fresh coffee and frying bacon. He rubbed his eyes and glanced at the clock on the dresser by his bed and saw that it was barely after 5:00 a.m. He dressed quickly, wondering who he'd greet downstairs as his phantom cook. He went down, then stopped motionless when he saw Tabitha at the stove, his *mamm*'s ample apron wrapped twice about her slim waist.

"Tabitha? What..."

"It was either me or Barbara Esch. I practically had to beat her off with a stick," she said briskly. "But when she saw I had the biscuits set, she gave up and went home."

"Really?" he asked, a smile coming to his lips.

"*Ya*, really."

He watched her move easily between the stove and the

table and was glad for once of Matt's late sleeping habits so that he could have a bit of time alone with Tabitha, though he knew it was wrong to want the stolen moments with Rob's beloved.

"So, I guess you won't be leaving for a time," Tabitha asked softly, clearly uncomfortable in bringing up the obvious point.

"*Nee*—not until *Daed* is well, and that could take weeks." He went on, wanting to say the right thing. "Perhaps Rob will be back by then."

"*Ya*, I'm sure he'd be a great comfort to you now," she murmured, setting a glass jar of bright orange marmalade on the table.

John watched the movements of her slender hands, confused by her response. *But what about you? Won't Rob be a comfort to you? Coming back...courting you...marrying you.*

"I think everything's ready. Do you want to get Matt? I heard that Esther stayed with your *mamm* at the hospital."

John shook his head. "Matt sleeps in and works late. *Sei se gut, kumme* and sit down yourself."

He indicated a place at the table, and she slipped off the apron and then sat down on the bench. He sat beside her, deciding to allow himself this slight luxury, but he soon realized that it was a mistake when he caught the sweet fragrance of her soaping and found himself unable to concentrate on his food after their moments of silent grace.

Yet, as they quietly ate and talked, he couldn't help thinking that it should always be like this. *Like this... together...forever.*

❧❧

Tabitha couldn't help thinking that it should always be like this. *The two of us together, eating, talking, living life with whatever blessings or sorrows* Derr Herr *sees fit to give us.*

But she knew that it was enough to be content with the moment, even as she thought prayerfully of John's *daed*.

"Everything is delicious," John praised, and she tried to hide the blush she felt staining her cheeks by getting up to fetch the cinnamon sugar for the toast.

She knew that *Gott* had given her the idea of revealing her love for John through cooking delicacies for him while his *mamm* and Esther were away. It seemed so simple— the proverbial saying that "the way to a man's heart was through his stomach"—but she knew it was more than simply a passing thought. *Derr Herr* had given her the idea, and she would follow through, letting her heart speak through her cooking and baking. Of course, John might never know, but she had faith enough to try.

"I'd like to make you—and Matt—lunch on a regular basis, if you'd allow it," she said after taking a sip of peppermint tea. She knew that John had only to spread the word that lunches were covered, and the community would arrange for food at other times.

But then she noticed that John seemed to hesitate over her offer, his dark blue eyes lowered to his plate and his firm jaw set. She waited, her breath held, until he looked up at her and finally nodded.

"*Ya, danki*, Tabitha. I will tell Matt to let the other womenfolk know."

She couldn't suppress the smile of joy that came to

her lips. "*Nee*, thank you, John. I want to be able to help during this stressful time, and I—"

"Now, what's all this?"

Tabitha looked up as Matt entered the kitchen with a cheerful laugh. She smiled in return though she was disappointed that this stolen time with John had come to an end. She started to rise to fill his plate, but John caught her hand briefly, then let go. "Let Matt get his own food. You cooked—that's more than enough."

"*Ach*," Matt joked. "I can see that you will one day be a gift to your no doubt sweet future wife, big *bruder*...whoever she may be."

Tabitha wondered briefly at Matt's words, then realized that, as one of the youth, Matt must believe that John and she were courting, even though John had elected to move away. She shook her head a bit, confused by all of the social logistics, then remembered that she had never made the call to Rob to tell him about her and John's fake courting. But still, she recalled, John was supposed to have written to his best friend, so hopefully, all would be well except for the fact that she'd have to tell Rob that she no longer wished to court. If *Gott* willed that she could not have John in her life, then perhaps she would be content as a woman like *Aenti* Elizabeth, because she couldn't imagine ever loving another man so long as John walked the earth. Yet her life belonged to *Derr Herr*.

She rubbed at her temple, and John brushed her sleeve with his fingertips. "Are you all right, Tabitha?"

"*Ya*, of course...I was thinking—I must get home for *Aenti* Elizabeth, but I will be back with lunch today. I'm making a rhubarb pie."

"We'll be here," Matt said, licking his lips. "And I love rhubarb pie."

"And what about John?" Tabitha couldn't help but ask.

Matt smiled. "*Ach*, he—"

"He loves rhubarb pie," John said, cutting Matthew off neatly.

Tabitha nodded, avoiding the knowing dark blue eyes bent upon her. "*Gut*," she whispered, then left the warm kitchen for the early morning chill outside.

CHAPTER 25

J OHN WANDERED OUT to the wood shop, determined
to keep working, while waiting for word about his
father. Bishop Esch was due to go to the hospital this
morning while John and Matt decided to visit in the evening, using the local van drivers who usually helped the
Amish travel far for a small price.

John thought of the pleasure he felt in seeing Tabitha
working in his home kitchen and looked forward to the
promise of pie and her presence that afternoon. He gazed at
some cherry wood his *fater* had got in not that long ago, and
an idea came to him, resounding and simple. He wanted
to make something for Tabitha, to say a thank-you for her
willingness to serve Matt and him while his *daed* was ill.
*But not only thanks...I want to tell her how much I love her
without words, to say what I cannot, what I will never say.*

He pushed aside the dark thoughts with determination and walked over to the long pieces of cherry, already
seeing in his mind's eye what he wanted to make—the perfect gift—a pie safe. A pie safe went back more than a hundred and fifty years in Amish American life, and although
it had no padlock on it, the free-standing cupboard was
used to keep household critters out of pies and other baked
goodies. Some Amish women, like his *mamm*, also used
it as a pantry of sorts while others kept it for dishes or

different ready-needed kitchen items. And although John could see the obvious quality of the wood that he had, he was more interested in the tin-punching required to make the traditional doors on the safe. Intricate designs or pictures of everyday objects were often punched, and even fancier punchings were allowed in the Amish community. But, he realized as he gently fingered the wood, all of his plans would have to wait as he knew he had to finish the desk he and his *fater* had started on before his *daed* fell ill.

John sighed as he picked up a piece of sandpaper and tried to concentrate on his work instead of the sweet thoughts of Tabitha sharing his early morning breakfast.

⤳⤳

Tabitha hurried to the cold frames to pull the carrots left over from the winter. Cold frames were an ingenious way of keeping bumper crops coming, no matter the season, and she had enjoyed experimenting with the greenhouse-like effects of the low, angled, miniature gardens.

She'd loved every minute she'd spent with John that morning, feeling a peculiar intimacy in the simplicity of breaking bread together, but now, she knew that *Aenti* Elizabeth wanted to make carrot jam.

"And I'd better hurry if I hope to have time to do the rhubarb pie," she muttered aloud to herself.

She took the bunches of pulled carrots to the outdoor water pump and cleaned off most of the dirt, then she hurried inside.

Fortunately Fram had gone fishing, and Tabitha was left

in the companionable silence that usually existed when she worked with *Aenti* Elizabeth.

She'd already gotten the jars ready, glistening glass atop several tea towels, and now she put the cleaned carrots in a large pot atop the stove to boil.

"How were John and Matthew this morning, Tabby?" *Aenti* Beth asked suddenly.

"*Ach*...fine. I told John that I'd make their lunch for as long as his family's gone—with your permission, of course."

"Certainly, child, and I do pray that Daniel makes a full recovery. I know you must feel the same for John's sake."

Tabitha stilled for a moment in confusion. "For John's sake...of course, but I—"

Aenti Elizabeth gave a rueful laugh. "*Ach*, Tabby, forgive me. *Nee*, you've never said anything about you and John courting, but I've got eyes, haven't I? And I've known you since you were a wee *maedel*...there's not much you can hide from me."

"Oh, but *Aenti* Beth," Tabitha cried, putting down the colander she held ready to drain the carrots. "It's not...I mean, John was planning on going away to his *onkel* Samuel's to work. He was due to leave today even."

"Then you're not courting?"

"*Nee*...I mean...it's rather complicated," Tabitha finished lamely. Then a sudden conviction came from her soul, and she knew that she couldn't keep prevaricating to her beloved *aenti*. She opened her mouth, prepared to cleanse herself of the lies that had haunted her of late, when her *aenti* spoke.

"Love is never easy, child, and I won't question you further. Let's finish the jam so you can set about lunch."

Tabitha sighed, then fetched the sugar and lemon juice and was about to add it to the carrot pulp when there was a knock on the back door.

She went to answer it and was surprised and overjoyed to see Letty standing there.

"Why, Letty, I'm so happy to see you. *Kumme* in."

But Letty's plump cheeks flushed and her eyes welled with tears. "*Ach*, Tabby...I can't. Not when I've made such a terrible mistake."

"*Ach*, but it was only a misunderstanding between us and I—"

"*Nee*," Letty shook her head. "You don't know. I've done something that will really hurt you."

❧❧

John was finishing the varnish on the back leg of the desk and Matt was sawing maple wood when Bishop Esch drove up in his buggy. Both of the *bruder*s immediately stopped work and went to where the bishop was tying off his horse.

"*Gut* day to you, sir," John said. "Do you have word of *Daed*?"

"*Ya*." The bishop looked up at the taller men and stroked his long grey beard. "Your *daed*'s to have a second surgery this afternoon. The doctors are to try to put a stint in the heart vessel that's positioned oddly—they'll give it a *gut* go, they say."

"What about the risk?" John asked.

"There's always risk in life, *sohn*. You must *kumme* to know that."

Yeah, thanks for the cryptic word of support...that's all

I need right now. The wise bishop apparently sensed his thoughts though, because he abruptly gestured to Matt.

"Matthew, I need a bit of firewood. The *nacht*s are still chilly. Do you mind?"

"Uh...sure."

John watched Matt stride off, knowing his *bruder* understood as well as he did that the request for wood was really a simple excuse to get John alone to talk.

"Let's go inside the *haus*, shall we, John?" Bishop Esch asked, already mounting the steps to the front porch.

John followed, knowing that it was no request of the older man—if the bishop asked you for something, you usually did it, and John had been too well trained in the *Ordnung* of his community to do anything differently.

Bishop Esch sat himself down at the table and John did the same, watching the other man idly lift a molasses cookie from the plate that Tabitha had brought for breakfast.

"*Gut* cookies," the bishop muttered, brushing the crumbs out of his beard. "Your *mamm* make these?"

John felt cautious for some reason but responded truthfully. "*Nee*, sir, Tabitha Beiler provided breakfast this morning."

"Hmmm...she'll be a fine wife one day as her cooking matches her comeliness."

John didn't say anything, and the kind old eyes of the bishop twinkled in his direction. "Perhaps a wife for you, John?"

John sighed. "What gossip have you heard, sir?"

Bishop Esch laughed. "I must admit that my Barbara

is not the most discreet of *Gott*'s creatures. She has mentioned that you and Tabitha are courting."

"Rumors," John said, "never come to any good."

"John, I've been bishop of this community since before you were born, and I've watched you and Rob Yoder grow up, side by side, friend by friend, into fine young men. Men I will, in vain, say that I am proud to know. It's only that I wouldn't want anything to destroy that friendship—one, not unlike David and Jonathan in the Bible, I think. Is not Rob 'closer than a *bruder*' to you?"

John bowed his head, and a rush of memories flooded over him—hunting, fishing, scrambling for wintergreen berries with freezing hands and then tramping home for marshmallows in hot cocoa. And then later, serious talks about life and living in the Amish community. Rob truly was closer than a *bruder*, but John could not deny his love for Tabitha.

"*Ya*," he whispered finally. "So you know that Rob has his heart set on Tabitha?"

"Again, Barbara heard something from Letty—and there we have it. I only want you to think, John. Perhaps to remember Phoebe Graber as well."

"Why Phoebe?" John's tone bordered on the defensive.

"What did you learn from that situation—from that—love?"

John frowned, beginning to feel mired in the conversation. "It's not the same," he bit out.

Bishop Esch lifted a gentle hand. "John, it's not my intent to trouble you or to make you doubt your feelings—I only want you to consider Rob—who is not here to speak for himself."

"I know that," John said low and with a troubled look at the older man. "I know."

"*Danki*, John. I only wanted a minute of your time."

Yeah, but you just ruined my whole day... and possibly my life.

CHAPTER 26

ROB WAS STILL familiarizing himself with the layout of the rehab center and its work in patients' lives. To him, it seemed like workers were more intent on paining the patients than helping them out. But then he looked to where his *da* sat panting in a chair after doing a short walk on his new leg.

"Are you all right, *Da*? Are they pushing you too hard?"

His grandfather laughed, a sound Rob hadn't heard in a long time. "It takes pain to produce growth, sometimes, Robbie. Remember that."

Rob nodded and spoke low. "You mean the pain I caused you when I told you about Katie and Clara and me leaving the Amish?"

Da cleared his throat. "Nope, that's not pain; that's love, and how *Derr Herr* works it is His own business. Besides, I like Katie. She took real *gut* care of me."

Rob couldn't help the surge of pride he felt in Katie's skills as a nurse and her compassion as a person.

Then his *da* spoke again. "Though tellin' your *mamm*—well, she might not see things as being all right in paradise." The old man laughed wryly at his own joke, and Rob frowned a bit. *How exactly am I going to tell my mother?* It was a question he still needed to pray on.

❦

Tabitha led Letty upstairs to her room so that they could speak in private, but her heart was pounding in distress as she tried to imagine what her friend had done.

They entered her bedroom and Tabitha went to open the window, letting in the cool spring breeze that refreshed her for a moment and gave her renewed strength. She turned to Letty and sat down on the edge of the bed, patting a space beside her.

"*Kumme*, Letty, sit down."

But Letty had pulled out a white handkerchief and was wiping at her cheeks. "*Ach*, I can't."

Tabitha frowned slightly. "Letty, what is it?"

"Oh, Tabby, I didn't realize...I thought she was changed and truly being my friend, so I told her."

"Her, who?"

Letty sank to the floor. "Barbara Esch," she whispered.

"What?"

"*Ya*," Letty sobbed.

"Well, what did you tell her?" Tabby demanded.

"Everything."

"You mean about me and Rob and John and—"

"*Ya*," Letty mumbled miserably.

"But you don't even know the truth, Letty!"

"I thought I did."

Tabitha bounced on the bed in temper. "Well, you didn't." Then she drew a deep breath and realized that this was her best friend sobbing on her floor, and she came off the bed and sat down next to the other girl.

"Letty, why didn't you simply ask me what the truth was? Don't you know that I love you, no matter what?"

Her friend regarded her seriously for a long moment. "Tabby, would you have told me the truth if I asked for it?"

Tabitha bowed her head. "*Nee*, probably not at first. I became ensnared in lies, like a moth in a barn spider's web. But I'll tell you everything now because I want nothing more between us."

Letty flung herself against Tabitha in response, nearly knocking them over together.

Tabitha had to laugh as she hugged her friend, knowing that no matter what Barbara Esch thought she knew, she'd never come between the love that Tabitha and Letty shared.

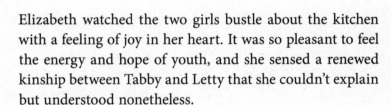

Elizabeth watched the two girls bustle about the kitchen with a feeling of joy in her heart. It was so pleasant to feel the energy and hope of youth, and she sensed a renewed kinship between Tabby and Letty that she couldn't explain but understood nonetheless.

Tabby was intent on making a feast for John and Matt Miller, and more than once Beth's eyes strayed to the well-worn recipe box, sitting on the table. She hoped that John Miller was the love of Tabitha's heart, but she still didn't know for sure. She idly stroked Rough, the puppy sitting on her lap, as she called out ingredient amendments to Tabby's casserole of pork-stuffed apples.

"All right, *Aenti* Elizabeth, we've got the apples ready... how does the stuffing work?"

Elizabeth smiled to herself as she remembered the day she was twelve and had learned to make the hearty dish. Her *grossmuder* had been lovingly firm when giving directions and had not even scolded when Beth had forgotten to core two of the robust apples.

Now her smile extended to Tabby. "The stuffing is simple, really. Just chop up that pork we had the *nacht* before last—make it real fine, as fine as you can. And Letty, you fetch the raisins and bread crumbs."

"What do we moisten it with?" Tabby asked. "Milk?"

"*Nee*," Beth laughed. "Maple syrup, and don't be light on the hand with it either. The more the better. You can always add a bit more pork."

She watched as they scurried to do as she instructed and noted that Tabby kept glancing at the clock. "Don't worry, child. You've got plenty of time for the getting of lunch, or dinner as they used to call it in my day. Supper was at evening."

"I promised them rhubarb pie," Tabby admitted.

"Then they'll have it," Elizabeth smiled. "Say a little prayer that *Derr Herr* will slow the clock down for you to finish your handiwork, and you'll see that you get everything done."

"*Ach, Aenti* Beth." Tabby bent near her. "I do cherish you."

"And I you, dear. Now keep on!" Elizabeth encouraged just as Fram entered with a string of perch.

"You'll clean those outside, Fram. The girls are working in here to minister to the Miller family and we don't have time for blood in the sink," Elizabeth asserted, ignoring her *bruder*'s stamping feet as he turned and went back outside without a word.

All three women in the kitchen giggled faintly and then returned to work. By 11:30 a.m. Tabby had everything loaded in a large wicker picnic basket.

"Add a thermos of that fresh lemonade, child," Beth instructed. "And then everything will be perfect."

Tabby obeyed, and the girl left with Elizabeth's approving blessing upon her.

Everything looks perfect, John thought glumly. *Yet how am I supposed to eat when Bishop Esch left here with my heart and appetite with him? I have got to leave here as soon as Daed is well.* Then the insidious thought came to him that his *fater* might not recover, and it would be left for John to be the main supporter of the family and he couldn't do that living a hundred miles away. Yet how could he live in Paradise if Rob and Tabitha married?

"John." Her soft voice made him turn from where he stood by the table.

"*Ya?*"

"Are you troubled about your *fater*? You're going to go tonight and visit, right?"

"Yes, that's all, Tabitha. I'm only thinking of *Daed*—and how *gut* everything looks, of course."

"I'll say," Matt observed, completely oblivious, John knew, to the turmoil he was in.

John helped with almost mechanical hands to unload the hamper as dish after dish appeared, each assailing the senses with both delicate and rich scents. When they were finished, Tabitha brought the silverware and the blue-rimmed white dishes from the cabinet. John told her where the cloth napkins were kept and tried not to study her trim form as she moved between the table and the drawer of the oak hutch.

They sat for silent grace, and then Matt enthusiastically began to fill his plate. "I'll take this with me out to the wood shop," he announced, and John threw him a desperate look that he seemed to ignore or misinterpret. And then Matt was gone out the screen door, leaving John exactly where he both did and did not want to be—alone with Tabitha.

Matt came in for seconds while John had barely seemed to touch his plate, Tabitha noticed worriedly. She wanted to ask if the food didn't meet with his approval but felt the lump in her throat was too tight to actually speak.

"John, some *gut*-lookin' English woman's out there," Matt mumbled, his mouth half full. "About the desk."

Tabitha couldn't help but meet John's blue eyes and noticed that they'd darkened at his *bruder*'s slang. Then John looked straight at her. "Want to *kumme* with me?"

"*Ya*," she said, feeling breathless. "Of course." *But why did he ask me? How am I supposed to deal with some woman who's* gut-lookin'—*and what does that mean exactly to a man?*

She followed John outdoors into the sunshine which glinted reflectively off the bumper of a shiny red car.

Tabitha then saw the woman—a girl, quite a bit older than herself, she imagined, but wearing a fitted T-shirt and faded blue jeans. Her blonde hair was loose and hung past her shoulders and her brown eyes were darkened with makeup—which Tabitha had to admit she found a bit intriguing.

The woman extended a hand to John, which Tabitha saw he took in a brief grasp. Tabitha merely got a nod.

"I'm Joy Evans," the woman's red lips seemed to purr as she gazed up at John. "I've come to check on my desk."

Tabitha watched John nod and realized for the hundredth time how truly handsome he was—apparently even to a woman from the English world. *But he has so much more than looks—a kind heart, a loving attitude toward his family, a loyalty to his friend.* Tabitha derailed her thoughts and trailed along after Joy, feeling like she'd rather be in the house, especially when the woman stopped for a moment to gaze critically at her.

"Is this your wife?"

"I'm not married," John replied, inching a neatly carved desk forward.

"Oh…that's nice." Joy smiled with a brilliance that Tabitha found unnatural somehow. "I must admit that this little girl looks hardly more than a child—certainly not like a wife, though I've heard that the Amish marry young."

Tabitha immediately resented the question and answered coolly before John could speak. "Some Amish marry young—others wait late to marry until they're about your age." She regretted her unkind words as soon as they were spoken but also didn't miss the laugh John quickly suppressed into a cough.

Joy merely looked annoyed. "Well, thanks for letting me know, honey. Now why don't you run in the house while I discuss price with this fine man?"

Tabitha turned to go, not meeting John's eyes—she'd been naughty enough to mention the other woman's age and felt that the least she could do was go and clean up as penance.

Matt was still eating when she stepped inside and shut the screen door with a click.

"That woman have a go at John?" Matt asked, munching pie and gesturing with his fork.

"Wh—what do you mean?" Tabitha asked as she started to pick up the napkins to take home and launder later.

"*Ach*, you know—think she could get a date out of him or whatever..."

Tabitha shrugged. *Yes, that's probably exactly what Joy was doing even now.* "I don't know."

Matt laughed. "Well, shouldn't you know? I mean—you are courting, right?"

Tabitha handed him the plate of raisin-filled cookies that complemented the stuffed apples. "I forget that all the youth know that."

"Right about now, everyone probably knows that— except my *bruder*, who's heading off for the hills as soon as *Daed* gets better. You know, you could learn a trick or two from that English woman and not let him go." Matt pointed his fork at her.

"Like what?"

To her bewilderment, Matt's incorrigible face flushed red

and he dropped his gaze. "*Ach*, never mind, Tabitha...Here, let me help you clear up. This was a *wunderbar* meal."

Tabitha puzzled over his words in her mind and wondered to herself if there truly might be a way to get John to stay in Paradise, but without resorting to the worldly tricks Matt had pointed out to her.

CHAPTER 27

S O, WHAT DID you say to Tabitha to make her light
out in the buggy before I even had a chance to
thank her for lunch?" John asked his *bruder* as they
bounced around, legs sprawled, in the back of the van that
evening, headed for the hospital.

Matt shrugged. "Nothing. Just told her she could make
you stay."

John shot him a dark look. "Lay off her, Matt."

"But I'm right, aren't I, big *bruder*? She could make you
stay—"

"*Nee.*"

Matt stretched his long arms above his head and yawned.
"All right, then she's the reason you're leaving, and for the
life of me, I can't figure out why."

"Just never mind. We're here. Let's focus on *Daed.*"

"Okay—don't be so touchy."

John didn't reply as they went through the sliding glass
doors and navigated their way through a maze of corridors
and several elevators until they got to their *daed*'s room.

John was disconcerted by the barrage of machinery and
tubes that seemed to protrude from his *fater*'s chest and arms,
but his *daed*'s bright eyes were open and he looked alert.

"*Ach*, John...Matthew...I'm so glad you're here." Their

mamm rose from a bedside chair to hug each *bruder*, and Esther did the same.

"How are you, *Daed*?" John asked, feeling his throat tighten. His *daed* had been strong for as long as John could remember—never ill in bed and had even been able to avoid colds and the influenza. To see him in the hospital bed beneath the white sheets, he somehow looked smaller and more vulnerable, and the sight made John's heart ache.

"I am as *Gott* wills, *sohn*, but these English doctors say I'm 'stable,' so that's a *gut* thing."

John nodded and his *fater* cleared his throat. "I wonder if you all might wander down to the cafeteria—I'd like to talk with John alone for a few minutes."

Everyone hastened to comply, and John was soon seated where his *mamm* had been and reached to pat the back of his *fater*'s tanned hand. His *daed* caught his fingers, and John's lashes felt damp with tears.

"John, I must speak to you in all seriousness for a few minutes."

"*Ya, Daed*?"

"John, you are a dear *sohn* to me, perhaps too strong at times for your own *gut*, but honorable—a *fater* couldn't want for more."

"*Danki, Daed*." John was deeply moved by the words of praise.

"But now I must speak of what would happen should I not leave this place."

"*Daed*—"

"Now, John, we must talk of this. It upsets me more to think that things would not be arranged right, and one thing that's on my mind in particular is your sudden wanting to leave to work in the mountains."

"You know I'd never leave the family, *Daed*, if you—"

"I know that. But what of your own family one day, *sohn*?"

John shook his head. "You needn't worry."

"*Ach*, but I do...because it comes to mind that you've been spending quite a bit of time at Tabby Beiler's *haus* and there's only so much carpentry that can be done in one location."

John shrugged. "Everything is fine, *Daed*." He drew a deep breath. "*Nee*, it's really not fine. I've been keeping things from the family, from you, and I don't like how it feels."

"So, there'll be a wedding *kumme* this fall, John?"

"*Nee*—at least, not a wedding for me."

"*Sohn*, when a man has time to lie in a bed all day, he thinks, especially when his heart has not been working the way it should. I know you were going to Samuel's in the mountains to run, and that's not like you, John. Don't run away from love, *sohn*, because it tends to pursue you, no matter where you go."

"I won't leave, *Daed*," John said after a long pause. *I won't leave, but I'll be trapped forever...tortured in body and spirit by seeing Rob and Tabitha together.*

His *fater* smiled wryly. "That's not what I'm asking of you, *buwe*. I'm asking you to remember that *Gott* is love and is the One who places us in families and the One who gives us love. Forget when you were nineteen, John, and live for this time, the moments *Derr Herr* has given you."

"That's not always easy to do, though I see the sense

of what you say." John smiled ruefully. "And I'm afraid Bishop Esch might not agree with your advice."

"Hiram Esch is a *gut* leader, but he is a man, John, and can be wrong the same as you and me."

John looked up as a nurse came in. He rose then bent to kiss his *fater*'s head. "I'll remember your words, *Daed*. I promise."

Then he walked softly from the room, his heart full as he tried to process what his *fater* had told him in love.

Tabitha chose to walk in the twilight that evening after both *Aenti* Elizabeth and Fram were abed. She had first sat at her bedroom window though as she often did, thinking and praying. But tonight she was restless, wondering how things were going for John at the hospital and if his *fater* was improving. But then she realized that if his *daed* was better, then John would leave Paradise. She sighed at her own realized selfishness and said a quick prayer of repentance.

She toyed in her mind with the words Matthew had spoken at the end of lunch that day. *Could I make John stay somehow, bind him to me? But how? Surely not by being a "gut-lookin'" Amish girl.* She giggled aloud a bit at the thought, then put Rough down on the ground to see to his small needs. She watched the puppy nose around a bit, then smiled as he began to chase his tail.

She knelt to the ground as the puppy circled her and thought back on the kiss she'd shared with Rob. At the time his smooth peck on her cheek had seemed like the most wonderful thing in the world. But the thought of kissing John, his firm mouth on hers, his thick, dark lashes hiding the intense blue of his eyes, made her shiver with delight.

Then her thoughts focused on what she might prepare for him the next day; she'd need to search *Aenti* Elizabeth's recipe box. Rough nosed her hand and she scooped the puppy up, hugging its tender warmth close. She stared up at the star-filled sky and knew a momentary peace in her heart that resounded with the command to "be still and know that I am God."

∽◎◎◎◎◎◎

Elizabeth was dreaming. She was walking across an open meadow where deer lay in the shadows and flowers bloomed with vibrant color. Her hair was loose, but instead of being gray, it was the brown of her youth, honey-stranded with natural highlights as if kissed by the sun. She could feel the grass beneath her bare toes and the brush of the blue skirt of her dress against her knees. She spread her arms wide and twirled in the sunshine, feeling more content than she could ever remember. And then there was a striking pain in her head, one that slashed through the dream and made her gasp aloud as she came awake, clutching her head. She gazed around the darkened room and knew a brief fear in her heart. Waiting for the headache to recede, she drifted back to praying, as was her habit, before falling back into a fitful sleep.

CHAPTER 28

JOHN WOKE TO a strange squawking sound that rang through the house and forced him reluctantly upright in his bed. He glanced at the clock, saw that it had gone five o'clock, and rubbed his eyes tiredly. Then his door burst open and *Frau* Mast, a wizened, toothless widow, appeared like some deranged apparition. He rubbed at his eyes once more. Then Matt appeared beside *Frau* Mast, his hair on end and his shirt undone.

"What is going on?" John asked finally as the old woman squawked again.

"There be a bat in this *haus*, and I cannot abide bats, John Miller," *Frau* Mast cackled.

"A—bat?"

"*Ya!* I be trying to make your breakfast and there it came, right over my head, swooping and swirling—get up, *buwe*, and do something about it!"

John slid to his feet, careless of the fact that he wore no shirt or socks. "Matt, could you—"

Matthew held up protesting hands. "You know I cannot stand bats, John, not since I got bit by that one lying on the buggy seat. I thought it was a candy bar in the dark and took a lot of pain for my troubles—rabies shots—bite marks—*Mamm* hollering—"

Matt and *Frau* Mast suddenly cried out in unison as John saw the bat flap past them in the hall.

"All right," John sighed, reaching for a shirt. "Matt, at least go fetch me a fishing net and take *Frau* Mast downstairs."

He shook his head as the two bat haters fled, leaving him alone to deal with the poor monster.

✤

Tabitha hurried to brew some peppermint tea for *Aenti* Elizabeth, who said she hadn't slept well.

"Should we visit a doctor?" Tabitha asked worriedly as she noticed her *aenti*'s pallor in the dawning light of the cheerful kitchen.

"*Nee*, child. I'm fine, truly. Now tell me what you're planning on making for John Miller at lunch today."

Tabitha sighed, knowing it was a tempting distraction her aunt offered from discussing her health, but Tabitha promised herself that she'd get *Aenti* Beth to a doctor or at least the local healer soon.

"Well, I thought of noodles with buttered crumbs and creamed peas and potatoes and an apple pie."

To Tabitha's surprise, her *aenti* frowned briefly. "Everything sounds *gut* but the pie, dear. You know, the first dish can be heavy, so why not balance out dessert with—say, soft ginger cookies with an orange glaze?"

Tabitha smiled. "Mmmm, now you're making me hungry! I'll have to run over to the Loftus's store to get some powdered sugar for the glaze though."

"Well, I'll feed Fram when he *kummes* down and suggest he goes fishing again."

"Are you sure you feel up to it?" Tabitha asked.

"*Ya*, run along. You know Chester Loftus opens at the crack of dawn."

Tabitha bent and kissed her *aenti*, then did as she was told, her mind filled with thoughts of ginger and orange and how the delicious cookies might be received by John.

John had managed to get the bat outside after a frustrating two hours. Feeling hot, tired, and irritable, he skipped breakfast, despite *Frau* Mast's efforts. He escaped to the wood shop and was half glad when he saw the old woman drive her buggy away.

"Is it gone?" Matt asked, suddenly appearing from the direction of the barn.

John looked up from the business book, where he was studying an order for a table and chairs. "Are you referring to *Frau* Mast?"

Matt laughed. "*Nee*, the bat—though they both might be the same except one makes excellent bacon."

"Nice. But I'm afraid your very real bat came from a sleeping colony in the attic."

"What?" Matt looked appalled.

"Yep. I found a small hole near the window up there where they've gotten in. I'm surprised we haven't heard them moving about more." John was amused to actually see his *bruder* pale a bit.

"What are we going to do?"

"Seal up the hole tonight when the colony leaves for their feeding. They'll find somewhere else to roost."

Matt held up his hands in protest. "Not me, *bruder*. I am not going anywhere near a bat colony."

"*Ya*, you are—that hole repair is a two-man job."

"We—we've got to *geh* see *Daed*."

John shook his head. "*Boppli*... all right, I'll do it myself. You can ride in and check on *Daed*. But you get to clean up the droppings tomorrow when they're gone."

"Bat... droppings?"

"*Ya*. Now let's start on this table."

John hid a smile as Matt began to work, for once quiet and clearly concerned.

❧

Tabitha decided to take the buggy to the store rather than walk. She filled a bucket and gave Swopes a drink before starting out for Loftus's. She got up into the buggy and swung Swopes out onto the drive and down toward the main road that led to town. It was a cloudy but comfortable morning. A light wind caressed her face as she hawed the horse to reach a trotting gait. The road was not busy save for a stray, colorful English vehicle zipping by, but they were respectful enough today and kept their distance from the buggy. Some days, though, she felt her heart up in her throat when a car would cut in unexpectedly. She thought back to the near miss with the van when she was with John. "John has good horse sense," she murmured aloud fondly. She thought back to the tension in the muscles of his forearm as he had steadied the reins. A car passed by and jolted her out of her developing daydream.

She resolved to focus on the road, and before long she and Swopes had arrived at the store. She urged Swopes off the road and over toward the hitching posts, reining the horse to a stop neatly in place outside the front of the store.

"That's how we do it, Swopesy," she said to the horse as she tied the reins neatly to the post.

The store was a large, barnlike structure at least a hundred years old, with wooden planks aged a light grey. There was a sign with the words "Loftus General Merchandise" painted in fancy yellow block script just under the roof and above the entrance. She wondered who Chester Loftus, the owner of the store, had contracted with to make the sign. It was by far the fanciest thing about the building. The rest of the structure looked its age and could have used a good painting, she thought.

As she entered, the smell of spices and cedar wood greeted her. She gazed around with comfort at the familiar surroundings: rustic shelving lined with dry goods mostly in clear plastic bags with white typed labels, funnel cake mix, trail mixes, nuts, dried fruits, sesame sticks, spiced pretzels, noodles, baking mixes, flours, clear gel, baking powder, cornmeal, baking soda, salts, maple syrup—from the small glass jars in maple leaf shapes all the way up to milk gallons full, raw honey, a sign for raw milk, candies and homemade fudge, homemade scented candles, a whole section of homemade salves, tinctures, and a wall full of dry goods to boot.

She liked shopping here both for the quality of the goods and for the good nature of the owner. The store had a welcoming feel, mainly because Chester Loftus made it his mission to make his customers feel welcome. She spied him ringing up some bolts of cloth for *Frau* King and her daughter, Miriam. Above the ladies' heads was a sign affixed to the ceiling with two thin metal chains. The sign read "Cashier," which to Tabitha seemed completely superfluous, because from just about any vantage point in the store, you could see the huge metal register at which Chester now worked.

"Hello, ladies," Tabitha observed. "My, that's a pretty shade of blue." She reached over to one of the bolts on the counter, rubbing it between her thumb and forefinger. "It's got a good feel to it too."

"I get my fabric from a good English supplier down in Lancaster," said Chester. "Brings me good quality at a fair price."

"*Mamm* and I are making some dresses and shirts," Miriam chimed in. "What would you call this blue, Tabitha? I say sky blue, but *Mamm* says just plain blue."

"Hmm." Tabitha mused. "It's somewhere in between I think, but I would have to agree with Miriam," she said, addressing the mother. "There's some very light airiness in the mix here."

"Yup," Chester agreed. "Sky blue it is, said so on the bolt tag. And it'll make a pretty dress, but I'm not sure a man'd like it for a shirt. Maybe a Sunday shirt though."

"We'll have to see, Chester," *Frau* King said, ending the conversation. "Nice to see you, Tabitha. Tell Elizabeth that we said hello."

"I surely will," she replied graciously, grateful that

neither woman had made any reference to her courting—in any context.

"What'll it be for you, Miss Tabitha?" Chester asked. "Would you like some of my fabric here, or are you up to some of that good cookin' I hear about that comes from the Beiler kitchens?"

"No fabric today, Chester. It's the cookin'—I mean, I'm making a meal for the Millers."

"How's Dan doing? I heard about the heart trouble."

"I believe he is stable and in *Derr Herr*'s hands, of course. He'll probably be in the hospital for a while, though, in any case."

"Well, be so kind as to tell the family that they are in our prayers, and you'll not be payin' for the goods that go into that meal. The goods will be a gift from the Loftus family. You just provide the cookin', young lady. And don't argue, I'll have none of it...just tell me what you need."

Tabitha could see by the set of Chester's countenance that indeed there would be no use in arguing, so she just smiled and nodded her head.

"*Danki*, sir. I will be sure to give the Millers your regards. I'll need a bag of flour, powdered sugar, and some ginger."

As Chester was doling out the sugar and flour into plastic bags, Tabitha gathered the rest of the supplies for the meal into her bag.

She thanked Chester again and trundled her supplies out to the buggy.

Tabitha soon returned from the little Amish store, which was hidden from most English eyes in its large, plain building. Herr Loftus had even pressed to know what she was baking.

She'd told him with a smile and had gone to her buggy with a glad heart that she lived in a community where others were interested in little things like cookies...but, she considered, that also meant they knew the big things too, or at least wanted to.

Now, as she entered her home, she noticed with some dismay that *Onkel* Fram was still present. He sat at the table drinking a cup of tea, while *Aenti* Elizabeth looked tight-lipped and tired.

Tabitha decided to act positively and set her purchases on the table.

"We just had breakfast, girl. What are you cooking now? I could still probably hold down a bite or two." Fram smiled toothily.

Tabitha glanced at him. "I'm sorry, *Onkel* Fram, I'm preparing a lunch for the Miller family—there might be a bit of leftovers when I'm through, which of course you and *Aenti* Elizabeth can have. But I'm afraid I must get down to cooking now."

She tied on her blue apron and sought for the yellow mixing bowl.

"Well then, I'll just entertain you while you're cooking, Tabby. You and Lizzie might like to hear a joke or two."

Tabitha glanced at her *aenti*, who gave her an encouraging wink.

"Of course, *Onkel* Fram...I'll—um—listen while I cook."

Fram slapped the table top. "All right then. Have *ya* heard the one about the young Amish teacher who sent a note home with a *buwe*? She said, 'Your *buwe*, Mark, shows the signs of astigmatism. Will you *sei se gut* investigate and take the necessary steps to correct it?' The next morning, she got a note from the *daed*, who wrote: 'I don't really understand what Mark has done, but I've given him a *gut* walloping and you can wallop him tomorrow. That oughta help some.'"

Tabitha laughed, and even *Aenti* Elizabeth smiled.

"That's an *auld* one, Fram."

"You're right, Lizzie...and how about a poem—let's see if I remember it right. It's something about a cookbook a *mamm* gave to her *dochder*.

> My dear, here's a wee book,
> That tells *ya* how I bake,
> The pies and cakes and other *gut* things.
> His *mamm* used to make.
> For men are hungry fellows, dear,
> But this we know about them,
> That cookin' wouldn't be such fun
> If we had to eat without them...
> So take this book with my dearest love,
> And the thought I now impart;
> When you feed a husband,
> Keep in mind—
> His stomach's near his heart.

Tabitha stopped and stared at her *onkel*. *Was this* Gott *speaking through a grumpy* auld *man to give me encouragement that John would see my love for him through my anxious efforts to cook for him?*

A smile of joy touched her lips. "*Danki, Onkel* Fram. That was truly wonderful."

Something of her demeanor must have translated itself to the gruff man, because his face colored and he rose abruptly. "Just some sayin's, that's all...well, think I will *geh* fishing once more. But I'll be back in time for lunch."

Tabitha watched him leave the kitchen, then turned to *Aenti* Elizabeth. "I think I'll make the ginger cookies first."

Her *aenti* nodded in bright agreement.

⌒⊃◉⊂⌒

As it grew near to noon time, John watched Matt slip away from the workshop to clean up and John decided to follow the idea.

He went up to his room, eased down his suspenders, and changed his blue shirt for a burgundy one, then glanced in the small looking glass above his dresser. He realized his black hair had grown overlong of late and decided to run down to the shed and give himself a quick trim before Tabitha came.

Not that it matters to her how I look. No doubt she's missing Rob's face and form, but I might as well not look slovenly.

He was standing outside of the shed, fooling with the scissors and his bangs, when Tabitha drove up a bit early.

He turned to greet her and walked over to the buggy, feeling foolish holding the pair of scissors.

"Hiya," he said, offering a hand to help her down.

She touched him with light fingertips and jumped easily to the ground.

"Are you doing a haircut, John? I—I'm a dab hand at cutting hair, if I do say so...I could help you, if you like?"

He saw the hesitancy in her beautiful blue eyes, almost

as if she was afraid he'd reject her offer. "Uh—sure. That would be great, if you really want."

"*Ach, ya*...let me have the scissors. We can do it on the porch, if you have a sheet and a chair."

"Okay." John led the way to the porch, noticing that Matt was unloading the food.

"Mmmm-mmm," his *bruder* raved. "You two don't mind if I have a bite first, do you? I've got to get going on that delivery of the hope chest to the Fosters'."

"Go ahead," John encouraged, not especially thrilled with the idea of Matt observing when Tabitha cut his hair.

He got a chair set up on the porch and one of his *mamm*'s old sheets, then sat down, feeling suddenly too tall and awkward as he bent his legs tensely in front of him. He laid his hands on his thighs as she flung the sheet out, then wrapped it around his neck.

He shivered involuntarily as her fingers grazed the back of his neck, then his heart started to pound as he was lost in a daze of sensory delight. She ran her fingers through his hair as if testing for its weight, then set about with the scissors, quietly stroking, brushing, and touching him until he felt like he was coming apart into pieces that might never fit back together again. It took all he had as a man to sit still under her gentle ministrations, and then she bent close to do his bangs and her lovely face was mere inches from his own. He couldn't help but focus on her mouth and the petal pink softness of her lips.

It would be so easy to kiss her—just one touch of her mouth to his—like water to a working man. He had to close his eyes when he felt her sweet breath mingle with his own as she leaned closer as if to get one more cut right.

"Well, well, isn't this a cozy scene?"

John's eyes snapped open at the insinuating female voice and looked down off the porch to see Barbara Esch standing, watching, with a sneer on her lips.

He felt Tabitha tense beside him and his lips set in a grim line. "Hello, Barbara, what can we do for you?"

CHAPTER 29

TABITHA GAZED DOWN at the other girl and felt nervous tension flood her body. It was such a different feeling from what she'd been experiencing only a moment before—heady pleasure and the warmth of love— so that she'd felt slightly dizzy standing next to John.

"I've *kumme* to put the ham in, John. I'll be baking it for your supper, and I thought I'd come a bit early in case there was anything you...wanted."

"*Danki*," John said, sounding short to even Tabitha's ears. "There is nothing that I want."

Tabitha swallowed and decided it would be better if she were kind to Barbara, even though she found her to be as sneaky as a barn rat. "Barbara, if it's all right with John, won't you *kumme* inside and share lunch with us after you've put your dish in the oven?"

John rose and yanked the sheet off his neck, then turned to her with a gentle smile that belied the anger of his movements. "You are both graceful and kind, Tabitha. Thank you for my haircut." He turned to stare down at Barbara. "By all means, *kumme* in."

Tabitha watched the other girl flounce up the steps, then enter the screen door without any permission.

John smiled down at Tabitha and caught her wrist when she would have turned to follow Barbara. "I really do appreciate my haircut, and I'm sorry your no-doubt-delicious lunch has to be interrupted in this manner."

Tabitha nodded. He was staring at her so intently—she wondered if her *kapp* was on crooked. She thought he might say something more, but he let go of her wrist and they walked together to the door.

Inside Tabitha put down the scissors and washed her hands at the sink while John sat down with Matt, who was finishing his own meal at the table. Tabitha hoped there would be enough food, as Matt seemed like he had torn through the buttered noodles with ruthless appetite.

She was surprised when Barbara sidled next to her and spoke in an undertone beneath the cover of the *bruders* talking.

"You don't fool me one bit, Tabitha Beiler—you and your false piety. Letty told me all about poor Rob Yoder and your betrayal. Wait until he comes back..."

"Tabitha," John called from the table. "These noodles are wonderful; just as *gut* as my *mamm*'s, and I wouldn't be afraid to say so."

Tabitha moved away from the hiss of Barbara's voice and sank down on one of the benches opposite John. "Thank you." She knew her smile trembled on her lips because she was unused to such a blatant attack from another.

Both Matt and John must have noticed, because they asked in unison, "Are you well, Tabitha?"

She had to laugh then, her confidence renewed as she nodded, deciding that *Derr Herr* would protect her from Barbara's sniping. She was even able to call Barbara away from the stove when she took the tinfoil off the cookies.

"Will you have one, Barbara? They're soft ginger with orange glaze."

The other girl sniffed. "*Nee*, I've my figure to think of."

John took two and Tabitha smiled, taking one herself then joining in with both *bruders* to enjoy the tasty treat.

When they'd cleaned up, Tabitha moved to pick up the wide picnic basket, and John took it from her hands. "I'll carry it to the buggy for you."

"And then you'll be back, John?" Barbara asked in a sultry tone.

"*Nee*, we've deliveries to make. But do be comfortable as you cook…although I'd watch out for bats if I were you."

"Bats!" Barbara screeched, scrunching down. "What do you mean?"

"Big bats," Matt mumbled, chewing a cookie as he shouldered out the door. "Colony in the attic, John thinks."

Barbara straightened and put her hands on her hips. "Well, I am certainly not going to stay in a *haus* with bats! I'll see you at the next singing, John. The ham should be done at five." She marched past the other three, and the screen door slammed behind her.

"Bats?" Tabitha inquired softly. "I love bats. They're so graceful even though they're blind. They display *Gott*'s artistry so well."

John smiled down at her. "I have to seal the hole when the colony is out tonight—would you like to help me? Matt's scared."

"I am not!" Matt hollered through the screen door.

"I'd love to," Tabitha said, feeling her heart race a bit at the thought of spending more time with him. "I'd really love to—*danki*."

❧◈❧

Tabitha gently stroked the pussy willow branches that filled the simple vase in *Aenti* Elizabeth's bedroom.

"*Danki*, child, for bringing the outside in to me."

Tabitha turned to face her *aenti*, who was sitting up, ready for bed. "I wish I could do more for you, *Aenti* Beth."

"Like what?" the old woman laughed. "You are a joy to me and always have been."

Tabitha sighed and pulled a small chair closer to the bed, sitting down on the edge of the woman's rocker.

"*Aenti* Elizabeth, I have to tell you. I—I've been deceiving you—outright lying, in fact, and I want to tell you the truth." Tabitha reached for the hem of the bed quilt and began to play with it nervously.

"I've always found that the best place to begin is whatever comes to mind first when you've got to have a difficult talk, and I promise you that whatever you say, I will always love you, Tabby."

Tabitha met her *aenti*'s kind eyes, and then the whole story came tumbling out in what seemed like confusing bits and pieces, but somehow *Aenti* Elizabeth seemed to make sense of it all. She smiled gently and caught Tabitha's hand. "So, child, John Miller is the true love of your heart?"

"*Ya*," Tabitha half-sobbed, the truth rushing through her like a cleansing spring.

"Well, the truth, my dear, is the best place to start in any relationship, and I am so blessed that you chose to share this with me. You know I've never been married, but the Bible teaches a great deal about marriage that I think you should study upon."

"I know some," Tabitha admitted shyly.

"*Ach*, I'm sure you do, child. But what about applying what you know from *Gott*'s Word to everyday life in a marriage?"

Tabitha shrugged helplessly, and *Aenti* Elizabeth squeezed her hands. "I think that love and grace and mercy—extended to your husband or to any children who might come along—that is the key application and one that will always safeguard your relationships. Now, would you do me the honor of both you and John coming in for a moment to see me before you leave this *nacht*?"

Tabitha nodded in confusion. "*Ya*, surely, *Aenti* Beth."

"*Gut*. Now run along and tidy yourself. I love you, dear child."

Tabitha caught her in a fierce hug. "And I love you, *Aenti* Elizabeth, with all my heart."

⤜◎◎⤛

After his supper of not-so-tender ham, John waved Matt off in the van, then set about grooming Tudor to go and pick up Tabitha. He couldn't deny that he had been moved by the tenderness and delicate workmanship that Tabitha had displayed while cutting his hair. Even now he touched the black strands with a sense of wonder.

Then he shook himself, tossed the horse brush back with the other tack supplies, and hitched up. There was only so much time, really, for the bats would leave at twilight to hunt, then come back as a group when it suited them, so he urged Tudor into a trot and made his way down the short mile to the Beilers.

He set the brake, got out, and tied Tudor to the

hitching post, then he mounted the steps to the door, feeling his heart start to thud a bit as he realized that it felt a whole lot like an English date and he knew he was playing with fire.

Fram Beiler opened the door though, a sad contrast to John's expectations of the beautiful Tabitha.

"Well, *kumme* in, don't just stand there lollygagging all *nacht*, *buwe*."

John suppressed the desire to roll his eyes and responded politely instead. "*Ya*, sir."

"The womenfolk are in Lizzy's bedroom. Said to knock on the door when you got here. Heaven only knows what they're up to."

"Okay." John nodded and made his way to the master bedroom door as Fram retook his seat in the living area with a grunt.

John knocked tentatively on the wood, not knowing what to expect, as he'd certainly never been invited to an elderly woman's bedroom before.

Tabitha opened the door, her eyes meeting his once, then her lashes lowered demurely, their light fullness resting on the cream of her cheeks.

"Hello," he said, feeling awkward. "Am I invited here, or is Fram having a *gut* joke at my expense?"

She smiled then and widened the door. "Of course you're invited. *Aenti* Elizabeth actually wanted to say good *nacht* to us together before we go on our bat adventure. I've just gotten her into bed and settled with her Bible. *Sei se gut*, come in."

John entered a bit nervously but then relaxed when he saw Beth Beiler sitting upright against some comfortable pillows, swathed in a double wedding ring quilt and with her gray hair still kapped, for it was the privilege of only a husband to see his Amish wife's hair unbound. The old woman smiled graciously at him and extended her hand. He took it easily, then bent and kissed her cheek, still as soft as a rose petal and as delicate.

"John Miller." She smiled, her eyes bright. "*Danki* for making an *auld* woman happy. I like your haircut."

He sat down on the edge of the bed. "I'm afraid I have nothing to do with how well it looks." He heard Tabitha laugh softly behind him and smiled.

"*Ach*, but you would be a fine figure of a man, even with a bowl on your head," Beth laughed.

"*Danki*," he acknowledged with a grin.

"Well, I called you both in here to bid you *gut nacht*. I hope that you have a successful time sealing up the entrance, though bats can be tricky as well as wondrous...but I know you'll both have a *gut* time together."

John leaned forward and kissed her cheek again, feeling in some strange way that she was giving them a blessing through her commonplace words, though he couldn't understand why. Tabitha came round the bed then and he rose and stepped out of the way, but not before he caught the simple mint fragrance that seemed a natural part of her, and one that played havoc with his senses.

He watched the two women embrace, then looked down at the pegged hardwoods on the floor, feeling again like he was witnessing something special, though he couldn't put his mental finger on it. Then Tabitha was by his side and they left the room, leaving *Aenti* Beth reading her Bible.

Fram grimaced when Tabitha bid him good night, and John had the unholy desire to wallop the man, though he doubted it would do any good. Fram Beiler seemed miserable enough as it was. But he was not about to let the older man ruin his time with Tabitha.

CHAPTER 30

JOHN HELPED HER up into the buggy, then untied the reliable Tudor and climbed in beside her. The evening air was lush with the glow of a full moon. A stray fox slinked across the road in front of them, intent on the hunt and silver-tipped in its tail by the moonlight.

"The bats should have just gone," he said, struggling for something to say that would make him feel normal. He truly lost his senses with her close beside him. *But there's none of that, old boy. Absolutely not. Rob has got to be home soon, and needless to say, that's who she's dreaming of in this romantic light. Not you—never you.*

He suppressed a faint sigh and set his mouth, staring ahead, concentrating on the road.

"Is everything all right, John?" she asked.

Was it his imagination, or did his name escape her lips like a savored caress? He shivered in spite of himself and shook his head. "*Ya,* surely. It—it was a pleasure to say *gut nacht* to your *Aenti* Beth."

"She likes you."

"And I like her," he affirmed, swinging Tudor into the narrow lane that led to his family's farmhouse.

They were both silent as Tudor ambled to an easy stop, waiting patiently to be hitched. Then John was surprised that when he offered a hand to Tabitha, she put out both her arms. He automatically switched his position to gently swing her to the ground, her body as light as thistledown, though he quickly released her and stuffed his hands in his front pockets to avoid the unknowing temptation she presented to him, her beautiful face tilted upward in the moonlight.

"I'll show you to the attic," he finally managed, and she nodded with seeming pleasure.

He picked up the wooden bucket of supplies that he'd assembled previously from the kitchen table and took a kerosene lamp and offered one to Tabitha, who fiddled with it expertly. Soon they were moving through the house, in both a cocoon of inky darkness and a halo of warm light. It was one of the most intimate things John had ever experienced, this walking together through the familiarity of his home with the one he wished he could share the place with forever. Again, it would be so easy to turn to her, to tell her how much he loved her, to hold her close in the place between light and darkness and promise to stand beside her forever.

But he kept walking, leading her up the back flight of stairs that wound its way in a curved fashion to the attics. "It's a long haul," he commented. "This place once housed thirteen children, I guess—way back in the fifties, before *Mamm* and *Daed* bought it."

"It's a wonder that none of them remained to take over the home and farmstead," he heard her say. "It's so beautiful."

"*Danki*, we rarely use these back stairs, but Esther is a polishing fiend, as you can tell by this smooth balustrade."

"Esther and your *mamm* keep a lovely home."

He smiled in the dark. "And you and Beth Beiler do the same." They'd reached the last step. She swung her lantern out over the downward spiral, and they both stood and looked for a moment at the long shadows in the play of half-light. "You're not spooked by this?" he asked softly.

"*Nee*," she replied. "I think of that Bible verse that says that darkness and light are the same to God—so they must be for us as well."

He turned to her then turned up his lamp. They stood in the circle of light, poised on the precipice of time and turning, and then he shook himself and moved back to open the small door, the handle of his bucket over his arm. "I present, the attic..." He opened the door with a flourish. "I'll go first, in case there are any stray bats. I think the colony is actually located in the left side room. You know these *auld* farm *haus* attics are vast—so there's the big middle trunk room, a room for drying vegetables and the like, and then an *auld* office or garret—which is where I believe the bats are nesting."

They started through the trunk room, which was well organized and even clear of dust, containing old trunks of every size and shape as well as odd pieces of furniture and a giant spinning wheel. "Watch your footing," John warned, stepping over an old red scooter that had been his, then Matt's.

"*Ach*, I'd love to spend a day going through these trunks and seeing what mysteries they contain," Tabitha whispered.

He realized that she'd stopped beside a particular trunk and came back to look at it with her. Her slender white fingers traced the clearly carved outlines of the letters—R A C H E L—and he felt a knot in his throat.

"Who was she?" Tabitha asked gently, almost as if she knew there was something special about the trunk.

"My baby sister—I don't really remember her clearly. She died when she was seven months *auld* of pneumonia. The doctor who came to tend her was English, and he'd been drinking before he got here. He tried to do a tracheotomy to open her throat so that she might breathe, and he merely thrust the tube through her skin, not even bothering to make an incision. She died on the kitchen table..."

"Ach," Tabitha cried softly, sympathy evident in her voice. "I'm so sorry, John, so sorry for your *mamm* and *daed* and the story that has become part of you." He saw her reach out a hand to him, and he put down his bucket and lamp and took it tenderly, caught between the painful past and the promise of the present. He knelt, still holding her hand, and used his other to open the lid of the cedar trunk.

The rich aromatic smell of cedar chips rose up to confront the darkness, and he felt Tabitha kneel beside him. He reached into the trunk and took out a small green and red baby quilt, lifting it gently, then putting it over their clasped hands.

Tabitha bent over the fabric in the light of the lanterns, her golden hair shining where a few errant tendrils had escaped her *kapp*. "Why, it's a Christmas Roses pattern," she exclaimed.

John nodded. "Rachel was a Christmas *boppli*. I believe this was the first quilt that swaddled her."

He let her hold the fabric as she seemed entranced with it, then broke their hand clasp to reach again into the trunk, this time withdrawing a paper envelope that had yellowed with age. He opened the paper and withdrew two bright, soft yellow baby curls.

"Oh, John...they're so beautiful. She must have been a lovely *boppli*."

Almost by instinct, he lifted the baby curls to one of Tabitha's own curls in the play of the light. He watched her look down, and they both saw that the golden colors were almost an exact match. "Your *dochder*s will be as lovely as Rachel was, and may *Derr Herr* bless them with long life upon the earth," he said hoarsely, thinking with *gut*-wrenching clarity of what it would be like to see Tabitha's daughters and not have one of those tender children be his own.

"Perhaps *Gott* will not fill my lap with *kinner*, as our people say." She reached to touch the baby curls with a gentle finger.

John shook himself. He couldn't do this—to her or to himself, but most especially, to Rob. He slid the curls back in the envelope, took the quilt from her, and closed the trunk.

"*Kumme*," he said, helping her briefly to her feet. "We must get to that bat issue."

"All right—but John." Her fingers slid down the length of his arm. "*Danki* for sharing Rachel with me. I—I'll never forget."

He steeled himself against her touch and nodded, picking up his bucket and lamp, then turning to the smaller room on the left where the wild things moored.

༺✿༻

The full moon shone over the kitchen garden, making it a hallowed pool of shadows and light that seemed to invite her to dive in with a wondrous dismissal of the head pain that now had receded to some subconscious part of herself. Elizabeth wheeled herself down the ramp and across the damp ground and set the brakes. She slid out of the wheelchair then leaned forward until she was able to fall onto her belly on the soft ground, pulling herself on her elbows, until her legs stretched far out behind her.

She slid over the grass, then into the softly tilled earth and smiled with joy as her fingers combed with the familiarity of an old friend through the curds of earth. She soon reached the first plants. Touching the ruffled leaves of the beets, she breathed deeply of the sugar onions further on ahead and plunged forward in delight, knowing her soul was content.

༺✿༻

Tabitha wasn't sure why the mood had suddenly changed so drastically between her and John as they had repaired the bat hole with quick-drying plaster. Certainly he had been courteous enough, helping her back through the attics and down the stairs.

But he'd been deeply quiet the last few minutes as they headed for her home and she broached the silence tentatively. "John—I—you sharing Rachel with me—it meant so much. I hope that you do not regret that action."

"*Nee*," he said, his deep voice hoarse, like stones rubbing against stone.

She glanced over at him in the moonlight. He'd left his hat back at his house, and a gentle breeze stirred the dark strands of hair that she'd only so recently had the pleasure to touch and shape. She knew the fine, proud shape of his head and the tanned, well-shaped bones of his face. She longed to know him more deeply, to know his secrets, his hurts, and his joys, but she also knew his honor and she would not ask him to betray his best friend.

They turned into her lane and she struggled to find something to say, but no words would come to her lips. She watched him draw rein and set the brake, then he jumped down and came around to where she sat. Her lips parted and she would have finally spoken when he swung her down without ceremony. Her hands found the breadth of his strong shoulders of their own accord, and she felt the sudden tension that seemed to shake him. Unbidden, Matt's words came back to haunt her—"You could make him stay." She suddenly knew the truth of this with a burgeoning woman's instinct, and her fingers convulsed against his shirt.

His handsome face was flushed and his lashes had lowered to thick crescents on his high cheekbones; she could feel the heated catch of his breath, the rocking forward of his body in slight motion. *It would be so easy to kiss him...to bind myself to him and perhaps force him to choose between Rob and myself.* Yet then, there was a calm, silent stillness in her soul—as if cool, living waters had sprung into motion and soothed her wildly chasing thoughts. She slid her hands from his shoulders and swallowed hard, taking a decisive step away from him.

"*Danki* for the evening, John—I—*gut nacht.*" And then

233

she fled into the house, not bothering to stop until she'd reached the sanctuary of her room. She knelt by the screened-in window, resting her chin on the sill, and listened to the combined sounds of her *onkel*'s snoring and the rampant chorus of spring peepers. And then she heard John's buggy go forward up the dirt lane, and she thanked *Gott* for speaking to her heart.

ॐ

John felt as though he had run miles through knee-deep snow. He'd known temptation in the last few moments that he'd never known with the blatant Phoebe Graber. He'd wanted to kiss Tabitha with a savage tenderness that had shaken him from his temples to the very tips of his boots. But the moment had passed, thankfully without him betraying either Tabitha's innocence or Rob's friendship.

"I've got to solve this somehow, Tudor," he said aloud, talking to the intelligent horse, which pricked up its ears and picked up its gait.

John drew a deep breath. "And prayer seems to be the best answer, at this point." And so saying, he bent his head a bit and began to speak to *Derr Herr*, asking for wisdom and discernment beyond himself.

ॐ

Tabitha's breathing slowed as she inhaled the night air and settled her mind through her prayers. Then a curious flash of light caught her eye down on the ground below her window. The moon moved from behind a cloud and suddenly illuminated *Aenti* Elizabeth's wheelchair, sitting empty alongside the edge of the kitchen garden. For a moment Tabitha thought she wasn't seeing correctly and she pressed her hand hard against the screen. Then she jumped to her feet and tore down the stairs and outside into the night.

She ran first to the wheelchair, then her frantic gaze swept the growing garden. About seven feet out, she saw *Aenti* Elizabeth, in her night clothes, lying on the ground.

A hoarse cry escaped her throat, and she ran and flung herself on the ground next to the old woman.

"*Aenti* Beth! *Aenti* Elizabeth!" Tabitha gently rolled her onto her back and saw the aged chest rise and fall. "*Ach, Aenti* Beth, I'll run and fetch help."

A gentle hand fluttered to up to touch Tabitha's face. "*Nee*, child...I—I am *gut*."

"*Nee, Aenti* Beth, you're not!"

Tabitha clung to her aunt's hand, stroking it again and again against her tear-stained cheek.

"You must listen..." *Aenti* Beth drew a strained breath. "The recipe box...your inheritance...only the carpenter will know its secret."

"All right, all right, *Aenti* Elizabeth—it's going to be okay." Tabitha gasped, then watched as a faint smile played about her aunt's lips and then her dear old eyes closed.

Tabitha understood, from a place deep inside of her, that she was in the presence of death, and there was nothing more to be done. Sobbing, she curled herself around *Aenti* Elizabeth's frail frame, feeling the ground beneath her and seeing the stars above through her blurred tears.

She had never felt more alone.

CHAPTER 31

THE NEXT FEW hours were a merciful blur to Tabitha as she struggled to maintain some sense of calm. *Onkel* Fram ranged between sorrow over "*gut* old Lizzie" passing to making sly references about his now ownership of the *haus* and land. But Tabitha didn't have time for his meanness when she knew she had to prepare for the bishop's visit and then the undertaker—an English Mr. Wesley—to arrive.

She had tenderly changed *Aenti* Elizabeth's dirt-soiled gown once she'd gotten her into her own bed with *Onkel* Fram's help. Now she had nothing to do but wait for morning. Sleep was out of the question, even though Fram somehow found a way to fall to snoring on the couch. Tabitha sat at the kitchen table, holding Rough in her lap and idly sipping at a cup of jasmine tea. She felt wide-eyed and beaten, and she knew that she had cried all of the tears that she could while in the garden. *I wonder if the salt will make the plants grow better.* She knew she was over-tired and then wished more than anything that John might appear and take her in his arms. She cuddled Rough closer on her lap with one hand, then lay her head down on her arm on the table, not realizing when she fell into a deep, fitful sleep.

❦

"She's completely worn out—poor thing," Ann Yoder whispered to John in the early morning gloom of the darkened kitchen.

"I'll carry her up to her bed if you'll accompany us," he said, already easing a sleeping Rough from her lap.

"Let me have the pup, and you lead the way with the poor girl. Heaven only knows how she managed to fall asleep with the likes of that man's snoring."

John carefully nudged Tabitha into his arms and lifted her with ease from the table. Her head fell back against his arm, revealing the bruise-like circles beneath her eyes, but he thought that she was still achingly beautiful, and he trod the steps to her room as if he were carrying a babe in arms.

Ann turned back the covers, then bustled out of the room. "This pup needs to pee," she whispered in a carrying tone over her shoulder. "And I'll not have my best apron soiled."

John heard her go downstairs, then gently laid Tabitha down. He decided there would be no harm in slipping off her sensible shoes and did so easily, but then she began to murmur and he put a reassuring hand on her brow.

"Mmmm—John, please. Please, *Gott*, send John..."

He almost withdrew in shock and amazement that she called for him in her sleep-drugged state. *She probably is only thinking that Rob is away and needs a strong shoulder to lean on during this difficult time.* But he could not deny that the sound of her speaking his name had brought raw tears to his eyes. He wanted so badly to ease her pain. He was so grateful that the bishop had stopped to tell him the news of Beth's death before taking the buggy into town to fetch Mr. Wesley—a man used to the Amish and their odd hours of action.

John gently stroked the hair that had worked loose from her *kapp* and wished he knew how to comfort her. The best he could do was ease the sheet and quilt up over her small frame and then leave her in peace, though he longed to stay beside her. But courting or not, it wasn't proper for him to be alone with her in her own bedroom. So, with another tender stroke of her pale cheek, he left her to get some sleep while she could.

Tabitha awakened to bright sunlight streaming through her window, and for a brief moment she wondered if the night before had been nothing but a bad dream. But then she saw the dirt stains on her sleeves and hands and knew once more the wash of sorrow that *Aenti* Elizabeth was truly gone. Tabitha rubbed at her eyes, then wondered how she'd gotten into bed, when there was a soft knocking at her door.

"*Kumme* in," she called, her throat still a bit hoarse from all of her crying.

To Tabitha's surprise, Ann Tudor entered bearing a tray with a mound of toast beside a delicate pot of tea.

"And before you say you cannot eat, think of all that you must do today. You'll need your strength, even with John by your side." Ann settled the tray on the bed beside

Tabitha, then moved to raise the simple window blind higher.

Tabitha winced at the onslaught of sunshine, then spoke slowly. "John?"

"He's been sitting downstairs for three hours now, waiting for you to waken. Why, how do you think you got to bed in the first place if it weren't for his strong arms?"

Tabitha combed her memory, trying to pick out any moments in John's arms, but she'd been exhausted and the time was lost to her. She picked up a piece of toast and Ann smiled.

"*Gut.* Eat. And in case you're wondering why I'm here—well, I saw the bishop passing and hailed him, with my nightgown on to boot. I figured since you've been bringing me pies and all that, the least I could do was help you out today." Tabitha chewed quietly, then asked, "Why pie?"

Ann laughed. "You mean, why is pie the key to having a friendship with me?"

Tabitha nodded, and Ann sat down on the side of the bed, careful not to disturb the tray.

"Why, child, pie is something that—that—look, you've heard of the English writer, Mark Twain, right?"

Tabitha nodded tiredly. "*Ya.*"

"Well, I read once that Mark Twain said "Pie needs no advertisement," and he's one smart *Englischer* for writing that. Pie is *gut* for breakfast, lunch, or dinner—it's far better than cake. And pie just seems to make people happier. I remember once when—" She broke off so suddenly that Tabitha was intrigued against her will.

"You remember when...what?"

"Never mind," Ann sniffed. "It's nothing."

"It's about my *mamm* and *daed*, isn't it? *Aenti* Elizabeth—she—she told me how you were once all three *gut* friends, but now they're gone, just like *Aenti* Elizabeth."

"*Ya*, child, and I'd give anything to have them back. You see, I was jealous when your *fater* chose your *mamm*—your *mamm* and I were real close. And we tried baking different pies to win the attentions of a certain gentleman, but in the end, he liked your *mamm*'s apple far better than my huckleberry with a spiced crust. We fought over pie. It seems so silly now. I'm sorry. I bet you won't want to speak with me now that you know the truth."

Tabitha didn't miss the ring of wistfulness in the other woman's voice, and she thought about her and Letty and how they'd made up. Tabitha reached out a hand and laid it tenderly on Ann's weathered palm. "I'll make you pie anytime, *Frau* Yoder."

The older woman smiled. "Call me Ann, honey."

⁖⁖⁖

John thought Tabitha looked so fragile, clad in a dress and pale blue blouse that matched her sorrowful eyes. She didn't wear all black, and he knew instinctively that this was in tribute to her *aenti*—who had died in all the vibrant color of an early spring garden.

Tabitha lifted her gaze to his, and he nodded as if to reassure her that she could get through the coming hour or so, for the bishop and Mr. Wesley had already arrived and were being admitted by Ann Tudor.

The bishop came, as he did to any death, to offer the condolences of the community and to bolster the spirits of the family left behind. Mr. Wesley came to take the body away to be prepared for burial, to be dressed in a white dress and *kapp*, and to be placed in an old-fashioned coffin that had a top half that opened so that those at the funeral might pass and look upon their loved one once more before burial.

All of this passed quickly through John's mind now that the men had entered the house, and Tabitha accepted their handshakes and words of kindness. There was, he realized, a certain spine of steel in her, as she stood slim and straight, speaking to the men. He admired this when he could also see that she shifted uneasily from foot to foot, as if in anxiety but determined not to show it.

The women of the community came too, bringing hearty food and casserole dishes that could be kept to eat late at night when sleep wouldn't come because of sorrow. Sometimes a woman would come and simply sit in silence in the living room as John and Tabitha sat too. There were no words spoken—as often the mere presence of a friend brought solace without unnecessary conversation.

And then John realized that Tabitha wasn't eating, and he sought in his heart to do something about the situation. He knew she'd feel better in the days to come, but he wanted to try his own hand at tempting her appetite. He decided he'd rope Matt into helping him and left Tabitha a bit early to set about exploration of the unfamiliar terrain of his *mamm*'s kitchen.

❧❧❧

"Now what is it you want to do?" Matt was chewing an apple and looking both doubtful and confused.

John blew out a breath of frustration. "Look, Tabitha didn't really eat today that I noticed and—"

"*Ya*, and her *aenti* just died, so who wants to eat? And with that creepy *Onkel* Fram hanging around, I'd lose my appetite too."

John chose to ignore his little *bruder's* excuses. "Matt, I want us to cook her some—well, *gut* things to have for breakfast tomorrow that might tempt her appetite."

"Exactly what kind of good things?" Matt chewed suspiciously. "You know neither of us knows how to do little but scramble an egg."

"I've been looking through *mamm's* recipe box and—"

"What?" Matt chortled. "I would like to have seen that."

John sighed. "Look, we're making her miniature raisin pies, all right?"

Matt choked on his apple. "As in—many pies? We couldn't even get the pie crust done correctly for one single pie, let alone many small ones."

"O ye of little faith." John smiled. "Let's pray and see how it goes."

John was glad that Matt held his tongue for the odd baking prayer. "Okay." John clapped his hands when he'd finished. "*Mamm* writes that a secret to mini-crusts is putting cream cheese in the dough. So, that's what we're going to do. Now wash your hands."

Two hours later John surveyed the messy kitchen table with satisfaction.

"Well, we did it, little *bruder*. *Danki*." John suppressed a grin; Matt looked like he'd been wrung through a flour mill. However, the reality was that twelve miniature and delectable-looking raisin pies sat on a simple dish, ready to be taken to Tabitha in the morning.

John clapped Matt on the shoulder, and a flurry of spices emanated from his younger brother's shirt. John did laugh out loud then. "I don't think there's ever any chance of either of us taking the art of pie making for granted."

"That's easy for you to say," Matt moaned. "You've got a girl to cook for you."

John nodded, the smile fading from his face. "*Ya*...look, Matt—" But the truth he'd been about to share was lost as his *bruder* made a dive for the nearly empty filling bowl and the moment was gone.

John slowly set about putting the kitchen to rights as he prayed that his small gift might bring on Tabitha's appetite and do her heart *gut*.

⤜◎◎⤛

Tabitha was up before dawn the next day. She felt too restless and keyed up to sleep much past 5:00 a.m. She wandered restlessly about the kitchen, touching things here and there and missing her *aenti* so much that she could feel the pain like a palpable thing within and around her. She had no desire to eat, and it was too early to start *Onkel* Fram's breakfast as he usually didn't rise until an hour or so later.

She walked into the living room and dropped onto the

couch with a disconsolate sigh, then started upright when the back door was eased open with a tiny squeak.

"Who's there?" she asked into the gloom, then breathed a sigh of relief when she saw John's tall form enter.

"It's me," he said softly, and she was reassured and comforted by his familiar deep voice.

She noticed that he balanced a tin-foil wrapped plate in one hand as he came toward her, and she gave him a wan smile. "Did someone leave more food outside?"

He eased down onto the couch beside her. "I bet you're sick of food, aren't you?"

"I don't mean to be ungrateful. I know that many people don't know what else to say or do, so they bring food. I—I can't seem to work myself up into eating though," she admitted.

He tugged the tinfoil off the plate with gentle fingers. "*Ach*, but this isn't any *auld* food, Tabitha."

She peered down onto the plate and saw the small circle shapes. "Miniature pies?"

"*Ya*, and I made them—at least, Matt and I did."

She felt a laugh bubble up unexpectedly in her throat. "You made them—for me?"

He gave a soft laugh too. "I know it might seem odd, but I was worried about you not eating and I thought maybe something small and dainty...might—well, tempt your appetite."

Tabitha stared at his strong fingers holding the plate. *To think, he yielded that strength to make something with tenderness and care so that I might eat.* She felt a pang of hunger in her belly for the first time since her aunt died.

She lifted one of the little pies and cradled it in her palm. "I'll have one if you do."

"Done," he agreed.

She watched him eat and then took a bite herself. "Mmmm—raisin. One of my favorites." She chewed thoughtfully. "It's really *gut*."

"Are you surprised?"

"Well," she smiled. "*Ya*." She felt shy suddenly, sitting there in the half light, sharing food with him. But he chose another pie from the plate and leaned back on the couch, and she did the same.

Then she felt like talking, in much the same way she had felt like eating—with a sudden pang. "John?"

"Hmmm?"

"How do you get over it—someone dying, I mean?"

She watched him shake his head. "I could tell you something of *Derr Herr*, I suppose," he said after a moment. "But even *Derr Herr* wept and mourned when He lost someone He loved." He spread his hands before him, then turned to her. "I guess you keep hurting for a while, maybe a long while. And maybe that hurt gets less after time, but it could be that it flares up in heartsickness—like a cycle. I don't think there's meant to be an easy answer."

"I want there to be. I'm afraid I'm not very *gut* at feeling pain, and it seems that it's one emotion that demands to be felt." She passed a hand over her eyes.

"That's true," he agreed. "And, of course, the emotional and spiritual pain starts to feel like something physical so that you don't want to sleep—or eat. But I think, I think life is waiting for you, Tabitha. I think it waits in all of the stars that will shine, all of the seasons to come, in the very garden where your *Aenti* Beth died—it waits for you to come and join again in the world *Gott* has given you."

She smiled faintly, feeling her heart respond to his encouraging words. "You're wise, John Miller, do you know that?"

"*Nee*, at least I don't feel that way much of the time."

She reached out an impulsive hand and touched his wrist, then let her fingers slip away. "You should, John. You've done my heart *gut*—with both your words and your pies." She picked up another raisin-filled crust and took a bite. "*Danki*," she whispered.

"You're welcome."

She told herself that she imagined the note of sadness in his voice and concentrated on finishing her pie.

CHAPTER 32

THINGS FINALLY SETTLED down to a tense normality for Tabitha following her aunt's simple funeral. She cooked and cleaned her home just as she would have done with *Aenti* Beth, and a week slowly passed. However, each day Fram grew more irascible, and finally, one afternoon, he bade her to come and sit down at the kitchen table for a talk.

"Now look here, girl, I can't complain about your cooking, though I could do with a few more pies here and there..."

"Is that what you wanted to talk about, *Onkel* Fram?" Tabitha asked with a faint smile, though her heart was beating fast at what must surely be coming regarding the house and land.

"Hmm? *Nee*...no, of course not. The point I'm trying to make is that I'm used to living alone. I like it that way."

Tabitha felt her heart sink and began to pray inwardly.

"But—" He paused significantly, as if he was about to bestow a favor. "I am a bit pleased, as I said, with your cooking and cleaning, and I wouldn't mind you living here as a hired girl, so to speak."

"A...hired girl?" Tabitha's lips trembled. It seemed the lowest of insults to not only want to rob her of a sense of home but also expect her to go on with its care and upkeep as if merely a servant. Hired girls, though still present in some communities, were becoming a thing of the past, yet here, her own uncle wanted to revive the tradition of a girl working for mere pittance even though she was family.

"*Ya*, you should be grateful I suggest it. You know you've inherited nothing but a recipe box—which proves old Lizzie was part crazy. But she did have enough sense to give me the land and *haus* as was my due. Now, I can see those big eyes of yours filling up, and I won't be swayed by any female theatrics. So, there it is. A hired girl."

Tabitha rose like a mechanical doll from the table, feeling like her arms and legs were leaden with each movement. "I think we need some fresh mint for dinner," she heard herself say in a surprisingly calm voice. "I'll go to the woods and hunt some up."

"Hmm? What's that you say? Mint? Why, I'll have your answer now or you can pack your bags and hire on with somebody else around here."

Tabitha looked at him steadily, though she was devastated inside. First *Aenti* Beth and now this. "I'll give you my answer when I come back with the mint, *Onkel* Fram. You wouldn't want me to make a hasty decision, would you?"

He stroked his long grey beard. "*Nee*, perhaps that's wise. But when you get back and not a minute later."

Tabitha blocked out whatever he was about to say and grabbed a basket from a hook on the kitchen wall. She slung the basket over her arm, nodded to her uncle, then managed to walk across the kitchen and out the door before she drew a desperate hiccupping sob, then took off at a run, like a doe pursued by hunters, toward the line of woods far on the other side of the fields. She ran as if she never wanted to be found or heard of again, and desperation gave her speed until she finally broke the line of pine trees and had to stop, panting with a deep ache in her side. She dropped to her knees on the pine-needled ground and let her tears flow freely.

Ach, Aenti *Beth, how I wish you were here.*

☙◌❧

John entered his *fater's* hospital room to find the bed empty and the sheets in disarray. For a moment he felt like his heart stopped because, in a rush, he saw what it would be to have his *daed* really gone from earthly life. He knew suddenly that he had to tell his father the truth about his life and why he wanted to leave while his *daed* was still present.

He walked out into the hall and caught sight of his *daed* moving slowly with a walker near the nurses' station. A nurse walked carefully beside his *fater*, and John came up to them silently, not wanting to startle his *daed*.

But the nurse noticed him and smiled broadly. "Your father's making great progress. Do you want to take over for me? Just make sure he doesn't overdo."

John nodded and switched places with her, touching his *daed's* folded fingers gently. The older man gave him a tight smile. "Like a *boppli*, I am."

"Sometimes we all have to start new."

"*Ya.*"

John watched his *fater's* face as he concentrated on each step, and he knew his *daed* was in pain. "That's enough I think, *Daed*. Let's turn and *geh* back to your room."

"*Ya.*" His *fater* breathed again, and John helped him slowly turn the walker.

It was strange, seeing his *daed* so fragile in his white hospital gown that was stretched with its wrinkled ties across his broad back. Strange and sobering.

Once he'd gotten his *fater* tucked up in the bed, John sat down in a nearby chair. His mother and Esther had gone to get supper, and he was grateful for this time alone with his *daed*.

"You've got something on your mind, *sohn*?"

"I'll tell you if you have a bite of whatever is under that plastic lid."

"*Ach*," his *fater* grimaced. "I miss your *mamm*'s food, *buwe*. Still, the meals aren't too bad. I imagine Tabitha Beiler hasn't been making you lunch now that Beth is gone."

"*Nee*," John rubbed at the back of his neck. "Look, *Daed*, I need to talk to you."

"As I asked, you've got something on your mind?"

"*Ya, Daed.*" John drew a deep breath. "I love Tabitha, but she loves Rob. And Rob, as my best friend, asked me to keep the secret of his and Tabitha's love and also to watch over her while he's gone. I've betrayed him and just about everybody by lying both this way and that to try and keep secrets from you and the family and basically everyone."

"Is that why you got it in your head to *geh* away to the mountains and work?"

"*Ya.* I thought...well, I don't think I could stand seeing Rob and Tabitha building a life together in Paradise."

His *fater* sighed and stroked his beard. "Have you told Tabitha how you feel, *sohn*?"

John groaned faintly. *"Nee*—I can't."

"John, I believe *Derr Herr* deals in truth, and as the Bible says, 'The truth shall set you free.' You may find that Tabby Beiler is not of the mind or heart you think she is. And, if I'm wrong, then you've taken back your life by risking to tell the truth. And I've got to say that I question Rob's judgment in asking you to lie, to conceal. It isn't right before *Derr Herr.*"

John closed his eyes as his *daed*'s words sank in. Then he looked at his *fater*'s kind face. "Maybe I should tell her—to have it out there. And to feel clean...right now it seems that I've got to keep track of a dozen stories depending on who I'm talking to."

"That's the way of a lie, *sohn*. It eats you up inside until you stand up to it."

John nodded. "All right, *Daed. Danki* for the advice—and for being my *fater.*"

The older man smiled gently, and John felt the warmth of love in the enfolding look and knew he could face the truth with both his *daed* and his heavenly *Fater* on his side.

<hr>

"You can let me out here," John told the van driver, then paid the man and walked down the lane to Tabitha's house, noting with pleasure the land bursting to vibrant life and strength under the recent rain they'd had. Today it was sunny and warm, and he had it in mind to ask Tabitha to go for a walk, if she wasn't busy in the garden. He'd made it a habit of late to drop in and see her for a short while each day, gently trying to cheer and comfort her for her loss.

He went to the back door to knock, as was his custom, and was surprised when Fram answered with a guttural greeting.

"*Ya*, what is it that you want?"

For you to be human, John thought, then reproached himself. *Fram is what he is—rotten*. "Is Tabitha home?"

"*Nee*, she's run off to the woods to think about what I told her."

John began to worry. "May I ask what you told her, sir?"

"*Ya*. I gave her my blessing to live on here as a hired girl. She said she had to think about it."

"A hire—" John had to break off and clenched his hands around the straw brim of his hat to keep from the unfamiliar and forbidden feeling to want to do Fram bodily harm. "How long has she been gone?" he gritted out.

"She said something about gathering fresh mint this afternoon...but it's past time for her to start on dinner. Now, if *ya* don't mind, I was taking a nap."

The screen slammed and bounced once in John's face. Then he turned angrily and started across the porch. His head was down, so he almost ran full tilt into the tall frame coming up the steps. He lifted his head and stared down into familiar brown eyes.

"Rob?"

⥼⥽

Tabitha finally gathered her thoughts as best she could and got to her feet on shaky legs, drained by all of her tears. She bent and picked up her basket, determined to collect some mint as long as she was in the forest.

She wandered along a deer trail, a slightly bent grass marking that, to the careful eye, led to a bed of rest for the animals. Then she moved deeper into the woods. The pines were aromatic and refreshed her, even against her will. She stepped over old pine cones protruding from the straw floor of the forest and listened to the majestic quiet that seemed to be a part of the place. Sunlight slanted through the pine canopy here and there, and as she walked, she began to feel more relaxed. She came to a grassy bank that bordered a bubbling stream and saw some sweet mint growing on the other side of the water.

She balanced her basket in her right hand, then set out, jumping from one dry rock to another and then testing the sturdiness of a sharp-angled stone when she saw no other way to pass. She put her full weight on it and it gave way, landing her in the creek with a sudden tearing pain in her ankle that made her forget her soaked clothing and everything else.

She had never fainted in her life, but now she knew a dizzy sickness and the water seemed to circle about through her brain. *I must get out of the creek*, she thought to herself, the throbbing pain in her ankle matching the beat of the words in her head.

She dragged herself over the rock-bottomed creek, feeling her hands bruise with the water up to her elbows. *Help me,* Gott, she prayed. Somehow she gained the stand of mint and grasped its sturdy stems, digging her finger-nails into the ground. Finally she managed to lie with her upper body on the bank while her legs and seemingly useless ankle still floated in the water with the hem of her dress. Then she did give in to the merciful pull of darkness that ate at her in red-black motions until she lay still, unconscious, on the damp of the earth.

☙ ❧

John was torn between two warring emotions as he looked at Rob—the desire to hug him and the fierce, forbidden feeling of wanting to grab him by the shirt front and shake him until his fine teeth rattled. He opted to do nothing and merely stared into the eyes of the person he thought he knew but whom he'd never really understood.

"John? You have an odd look about you..." Rob's tone was light and grated on John's nerves.

"And you look odd to me too," John said, as memories flooded his mind. *I'm going to lose a friend, but maybe I'll find something better in the loss.*

"I look odd?" Rob brushed down his immaculate shirt front and raised a questioning brow.

John smiled sadly. "You won't understand. It's my fault—my willingness to lie for you, to keep a false sense of honor."

"What are you talking about?"

"You asked me to watch over Tabitha—to keep your so-called love for her a secret from the community and your *mamm*, but you never considered the cost or the burden of the lie."

"Hey, John, you're talking out of your head. Anyway, I've got *gut* news. I'm in love—real love. Her name's Katie. She's a nurse and has a little girl named Clara. They're English."

John stared in mute dawning horror at his friend as

Rob rambled on briskly. "I realize that I was just playing at love with Tabitha, but what I feel for Katie—it's different."

John shook his head in amazement and disillusionment. "What are you going to do about Tabitha? She loves you, Rob. And I won't stand to see her hurt—any more than she's already been by your neglect and unfaithfulness. You never wrote her or called her or—"

"My unfaithfulness," Rob said, cutting him off. "Hey, John Miller, I happened to see Barbara Esch on my way over here, and she had a few secrets to tell. So you let me know who exactly is unfaithful."

"You didn't receive my letter?" John asked angrily.

"What letter? The kids around my *grossdaudi*'s liked to run get the mail and play with it at the same time. The letter was probably lost to the wind."

John sighed, knowing he had to explain, but at the same time he was anxious to go after Tabitha. "All right. I don't know what Barbara said, but I wrote that I was pretending to court with Tabitha to keep the other *buwes* away."

Rob seemed to weigh out the words. "And were you?"

"Was I what?"

"Only pretending. You didn't come to love her yourself?"

John felt a sharp stab in his spirit. It would be so easy to lie once more, to put this behind him. But he knew Rob deserved the truth—even if his friend might not understand its value.

John swallowed hard and nodded. "I love her, but she doesn't know, and I wouldn't have you tell her. I'd planned on going away to work at my *onkel* Samuel's as soon as *Daed* gets well and will allow it."

"Why?" Rob suddenly asked, and John was confused by the almost lightness in his friend's voice.

"Because I couldn't stand to see you two together—married, *kinner*...I...why are you smiling? And what about this...this English girl?"

Rob clapped him on the back. "You know, it's a strange thing, but I had a dream the *nacht* before last that you and Tabitha were married. My bet, old man, is that she loves you too. Let's go in and find out." Rob brushed past him and started for the door.

"What? Wait—she's not in there," John cried.

"Well, where is she?"

John blew out a breath of frustration; everything was upside down. He explained the situation quickly, in the way that a person can do with someone they've known forever. With few words the two men ran to the fields and then on to the forest—together in gait. And John began to pray for Tabitha, hoping that Rob was doing the same.

☙❧

Rob tramped through the woods, and his heart pulled at him as he thought of both Tabby and then John. His friend's face was bone white and lined by the gravity of the situation. Rob could only imagine how he might feel if it was Katie or Clara who was in the woods with dark soon approaching.

He stepped over a weather-felled branch and said a quick prayer in his heart that the situation would turn out well.

"Hey, John?"

"What? Did you find something?"

Rob shook his head, then hurried to catch up as John seemed to double his pace through the dense forest floor.

"John...I want to apologize."

"For what?"

Rob swallowed. "Maybe for not valuing you enough as a friend, as a person. I've learned a lot about life from Katie, and I know—well, I know I always haven't treated you fairly."

"It doesn't matter," John said absently, pushing ahead through some laurel overgrowth.

Rob caught the branches and kept going. "Hey, John?"

"What?"

"We'll find her. I know she'll be all right."

Rob saw John's nod and prayed in his heart that the words he spoke with such assurance were really the truth.

꩜

After an hour of searching and calling, John was deeply worried. "Anything could have happened...someone could have come along...or—"

"Don't think like that," Rob replied gloomily. "But perhaps we had best go back for lanterns. It's past supper time."

"You go and bring the men of the community to search. I'll keep looking," John said, already turning in a different direction toward a faint deer trail.

"All right," Rob agreed, turning to go.

Then John bent to study the grass as he heard the bubbling of a creek in the distance.

CHAPTER 33

TABITHA CAME AWAKE to a sick sensation of pain and the sound of a hoarse voice hollering her name. The sunlight no longer passed through the trees, and she could tell that it was near dusk and especially dark and cold where she lay.

She tried to answer back, filling her air with lungs to call "Help!" in the strongest voice she knew, but it seemed no match for the waters of the creek. She tried again, this time screaming as if her life depended on it. The cry ricocheted through her, and she sobbed aloud at the echoing pain in her ankle.

"Tabitha!"

She turned her head to see John splashing through the creek, racing to get to her.

"*Ach*, John." She couldn't help crying.

He knelt on the ground beside her and gently took her hand. "Tabitha—oh, praise *Derr Herr*. Where are you hurt?" She noticed his arms were shaking, and her eyes filled with tears. Ach, *he's so worried for me, perhaps he*—

"My right ankle," she sobbed.

"We've got to get you out of this creek or you'll catch pneumonia for sure. You're already shaking like a leaf."

He released her hand and moved back into the creek. She bit her lip as he knelt in the water near her ankle.

He looked up, and she saw both the fear and determination in his dark blue eyes. "I'm sorry, sweetheart. I'm going to have to hurt you to help you."

Sweetheart? He called me sweetheart—and then he lifted her legs, supporting her ankle, and she fainted once more.

☙ ❧

John had thanked the men who had come with Rob, bearing lanterns, to lead him back out of the forest as he carried the still unconscious Tabitha in his arms. He had felt odd holding her with Rob walking by his side, but his friend had made no offer to carry her. John had feared that she might awake and see Rob and then be confused, but she stayed deeply out, so much so that he thought they should take her to the hospital. But once they got to Tabitha's house, they found *Frau* Ebersol, the local healer, waiting on the porch.

"Her ankle," John said to the ancient-looking woman who knew much about herbs and disease, as well as bones and blood. She made no claim to being a doctor and often referred their people to specialists in Lancaster, but now she nodded.

"Take the child into the bedroom downstairs and put her on the bed so I can examine her before she wakes."

John hastened to obey, not even truly noticing Fram, who hovered on the edge of the bustling movement.

The other community men had gone to their own homes, but Rob went with John and *Frau* Ebersol into the room.

"I'll leave," John said in an undertone to his friend once he'd laid Tabitha on the bed.

"You'll do no such thing," Rob whispered back calmly. "It's your right to be here as the one who loves her. I've got to go call Katie. *Gut nacht*, John."

"Hey." John grabbed Rob's arm. "What about when she wakes up?"

"She has no idea I'm here." John felt him pull away and was going to stop him when *Frau* Ebersol called across the room.

"If yer done fiddlin', I need some help gettin' her some dry things to wear."

"I'll fetch a woman to help you," he said, shaking his head.

"I jest need *ya* to run over to her *aenti's auld* room and fetch a flannel robe, *buwe*, not look upon her."

"Oh—right... okay." He hurried to obey and returned to find Frau Ebersol examining Tabitha's ankle.

"Not broken... badly sprained," she said finally, looking up at him.

"You're sure?" John asked.

"*Ya*." She gave him a pointed look from her raisin brown eyes. "I be sure."

John nodded. "I mean no disrespect... I'm sorry."

"I'll tape up the ankle, then I'll brew her some tea that'll ease the pain. I've also brought some turmeric capsules for inflammation. You can *kumme* round tomorrow and pick up a pair of crutches. She'll be feeling better in a few days, though a bad sprain can often be more painful than a break."

She lifted what looked like a large flowered carpet bag from a dresser and brought out bandages and medical tape. "Go borrow some dry clothes from Fram, then come back and sit with her. I'll be about."

"All right." John couldn't help his gaze lingering on Tabitha's pale face, still beautiful, even in her pain. Then he stalked from the room, determined to be back before she awakened.

⊚)(⊚

Tabitha hovered on the gossamer strands between sleep and consciousness, not really wanting to wake. But then she remembered—*John called me sweetheart.* She opened her eyes and blinked several times, not quite believing that she saw him sitting next to the bed.

"John?"

He moved with alacrity, sitting up straight and then leaning forward to search her face with his dark blue eyes. "I'll get *Frau* Ebersol..."

"*Nee,*" she said, her voice hoarse. "Wait, *sei se gut.* My ankle—it feels better than when I was in the stream. But how did I get here?"

She watched his dark lashes lower. "I carried you back."

Tabitha swallowed back sudden tears. "You called me sweetheart."

He looked at her then, raw emotion and pain darkening his gaze. "I—I wasn't thinking."

Some instinct prompted her to not let go of his endearment, even with his reasonable response. "You were thinking...I know it, John Miller. You helped me, and you had to think to do that."

"Tabitha, don't," he almost implored.

"But you—"

"Rob's home."

"What?" Her voice quavered even to her own ears.

"Rob—he's back. He helped look for you."

She was quiet for a long moment, then something occurred to her. She looked directly at him. "Rob searched," she whispered. "But you—you were the one who carried me?"

"Tabitha, I—" He broke off as *Frau* Ebersol entered with a cup and spoon, and Tabitha heartily wished the old healer gone for a few moments that she might have heard what John was going to say. But he had moved from the side of the bed and appeared distant once more.

But Tabitha felt a growing confidence inside, a wash of flame and purpose that seemed to come from *Derr Herr* Himself that told her John had more truth to speak to her—perhaps much more.

She swallowed obediently what *Frau* Ebersol offered and closed her eyes to pray, then sleep.

John left Tabitha sleeping and was preparing to relax on the couch in the Beilers' living room when Fram suddenly came down from upstairs. The old man hovered on the edge of the room like some curious specter until John was forced to abandon the idea of rest. He sat up straighter. "You'd like me to be gone, perhaps, sir?" he asked, preparing to do verbal battle to at least stay a few more hours.

But Fram waved away his words. "What? *Nee, buwe*...stay as you like. I—uh—how is she?"

John frowned, remembering that it was Fram's talk of a hired girl that had driven Tabitha to her knees in the forest. "As well as can be expected—given the circumstances," he said coldly.

Fram came forward and perched on a chair, almost as if a stranger to the room. "It was my fault," he admitted after a moment. "Bishop Esch come over and we had a talk. The *auld* man is wise. A mite wiser than I'll ever be. He made me see that I owe—uh—Tabby an apology like... and that I don't need this *haus* or the land."

"What?" John blinked in surprise.

Fram sighed, rubbing his gnarled hands together. "You see, I got a fine *haus* and land back in Ohio, but it always rubbed me wrong that Lizzie got to live here first—I talked to her wrong too, *Derr Herr* have mercy on my soul... my own big sister even."

John was amazed when he heard what sounded like a half sob come from the old man. "So—what are you going to do?"

"Something right, for once." Fram took out a hankie and blew hard. "I'm leavin' this *haus* and land to Tabby and you, to build a fine home on together and raise *kinner*."

John shook his head. "But I'm not even—"

"Now, now, no lyin', *buwe*. I know the heart you have for my niece. You treat her well in the future, like a woman of honor and spirit—not like some—some hired girl." Fram got to his feet slowly, as if his admittance had aged his frame further. John rose also, extending his hand in gratitude, even though he knew that he would not share in the house himself.

"I'll be leavin' tomorrow, after I've told my niece the

same as what I've said here...I—I wish you well, *buwe*. Pray for me if you think on it."

"I will," John promised then watched Fram leave the room for the stairs, his steps slow and ponderous.

John sat back on the couch and ran a tender hand over Rough. "There's no telling what God can do," he whispered to the puppy. "No telling."

Chapter 34

F RAM LEFT THE very next day with as little ceremony as when he'd come, but Tabitha rejoiced after their brief, closeted meeting. *Of course, I cannot tell John what Fram said*, she thought, carefully adjusting her ankle on a pile of quilts.

But, ach, dear Gott, *what a pleasure it would be to build a life with John.* She leaned back and eased her breakfast tray away from her. *Frau* Ebersol had stayed on—"Just to make sure everything was doing," as she put it—and Tabitha was grateful for her pointed but still pleasant presence.

"Did *ya* eat?" the old woman demanded as she came into the room.

"*Ya, danki.*" Tabitha smiled.

"Well, I expect you can get up tomorrow. Doesn't do to baby an ankle too much, even with a bad sprain. Besides, there's a singing tomorrow *nacht* that I imagine John—or some fella—would like to take *ya* to."

Tabitha gave her an innocent look. She knew the healer was referring in an oblique way to Rob, but she wasn't about to confirm or disavow anything until she'd had the chance to talk to Rob himself. She owed him the truth that she no longer had feelings for him. *But don't I owe John the truth too?* She pushed aside the thought for the moment and sipped on the tea that *Frau* Ebersol had brought to ease her pain. Though only *Derr Herr* can ease the pain in my heart of not having John in my life forever.

⁓ ⊚ ⊛ ⁓

As it was, Tabitha saw neither John or Rob over the next day, and she didn't know whether to prepare to go to the singing or not. But in the end, with *Frau* Ebersol's help and an extra cup of the soothing tea she brewed, Tabitha was ready and waiting when John arrived, almost as if they'd planned it together.

He carefully lifted her into the buggy, crutches and all, and they set off at a brisk trot to Letty's house, where the singing was being hosted that night.

Tabitha was surprised at how little John had to say on the drive, though she herself could hardly find words. She knew she'd have a chance to see and possibly speak to Rob that night but wasn't sure of the setting as being appropriate.

And as John helped her into the Mast's filled living room, she couldn't miss the none-too-subtle whispers that seemed to abound around her. And then she realized why—Rob was standing in the place of honor as the leading gamesman for the night. It was he who would pick the songs and then decide the games they would play, and the fact that he would not meet her eyes made her slightly nervous.

As the evening progressed, Tabitha became aware too of Barbara Esch's vengeful gaze and wished that she might somehow have peace with the other girl, who seemed bent on doing her harm. But then Rob announced the first game, and Tabitha swallowed hard. An old Amish favorite, the game was called "Please or Displease?" and required the *buwes* to line up on one side of the room and the girls on the other. The leader would then ask a girl if it pleased or displeased her to do a certain action or speak a certain phrase to an opposite *buwe*. She could choose, and there was normally much joking and laughter involved.

John helped her into place on her crutches, then immediately left her for the row of young men who stood across the way.

Rob began with a charming smile. "Let's see—who shall it be first? *Ach*, I know—Ruby Loftus."

Tabitha watched as the dark-haired Ruby colored prettily as she awaited Rob's question.

"Ruby," Rob queried with a smile. "Does it please or displease you to walk with Henry Lantz once around the barn—alone—together?"

There was a flurry of suppressed giggles as Ruby flushed even more, then lifted her chin. "It displeases me."

Tabitha thought the girl's decision wise, especially after her own experience with Henry's attempt at kissing. Still, Tabitha wondered idly who it was that Ruby truly favored. But then she heard her own name called and snapped to attention.

Rob's gaze swung in her direction, and the room suddenly grew silent. Tabitha realized that Barbara had most likely seen fit to spread her poisonous gossip among the youth, but Tabitha could also not dispute the fact that Rob's eyes seemed to be twinkling at her.

"Tabitha Beiler," he said in carrying tones. "Does it please or displease you to admit…that you are courting…John Miller?"

Tabitha felt she would have fallen had her crutches not been holding her. It was one thing to have the youth suspect her doings but quite another to make such an announcement—especially with Rob present. Then the room erupted, and she saw the smile that passed between John and Rob and her heart soared. "It pleases me," she said clearly, and silence reigned once more. "I, Tabitha Beiler, am delighting in the courtship of John Miller."

Rob nodded and swung to the men. "And does it please you, John Miller, to accept such a statement from the beautiful girl opposite?"

Tabitha waited breathlessly, and then John smiled. "It so pleases me," he said, and cheers and well wishes echoed around the room.

Suddenly Tabitha was caught in a brief hug in John's arms and then John and Rob were shaking hands and laughing together. Tabitha knew she'd remember the singing for the rest of her life—with John.

☙❧

John glanced beside him in the moonlight at Tabitha's smiling profile as he navigated Tudor down the dark road. The singing had ended in a round of merry congratulations that still stirred his heart. He knew Tabitha's thoughts must be equally occupied by the evening when she jumped at his gentle query, "What are you thinking?"

"Nothing," she replied. "And everything."

He laughed low, his mind still savoring her clear, dulcet voice as she admitted to courting with him.

"Did you know?" she asked, turning her face to him.

He almost jumped, unsure if she wanted him to admit that he had any suspicion of her love for him. "What Rob was going to do?"

"*Ya.*"

He shook his head, easing his hat back. "*Nee*, I surely did not. But Rob's always been like that—unpredictable at times."

"Well, I'm glad he was tonight." Her pretty voice sounded shy, and John worked up the courage to gently cover her folded hands with one of his own. "I'm glad he was too. I had talked to my *fater* a few *nacht*s back and had planned on telling you—uh—how I feel, but I didn't want to keep you from your feelings for Rob."

"How you feel?" she whispered.

He swallowed hard and pulled the buggy off the road and beneath a low overhanging of tree branches, illuminated by the moonlight.

"*Ya*, how I feel..." He slipped his hat off and turned to face her. "Tabitha, I love you. I don't know when or how it happened, but I know that *Gott* wrought this love in my soul, in all that I am."

He waited breathlessly as the seconds seemed to tick by interminably, and then she slipped her tender young arms about his neck and he heard her whisper on a sigh. "*Ach*, John—I love you too. I knew the day you said you were going to leave to work in the mountains that I loved you." Then, as if she realized the spontaneity of her hug, she drew back and he wanted to throw his abandoned hat

273

up in the air and kiss her breathless. He settled instead for a chaste kiss on her forehead.

She sighed with a sweet smile "I guess we were at cross purposes all along. I didn't want you to know how much I loved you because I thought you'd never return the feelings out of your loyalty to Rob."

"What a guy Rob is!" John joked on a laugh. Then he grew more serious. "Tabitha, you know we give no pledge of jewelry to keep a promise between—couples. But I would have you know that I pledge you my heart this night and that it is my dearest wish that we would court with genuineness until we can marry. And, you know, Rob put you on the spot tonight with the idea of courting and all, but I want to ask you myself—will you marry me?"

He watched a beautiful smile play across her lips, and then he felt her lean her bonneted head against his shoulder.

He savored the sweetness of her voice as she whispered. "*Ya*, John. I will."

❧❧

The next day John looked up from where he worked on the pie safe for Tabitha and watched Rob ride his familiar big red roan down the drive. Rob tied the horse to the hitching post, then sauntered over to the wood shop.

"Well?" John heard him ask.

John laid aside the sand paper he held. "Well, what?"

Rob grinned. "Don't you want to thank me?"

John arched a brow and slid his hands to his hips. "For

that display last *nacht*? You were taking an awful risk with my heart if it had not pleased Tabitha to court me."

"But it did," Rob answered smugly.

John had to smile. "*Ya*, it did."

Rob clapped him on the back. "*Gut*, but now I need to ask you a favor."

"What?"

"I want you to help me tell my *mamm* about Katie and that I'm going to leave the Amish."

"What are you talking about?" John was floored.

"Katie...I told you. I love her. But she's English."

"Are you *narrisch*? You fall in and out of love so often I can't count, and now you think you're going to give up your way of life because of one woman?"

But John saw a new look in Rob's brown eyes—a seriousness and maturity.

"*Ya*, John. Because of one woman. The woman I want to marry and spend my life with."

John sank down on a nearby sawhorse. "I believe you," he said finally.

"Good. So, will you do it?"

John shook his head. "The last time you asked me for a favor I—"

"Found the love of your life?" Rob quipped.

John nodded. "All right. I'll help you talk with your *mamm*, but you're going to tell the absolute truth, and Rob, you're going to hurt her—you know that?"

Rob bowed his head. "I know."

John began to pray beneath his breath, determined to help his friend—but this time with honesty instead of lies.

CHAPTER 35

TABITHA WAITED WITH nervous excitement that evening, wondering when John might arrive for courting. He'd stopped by earlier in the day to tell her that he was bringing Esther home from the hospital to stay with her, as both company and chaperone to keep tongues from wagging over any courting done. When Tabitha had protested that his *mamm* and *daed* needed Esther, John had explained that his *fater* would thankfully be home later that week and Esther was happy to come.

Now, a spatter of pebbles against the window behind the catch made her jump then laugh out loud. Tabitha rejoiced in John's old-fashioned way of doing things and moved as quickly as she could on her crutches to open the door.

Esther entered first to give Tabitha a big but brief squeeze, and Tabitha understood that this was the way John's prickly but kind-hearted younger sister was welcoming her into the family.

Esther carried an old black suitcase, and Tabitha gestured to the stairs. "It took me some doing with the crutches, but I've got my *auld* room fixed up for you. But please, Esther, stay up awhile with John and me if you'd like."

Esther gave a lady-like snort. "When you're courting? I should think not. Besides, I'm tired of sleeping in the hospital suite. A real bed will feel *wunderbar*."

Tabitha watched her march off to the stairs, then turned to look up at John as he entered.

He smelled like spring and his light blue short-sleeved shirt showed the tanned muscles of his forearms from his work outdoors. She swallowed and gestured solemnly to the couch with the tip of one crutch. "Won't you sit down, John?"

He smiled. "After you, sweetheart."

She thrilled to the gentle endearment, then hobbled to the couch and collapsed, allowing her crutches to rest beside her. John sat down on her left, and she watched him work the brim of his straw hat through his lean fingers. She sensed his nervousness and felt the same way herself.

"I guess we've rather done things backward," he said finally.

"What do you mean?"

"Well," he half-laughed, "deciding to marry before courting properly and all that. You know our people use the courting time to get to know one another and decide if they're—we're—a *gut* fit."

"And do you think we are?" she asked softly.

He turned to look at her in the pleasant light of the kerosene lamp. "*Ya*, and you?"

She smiled. "*Ya*, John. And now that we have such important matters in hand, we—well—we could discuss our wedding and make our plans."

She watched him visibly relax as he scooped up Rough off the floor onto his lap. "All right, future *Frau* Miller, what would you talk about?"

"*Ach*, I forgot. I made us a snack. Would you go to the kitchen and bring in the plates from the table? We can eat here on our laps."

"Surely." John passed her the protesting puppy, then walked to the kitchen and back, balancing the plates she'd filled before his arrival.

"A snack?" he laughed, arranging everything just so. "I would say that it's more a small feast."

Tabitha laughed with him, nestling Rough against her side where he couldn't get at her food. She was pleased with the savory biscuits, pimento cheese spread, pickled eggs and beets, as well as the chocolate mayonnaise cake she'd made, and it pleased her even more to watch John enjoying everything.

When they'd finished, he cleared things away then came back to the couch to gently take her hand in his. Her heart beat fast in her chest at his tender touch, and it was difficult to concentrate on what they were talking about.

"So what do you think?" John asked, and she stared at him blankly.

"I'm afraid you'll have to repeat yourself." She felt her cheeks heat up, but his dark blue eyes twinkled merrily at her as if he shared her secret about their hand holding.

"I said"—he leaned a bit closer—"that perhaps we should live here and add on to the *haus* as needed. You know *Mamm* and *Daed* are right down the street."

She nodded, thinking. "But will your family mind? You know it's common for the *maedel* to come and live with the man's family. I might be able to help your *mamm* and Esther."

John stroked his chin. "I think, with us so close by, that they will not mind. But we shall see…" He sighed aloud as if lost in thought suddenly, and her hand convulsed in his.

"Is—is something wrong, John?"

He looked at her, and she realized now how tired he was. "Not much wrong," he soothed. "I did another favor for Rob today, and it was—difficult, to say the least."

"*Ach...*" she murmured. "Do you want to talk about it?"

He seemed to consider for a long moment then finally nodded his head. "*Ya,* I do."

She breathed a faint sigh of relief, glad that they would have no more secrets between them.

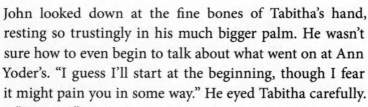

John looked down at the fine bones of Tabitha's hand, resting so trustingly in his much bigger palm. He wasn't sure how to even begin to talk about what went on at Ann Yoder's. "I guess I'll start at the beginning, though I fear it might pain you in some way." He eyed Tabitha carefully.

"How so?"

"Well." He paused then went on with determination. "When Rob returned, he told me that he'd come to love an English nurse—Katie—in Ohio."

"And?"

"This doesn't bother you?" he asked.

"*Nee*—it is no more than what I did—finding true love versus a mere feeling or the elation of falling in love."

He smiled at her sensibleness. "All right. I'll agree with you. But Rob asked me to help him tell his *mamm* about Katie and also to tell Ann that he plans on leaving the Amish."

"*Ach*, poor Miss Ann! But she doesn't have to worry that he'll be shunned—he hasn't joined the church yet."

"Another *gut* point, but it's his moving away to Ohio on

a permanent basis that's broken Ann's heart. You know how protective she is of Rob, and he is her only son."

"*Ya*, I know. Look, John, would it help at all if I went to see her with you? We've become quite *gut* friends, I think, and maybe I could help her in some way if *Derr Herr* allows."

John squeezed her hand. "I think that's a *wunderbar* idea, Tabitha. And, living so close, we can make sure, by all means, that she doesn't feel too lonely without Rob."

"She may, in time, even choose to move to Ohio," Tabitha mused aloud.

"Perhaps, but her community is here."

"I know, and that's so important. When *Onkel* Fram first spoke to me of being a hired girl—*ach*, I was so angry and afraid that I'd have nowhere to go or that I might have to leave Paradise."

John nudged close to her and bent his head to her ear. "Don't ever be afraid of that, sweetheart. As *Gott* wills, I will always make our home a haven for you and our—well, *sohns* and *dochders*."

He watched her touch his wrist in a squeeze of gratitude and knew a fullness in his heart as he prepared to welcome the days *Derr Herr* would lay out for them together.

EPILOGUE

THE NEXT WEEK Tabitha looked up in surprise as John and Matt pulled up in a long wagon with a tarp hiding something in the back. She'd been trying to balance on her crutches and water the porch plants at the same time. Now she put down the tin watering can to watch with interest and pleasure as the two *bruders* flung back the tarp and started easing the carved wooden piece of furniture from the back.

As they neared the steps, she recognized it for what it was—a pie safe with punched tin and a high gloss.

"*Ach*, my," she cried, then eased open the door and hobbled out of the way.

"A gift," John breathed, smiling, as they finally set it upright in the kitchen.

"And a *wunderbar* one!" she laughed, moving close to inspect the hearts on the tin.

"You know, *Aenti* Beth left me so many great recipes for pie, and now that I think of it, that night in the garden, she said something odd. I'd forgotten about it until now."

"What was it?" John asked.

"She said, 'The recipe box is your inheritance, but only the carpenter will know its secret.'"

"Well, John's a carpenter," Matt observed casually.

Tabitha looked at John in amazement. "You're a

carpenter," she repeated then hastened to hand him the recipe box. "What's its secret?"

John laughed then grew more serious as he took the box with careful fingers. "Perhaps it's all the goodness contained inside in the recipes themselves."

"I've thought of that," Tabitha said. "It has to be something only a carpenter would know."

John moved closer to the kerosene lamp. "Well, it is wood, of course...a nice *auld* walnut." He opened the lid and took the recipes out, laying them on the table. Then he looked carefully inside the box, turning it this way and that. "I can't see anything unusual...unless..." He turned the box over and studied the bottom. Suddenly he pressed something and there was a definitive click. Then he slid a panel from the base of the small box.

"*Ach*, my..." Tabitha gasped.

"It's a puzzle box," John said.

"Well, what's in there?" Matt demanded noisily.

"That's for Tabitha to find out." John handed her the box and she took it with shaking hands.

She peered into the tiny alcove, then lifted a folded piece of paper from the space. She opened it and read to herself, then she looked up at John with her lips set. "John, I'm sorry, but you're going to have to leave for two hours."

"What?" Matt exploded.

John obeyed Tabitha without comment, dragging his younger *bruder* with him.

Tabitha watched them go, tears sparkling in her eyes. Then she carefully lay the paper down on the table and turned to reach for the yellow mixing bowl and a pie pan.

❧❦❧

Two hours to the minute and minus Matt, John knocked at the screen door, smelling a sweet aroma coming from within the kitchen. Tabitha met him at the door and grabbed his hand, pulling him after her to the kitchen table.

"Now, John, *sei se gut*, close your eyes."

He did as he was asked, wondering with a smile what she was up to. Then he heard something being slid onto the table in front of him.

"All right, John," she called. "Open your eyes!"

He did and stared first at her beautiful smile then down at the table. "Apple pie!" he exclaimed. "My favorite. *Danki.*"

She shook her head.

"Not apple?" he asked in happy confusion.

She moved the recipe box next to the pie, then pulled a folded paper from her apron pocket. "Not only apple— you must listen. This...is my true inheritance from *Aenti* Elizabeth and from her *grossmuder.*" He watched her delicate throat work as she swallowed. Then she began to read:

For a woman who has found a devout man, and this man the true love of her heart, a secret recipe, never to be revealed to the man except through the tasting of the food—an "Apple of His Eye" apple pie. For the woman should always say, "Keep me as the apple of your eye; hide me in the shadow of your wings."

Tabitha lifted her head. "And then there's the recipe..."

"Which I'm to never know but through the tasting of the pie?"

She cast her lashes down demurely. "If you would like a taste, *ya*."

He stepped near her, ignoring the pie for the moment. "*Ach, ya*," he breathed, taking her in his arms. "I would indeed have a taste. For you, woman, are indeed the apple of my eye and the very love of my heart."

Then he bent and kissed her, once and hard, only to draw back and stare down into her eyes—which were twin pools of promise. And he knew, as a sure inheritance, that he was home.

AENTI BETH'S "APPLE OF HIS EYE" APPLE PIE

Preheat oven to 375 degrees Fahrenheit.

For the crust:

> 2 cups flour
> 1 teaspoon salt
> 1 cup of lard*
> 1/3 cup of milk
> 1 tablespoon vinegar

Put flour in a bowl then add salt.

In a separate bowl add vinegar to milk and set aside.

Cut lard into flour until it looks like crumbs (you may need to add more flour until mixture is crumbly), then add the milk and vinegar mixture. Add more flour if dough is too sticky.

Dust a flat surface with flour and separate dough into two equal-size balls. Set one aside.

Flatten the dough ball with your hand and then, starting in the center of the dough, roll each ball into a 10- to 12-inch circle. Turn and flour the dough as needed to make sure it doesn't stick to the surface. Once flat, fold the dough in half and place in a pie pan, then unfold to fit the pan.

Repeat process with the top crust and set aside.

---

* Or butter-flavored Crisco

For the filling:

> 6–7 apples, sliced thin and cut small (you want to use sour apples like Crab Apples, Granny Smiths, etc.)
> ½ to ¾ cup white sugar
> ¾ brown sugar
> Small handful of flour
> Cinnamon (several teaspoons to taste)
> 4 teaspoons of butter

In a bowl mix together white sugar, brown sugar, flour, and cinnamon. Add sliced apples (make sure they're not chunky) a little bit at a time. Mix with your hands until all apple slices are coated. Pour apple mixture into the bottom pie crust, then dot top of filling with pats of the butter.

Add top crust. Pinch edges closed and use a fork to create vents in the top.

Put pan on a cookie sheet and place in oven. Bake for about forty-five minutes or until crust has lightly browned.

Enjoy!

COMING FROM KELLY CALDWELL IN 2017

THE BLUEBERRY BRIDE

BOOK TWO IN THE AMISH PIE SERIES

CHAPTER 1

THE HOT SUNSHINE of the summer Thursday morning caught on the glassware and flower petals that gave special significance to the corner of the Miller kitchen where the *eck* table stood.

All that was needed was the bridal couple and their attendants to begin the special wedding feast where John and Tabitha Miller would receive the blessings and well wishes of both family and community.

But the wedding ceremony still went on, as it normally did, for a *gut* four hours, and Matt Miller was bored. He let his gaze roam over the profile of his handsome big *bruder* and then briefly paid attention to the sound of Bishop Esch's exhortation, only to idly glance across the row at his fellow attendant and the one he was to escort for the day—Letty Mast.

The girl's plump cheeks were flushed a becoming pink and her small hands were clenched in her lap, as she sat, as attuned as a baby hare to every moment of her best friend's wedding. *I've never realized how pretty Letty is,* Matt mused to himself, but then something went subtly wrong. Letty's face drained of color and she wobbled slightly in her hard-backed chair.

She fell, like a wilting rose bud, slightly sideways, fast destined for the floor, but Matt was faster. He caught her neatly, ignoring the circle of whispers behind him, and pressed the back of his hand to her forehead as he lowered her gently to the wooden floor. "Fainted only," he pronounced quietly, knowing Bishop Esch would continue with the ceremony whether one girl fainted or ten.

"She needs to eat," Matt hissed over his shoulder, aware that the girl had been most likely too focused on her duties as attendant to have any breakfast. Someone handed him a morsel in a white cloth napkin. *Pie,* he thought. Gut. He pressed some crumbs to her lips, and she opened her wide brown eyes in both dawning surprise and dismay.

"Blueberry pie... *ach,* my..."

Matt smiled down at her. "Oh, my, indeed."

GLOSSARY

ach—oh

aenti—aunt

auld—old

boppli—baby

bruder—brother

buwe—boy

da—grandfather

daed—dad

danki—thank you

Derr Herr— the Lord

dochder— daughter

eck—head bridal table

en der weldt—in the world

Englischer—non-Amish person

fater—father

frau—Mrs.

geh—go

Gott—God

gut—good

gut nacht—good night

grossdaudi—grandfather

grossmuder—grandmother

haus—house

hund—dog

kapp—hat

kinner—children

kumme—come

maedel—girl

mamm—mother

narrisch—foolish
nee—no
onkel—uncle
Ordnung—a set of rules
sei se—would you
sohn—son
was—what
weldt—world
wunderbar—wonderful
ya—yes

CONNECT WITH US!